Rand paused before going for the jugular. "Your choice, Ingebord."

She took a step backwards and he knew he had penetrated her disguise. "I... I... I no longer use that name. I much prefer Svanna."

He narrowed his gaze and saw the fear she tried to mask. So not quite the impervious ice maiden, but a woman with a secret, and one which he planned to unpick. He instinctively fingered his scar. "Don't lie to me. We encountered each other in Agthir. Eight years ago."

Her eyes widened and her hands played with the neckline of her gown. "You remember me? I mean, did we?"

"You were quite memorable." He made his voice purr, looked at her directly and willed her to believe the exaggeration. He had no memory of what happened preceding the attack or if they had ever conversed, but he'd never attacked a woman nor stolen a kiss from an unwilling one.

A frown puckered her forehead. "You will stay there until I come for you. Whatever you want from this place, you will not get it, if you fail to keep to my instructions."

Rand made his best courtly bow. He would find a way of getting what he wanted and saving his cousin's life. And Ingebord—or Svanna, as she now called herself—was going to ensure it happened, even if she failed to realize that. He looked forward to the realization dawning on her.

"To hear is to obey, my fair lady."

Author Note

One of my favorite Icelandic sagas, *Halfdan Eysteinsson*, inspired this book, because although I gave an HEA to my heroine Maer in *Secret Princess for the Warrior*, I could not get the woman who was forced into impersonating her out of my head. I wanted her to have a happily-ever-after because in the original saga, she doesn't. I thought that a shame, swiftly followed by *I can do something about that*. Cue my daughter moving for work to Dublin and I knew the sort of story I wanted to write. Among other things, the story gave me an excuse to do research. I do hope you enjoy reading Svanna and Rand's story as much as I enjoyed writing it.

As ever, thank you for reading my stories. If you'd like to get in touch, I love getting comments from readers and can be reached at michelle@michellestyles.co.uk or through my publisher or Facebook or X @michellelstyles.

VIKING'S ROYAL MARRIAGE BARGAIN

MICHELLE STYLES

Recycling programs for this product may not exist in your area.

ISBN-13: 978-1-335-83162-0

Viking's Royal Marriage Bargain

For questions and comments about the quality of this book, please contact us at CustomerService@Harlequin.com.

Harlequin Enterprises ULC
22 Adelaide St. West, 41st Floor
Toronto, Ontario M5H 4E3, Canada
www.Harlequin.com

HarperCollins Publishers
Macken House, 39/40 Mayor Street Upper,
Dublin 1, D01 C9W8, Ireland
www.HarperCollins.com

Printed in U.S.A.

Born and raised near San Francisco, California, **Michelle Styles** currently lives near Hadrian's Wall with her husband and a menagerie of pets in an Edwardian bungalow with a large and somewhat overgrown garden. An avid reader, she became hooked on historical romances after discovering Georgette Heyer, Anya Seton and Victoria Holt. Her website is michellestyles.co.uk and she's on X and Facebook.

Books by Michelle Styles

Harlequin Historical

Summer of the Viking
Sold to the Viking Warrior
The Warrior's Viking Bride
Sent as the Viking's Bride
A Viking Heir to Bind Them
Tempted by Her Forbidden Warrior
Secret Princess for the Warrior

Vows and Vikings

A Deal with Her Rebel Viking
Betrothed to the Enemy Viking
To Wed a Viking Warrior

Sons of Sigurd

Conveniently Wed to the Viking

Visit the Author Profile page
at Harlequin.com for more titles.

To KMS, who decided to live in Dublin
but still takes time to phone.

Prologue

839

Off the coast of Agthir
(Modern-day southwestern Norway)

Randolfr Fullrson's return to the land of the living came in slow, painful degrees of consciousness. First, he noticed the rocking of the boat, then the pins and needles attacking his limbs, and finally his sight returned. Instead of the royal hall or indeed the Queen's garden where he last remembered heading towards, he was lying on his back, looking at the swaying leather-covered shelter of a merchant ship.

He turned his head. A sharp pain shot through it, becoming embedded in his left cheek. A loud groan which embodied all the torments in the world echoed throughout the shelter, and he felt pity for the poor creature having to endure that sort of agony. Belatedly, he realised the sound had emerged from his aching throat.

'Worse than Fenrir the Wolf's embrace on a cold night,' he mumbled to no one in particular.

'You live, thank Odin and all the gods.'

'Thorarinn?' His own voice was a shadow of its former strength. The left side of his jaw refused to move in its normal way. He concentrated hard and tried again. 'Where are we, cousin? What new evil has befallen us?'

'Hush, Rand, for everyone's sake.' His cousin looked over his shoulder as if he were expecting to see ice giants with drawn swords bearing down on them. 'We're on a boat, going east. Putting water between us and Drengr and his sons.'

'Drengr, the King's advisor? Why is he concerned with the likes of us? Why do we have to leave Agthir?'

'With any luck, he won't have us declared wolf's heads. His sons, particularly the youngest, Turgeis, want your blood.'

Rand concentrated on the seam in the dark leather awning. Last thing he remembered was talking—no, sharing a kiss—with that blonde-haired serving girl with the flashing eyes and saucy tongue. Innocent, but eager to flirt. Her name… Svanna…even now seemed to be sliding into a great swirling black. They were supposed to meet, but where? The black hole appeared to reach out to him.

'Why?' he croaked out, trying to escape its clutches.

'Didn't know it was you, see. Turgeis offered a pouch of gold to any man who knew where the Queen's daughter dallied with her new lover. I took a gamble and said the Queen's private garden.' Thorarinn gulped hard. 'They paid me gold but…then someone said they'd seen you headed that way. And then I saw you being beaten.'

'The Queen's daughter?' Rand tried to think around the stabbing pain in his head. He'd only seen the young woman from a distance in the feasting hall, he and his cousin seated far too low on the tables to reach her exalted notice. Heard her sing-song voice once, asking where her dog Tippi was. Who in the royal household of Agthir hadn't as the young woman loved that dog? The story of how she'd charmed the current King with her innocent golden beauty and he'd married her mother, saving both their lives, was recited at every Agthir feast. 'Don't have a death wish. Meeting…' beneath the pain, he dredged up her name '…Svanna. Meeting that girl.'

'Ingebord, the Queen's daughter, was supposed to be meeting someone, and I lost at dice.'

Rand struggled to think how the two events were connected.

'Never spoken to her, Thorarinn. I swear this.' He'd gone to the garden because of… Now, all he could think of were her laughing eyes. He'd picked some flowers to make Svanna smile, and dropped them when the first blow came.

'Dreadful mix-up. Needed to pay my gambling debt or risk losing my fingers.' Thorarinn hunkered down beside him. 'Once I discovered you were in that garden, I went back, fought the King's advisor off, getting severely kicked for my pains, I might add, and carried you to this ship. I saved your life.'

Rand's brain buzzed as if a thousand bees had attacked it and the awning swung round in a dizzy-making series of circles. He concentrated on breathing and allowing the blackness to swirl about him. The world slowly righted itself. After another long while, he risked opening an eye. Thorarinn knelt beside him with his head bowed. The marks of the beating shone on Thorarinn's face and hands.

'You saved me?'

The creases in Thorarinn's face relaxed. 'I did. Drengr and his sons would have left your body for the crows to feast on.'

'Never met the Queen's daughter. Never touched her, kissed her or attempted to kiss her.'

He'd kissed the other one, the serving girl, but her face

and name were slowly going from his mind, like water slipping through his fingers. The sweet taste of her mouth and her silvery laugh lingered. He shook his head, trying to get rid of the incessant buzzing. Svanna.

'I know that! This is me, your cousin, remember?'

'That's the trouble. Not remembering, Thorarinn. All slipping away,' Rand whispered and the pain in the left side of his face throbbed to a crescendo.

'Your pretty face has altered but you breathe.' Thorarinn gave a quick smile and clapped him on the shoulder. The gesture from his normally undemonstrative cousin told Rand all he needed to know about how severely he'd been beaten. 'Safe now. Embarked on a new adventure.'

'New adventure?'

'No more Agthir. No more Queen's golden-haired daughter or murderous King's advisor and his sons. Eastward, cousin.' He bumped his fist against Rand's hand. 'Our past behind us. No need to discuss this ever again.'

Rand's fingers explored the bandage on his face. Thorarinn spoke true—he would carry the mark of that beating until he died. The irony of the Queen's daughter being in ignorance of his existence caused a bitter laugh to escape his throat. Some part of him could not help wondering what her lips would have tasted like. Would they have been as sweet as the woman's whose name was lost to the darkness of his mind? He doubted it.

'The next time something like this happens, I swear it will be for something I've done. If the chance arises, and the lady is willing, one day I'll kiss the golden-haired daughter of the Queen of Agthir.'

'That's my cousin.'

'I owe you, Thorarinn. I will have your back, always. I promise.'

Chapter One

848, nine years later

Sigmundson's steading, Islay, in the remnants of the Dal Riada Confederacy (modern-day Bunnahabhain, Islay, Scotland)

Svanna Guthardottar regarded the tables in the hall with their brightly polished goblets and trenchers laid in the proper order for the feast of thanksgiving later. This gathering was her final chance to ensure a match between Astrid, the former Queen of Agthir, and the lord of this steading, Sigmund Sigmundson. To ensure the happy event, all the preparation for this feast needed to be complete perfection.

A marriage between the pair would make it easier for her to remain on Islay rather than having to return to Agthir, where she'd spent over a decade impersonating the Queen's true daughter, Ingebord, to ensure all their lives would be safe. Even after Ingebord—now calling herself Maer—returned and claimed her place through a love-match marriage to the late King's son and heir, Svanna maintained the façade of being the Queen's daughter because it protected all concerned. Ingebord had been declared Astrid's foster-daughter, so Svanna's deception had protected all involved, particularly Astrid, from the late usurper King's fury at being deceived in that fashion.

Thus, it was only since she and Astrid had travelled to Islay shortly after the usurper King's death that Svanna had reclaimed that feeling of being who she was and had started using her birth-name of Svanna again, a name she liked far better than Ingebord.

She knew Sigmund sought a strong alliance with his fellow petty kings in Islay to protect them from the threat of invasion. To her mind, he'd make the perfect protector because Sigmund had once been Halfr the Bold, the legendary warrior who had whisked away Maer to the east when Agthir fell.

'My lady, the Queen, asks you attend her on the shore,' one of the servants said, rushing in. 'The petty kings are arriving, and she wants to ensure the proper hospitality is given before the church service begins.'

Svanna dusted her hands on her apron. The huge stone beside the high table which the Queen had had moved this morning to make the swearing of oaths easier appeared unsteady, but she agreed with Astrid about the move. 'I hope all the kings are prepared to swear the oath.'

'Once Lord Sigmund is proclaimed high King of Islay, becoming a king in truth, the entire island will be at peace.' The servant grinned. 'Then maybe he will marry Queen Astrid. Your foster-mother is good for him. His mood has improved no end since you both arrived.'

'An honourable peace works for everyone,' Svanna said, reciting one of Astrid's sayings before she left the hall. 'We must expend all our efforts to achieve it.'

Astrid had taught her all the tricks of ruling and being a peace-weaver, including negotiation, building alliances and the subtle diplomacy which came through hospitality, in preparation for Svanna ruling or marrying, but thankfully Maer had returned in time.

After her return, Maer had urged Svanna to only marry if she truly desired the match rather than for strategic reasons, but Svanna had never met a man she could love in the way Maer loved her husband, and she doubted she ever would. Her mind skittered away from what had happened to her in Astrid's garden nine years ago, and her narrow escape from the fate Turgeis Drengrson intended. *Young warriors must be allowed their fun*, her old nurse had claimed, but what he wanted to do to her was not Svanna's definition of a good time. Her nurse had often excused warriors who overstepped, feeling women should endure and not get themselves into precarious situations in the first place. Svanna had heard her give similar lectures to the serving girls in the hall. Caution and vigilance about potential danger were her watchwords.

Before she reached the harbour, the swineherd stepped in front of her, blocking her way. 'Lady Svanna, my new assistant has seen many ships, Northern ships, in the next harbour but one. Lord Sigmund says that the lad must be mistaken and as excitable as I was at that age, but he's wrong. The lad's as steady as they come. Make them listen, please.'

Svanna forced a smile and refrained from telling the excitable man that Sigmund had laughingly predicted that the swineherd would come up with nonsense about Northern ships, notorious for such predictions apparently. But only a fool would attack such a large gathering of warriors. 'The possibility of attack is why Lord Sigmund posted guards.'

'But not on the far harbour.'

'I'm sure they're simply merchant vessels who have

stopped to take on water. Does your assistant know the difference between a Northern merchant ship and a warship?'

The swineherd rubbed his chin. 'What you say rings true. I'll tell my lad.'

'You do that.'

'Lady Svanna—' the priest said, hurrying up to her after she had stopped to chat with a little girl and her mother. Although Svanna had accepted that she was unlikely to have children as she had no plans to marry, she enjoyed spending time with them. Sometimes she wondered what sort of mother she would have been if the fates had twisted her life's thread differently. 'If you are going down to the harbour, can you ask Lord Sigmundson to attend the service? He is refusing to speak to me about it.' He lifted an ornately decorated hand bell. 'I shall be ringing St Fillan's bell to call the faithful and it would gladden the other kings' hearts to see him there. Perhaps your foster-mother as well?'

'He didn't want to upset anyone as his beliefs are private,' Svanna said, giving the excuse Sigmund and Astrid had used several times. 'But I will mention it.'

'The additional weapons store for when they are in the service is full of hay, Lady Svanna. That swineherd said his boy would move the hay, but it hasn't been done.' The priest drew himself up to his full height, resembling a wet crow. 'I won't have weapons of war in my church. Not today. Not ever. Please tell Lord Sigmund that.'

'I'll ensure it is done,' Svanna said, mentally sighing.

By the time she'd finished supervising the servants and sweeping the weapons store clean, the shoreline was littered with coracles. Most of the kings and their entourages had made their way up to the church in preparation for the service of thanksgiving. The stores bulged with arrows, spears, a wide variety of knives and the occasional steel sword. Svanna set a single guard over the store, more as a sop to the swineherd and his assistant.

'Will we have enough food?' Astrid murmured as Svanna took her place beside her. 'The king from Kinsella has brought twice the number of men he said he would.'

'I took the precaution of ensuring another pig was put on to roast earlier,' Svanna answered with a small curtsey, and took the horn filled with mead from the Queen. 'You should rest before tonight. They will expect the great Queen of Agthir to shine.'

'They would be speaking of my daughter Ingebord now, not me.' Astrid's lips turned up into a tired smile. 'Always worrying about my health, Svanna. You should be thinking about getting married and having a family.'

Svanna allowed the comment to pass without remark. They both knew why she had remained unmarried. To avoid Svanna being forced to marry to install one of Drengr's sons on the throne, Astrid had taken Svanna's advice, and sent word to Sigmund requesting her true daughter's return.

'Is that all the kings?' Svanna counted the kings who'd arrived on her fingers. 'Where is the king of Gruinard? Surely he should be here by now, ready to swear his allegiance.'

'Ill, apparently.' Sigmund made an irritated noise.

'Always one or two who would find an excuse. Jealousy. But he will fall in line once the other kings pledge their oaths and you are proclaimed the high King of Islay, Halfr,' Astrid said with a shrug. 'Trust a woman's intuition for once.'

Sigmund wagged an indulgent finger at the name Astrid used, as if to remind her that they were in a public place. The late king of Agthir, Astrid's second husband, had put a bounty on Halfr the Bold's head which had never been fully rescinded.

Svanna shaded her eyes and looked at a *karfi*, a small

Northern warship which had nosed into the harbour, carefully navigating between the rocks and sunken ships guarding its entrance. 'I thought the Northmen from Dubh-Linn were not supposed to know about this.'

'They don't,' Sigmund answered with a frown. 'If anything, they think the gathering is set for next week. I did stress the importance of secrecy to all concerned.'

'Then why has that ship entered the harbour?' Svanna asked, fighting against the rising panic in her throat. Panicking served no one, but she couldn't help her stomach tensing. 'I don't recognise the sail or the yellow and green markings on the hull.'

'That much is obvious,' Astrid murmured. 'Focus on what is not, Svanna, and see if you can use that to your advantage. Which is what a trained peace-weaver like you does.'

Svanna focused on the ship and tried to spot something that might help, rather than remarking that she was unlikely to have to put her skills of peace-weaving to any meaningful use.

'The swineherd mentioned his assistant had spotted several Northern warships anchoring in the next harbour but one,' she said, shading her eyes and trying to pick out the motifs on the shields which still hung at the ship's sides. 'Could this be the start of a larger delegation from Dubh-Linn? Has news of the gathering reached Eire before Lord Sigmund wanted it to?'

'The swineherd was always excitable as a youth. Now he has been promoted and has acquired an assistant, he is even worse,' Sigmund said. 'I'm sure Maer kept you entertained with tales of him and his wilder fantasies back in Agthir.'

'He should have been a *skald*, instead of keeping pigs,' Astrid added. 'The tales were impressive on our journey over.'

Sigmund shook his head. 'I'd hoped that his new responsibilities would curb his enthusiasm for such tall tales, but my error.'

'He was very insistent,' Svanna said, stuffing the sense of unease back down her throat. 'Several ships, anchored in the next harbour but one. Why would he make a mistake like that?'

'It would be a foolish man who tried to attack us, particularly this large gathering of warriors. You worry overmuch, Svanna.' Sigmund's eyes crinkled as if he found her insistence amusing. 'I made my reputation as a warrior long before you were born and I know a thing or three about the men from the North who raid. It would be foolish to attack us with this veritable army of warriors in attendance.'

'We know which warship the swineherd has made into several,' Astrid said.

Sigmund suddenly stiffened and cursed under his breath.

'Have you worked out who it belongs to, Lord Sigmund?' Svanna asked instead of giving voice to her fears about the vulnerability of the church, or indeed the hall where the celebratory feast was due to take place.

'Relax and smile, Svanna. Halfr has all under control. Nothing will be allowed to ruin our...his day.'

Astrid and Sigmund exchanged significant looks and squeezed their hands briefly together. Svanna felt as if she was intruding on a special moment. Hope grew in her chest. A marriage between them would give her a legitimate reason to remain on Islay, where she found it easier to be herself.

'I will go and speak to the servants, Halfr. Gently find out the mood in case the swineherd has spread his tale of gloom to the others,' Astrid said in a quiet undertone, giving his hand another brief touch. 'Ensure all is well-guarded in the hall, even if I think it is an unnecessary precaution.'

He nodded, accepting the assessment. 'And your foster-daughter?'

'I'll wait with Lord Sigmund,' Svanna declared. 'Our unexpected guests should receive proper hospitality. No one will notice if I am at the church service or not.'

'You are good, Svanna,' Astrid murmured and Svanna knew she had said the correct thing.

Astrid always said that peace-weaving was a woman's business much more than a man's. Done properly, it prevented wars, but it was not celebrated in the sagas because men liked the thrill of combat instead of the hard slog of diplomacy.

'Any luck with the shields?' Svanna asked once Astrid had disappeared up the slope. 'What have you seen that I have missed? Are they from Dubh-Linn or somewhere further afield? What are you keeping from my foster-mother?'

'The shields proclaim the ship is aligned with the new high king of all Eire, Máel Sechnaill mac Máele Ruanaid, rather than Dubh-Linn. If he is aware of this gathering, everyone on Eire is.'

'Surely this Máel Sechnaill mac Máele Ruanaid must think that banding together of the Gaels to stand firm against the Northern raiders is a good idea.' Svanna stumbled slightly over the pronunciation of the King's name. Her Gaelic had improved considerably since she'd arrived, but the complicated names could make her tongue twist.

'He might, but Máel Sechnaill mac Máele Ruanaid makes Thorfi look straightforward,' Sigmund said, naming the late King of Agthir. 'He wants what is best for him and his family, and not for anyone else.'

Svanna tapped a finger against her chin. 'I doubt the high King will be on board and wanting to pay homage to you.

But should that unlikely event occur, then you must be gracious, Lord Sigmund, and not refuse the gesture.'

Sigmund laughed and placed a hand on her shoulder. 'You are good for me, Svanna. Simple truths. Yes, like you, I doubt he is on board. Shall we see who he sent instead?'

She smiled back at him. 'A good plan.'

Less than five breaths later, Lord Sigmund stiffened. 'I don't believe it. Of all the Northern warriors.'

'What?'

'Randolfr Fullrson. He now calls himself Lord Randolfr after Máel Sechnaill bestowed various large estates on him.' Lord Sigmund pointed to a tall man standing on the prow of the ship.

The wind blew the tousled curls of his golden hair from the man's face, revealing a jagged scar running down the left side of his face, the relic of some long-ago battle, but one which distorted his mouth and left eye. As he turned his head towards them, she could see that his right side remained unscathed. The contrast between the two sides, one strikingly handsome and the other ruined, was noticeable even at this distance. Silently she prayed to the Norns that her memory was playing tricks on her and that she'd never encountered him before.

'Is there anything else I should know about him?' Svanna managed to choke the words from her throat.

'Rand the Silver-Tongue, according to my foster-niece Maer when we travelled back from Constantinople together.' He shrugged. 'She was quite taken with him on board ship, but the scales fell from her eyes when we arrived at Dubh-Linn and she witnessed his naked ambition.'

'Maer is happily married to her new husband.'

Sigmund made an irritated noise in the back of his throat. Svanna knew from hints that he had initially been against the match Maer had ended up making, only giving in when he'd realised how much in love she was with the usurper King of Agthir's son.

'A small warning: you might've encountered Silver-Tongue years ago,' he said. 'My foster-niece confided that he and his cousin sought employment in Agthir as sell-swords once but left abruptly, having angered the usurper. Part of her initial attraction to him, in my opinion.'

Svanna's stomach knotted. She did know the name from over eight years ago. Randolfr, more commonly called Rand, as he'd laughingly introduced himself.

That feast had been full of rowdy behaviour from the younger warriors, something the usurper had appeared to endorse wholeheartedly. The Queen had retired early with a headache, freeing Svanna to sneak back in, dressed in her nurse's gown and cloak, taking risks like the true Ingebord once did, instead of behaving like the boring Svanna who often feared her own shadow. The light banter with Rand had made her tingle all over. Even now she remembered the laughing brown eyes, golden-brown tight curls framing a face almost too pretty to be a man's and a chaste kiss shared, before she'd heard several servants calling for Ingebord, wondering if any harm had come to her. She'd wriggled out of his arms, mumbling an excuse about needing to join in the search. They'd promised to meet the next evening in the Queen's herb garden. She'd barely slept a wink that night, hugging the encounter to her bosom.

Going to the appointed meeting place the next evening, Svanna had discovered a discarded posy of flowers which she knew had not been there before and had carefully tucked it away as a remembrance and a promise. When she'd casually asked her nurse the next day about why there were empty places at the table, she'd answered with a loud sniff that several had found reasons to travel east, leaving on the early morning tide, and she'd do well to think on that. A quick check on who had departed in such haste and she'd discovered one was Rand. Family business, someone had said, tapping their nose as if she should understand.

Unable to resist the lure, she'd returned to the appointed meeting place in Astrid's private garden to see if Rand had left anything else, even a few scratched runes, explaining why he'd left abruptly and when he expected to return.

However, amongst the flowering herbs, Turgeis, the youngest son of the King's trusted advisor, had lurked. He'd attacked her, pawing at her clothing and holding her down. She'd only escaped with her honour intact thanks to the bravery of her dog Tippi, who had come searching for her, leaping at the man with a fierce growl and taking a chunk out of his arse. He'd run off, muttering threats to her and Tippi. When she'd tried to explain the situation to her nurse, who'd appeared in the garden, her nurse exclaimed that a woman who found herself alone only had herself to blame if young warriors took advantage. After her nurse's reaction, she'd never dared to fully explain to Astrid what had happened, not even when her shouts from the reoccurring nightmares about the incident had caused Astrid to wake. Instead, she'd tried to deal with her shame and fear of being alone with any man on her own. In the first few months, she'd often take the drying posy out from her trunk to remind herself that not all men were like Turgeis and his brothers, and that had given her comfort.

Five years later, when she came across the dried posy, it crumbled at her touch. She knew then she'd been wrong to put any store by it. Her safety came through maintaining her icy demeanour and quashing any flirtation before it truly started.

Several times in the dead of night during her darkest moments, Svanna wondered if somehow she'd been spotted and the usurper had quietly suggested the departure to hasten the handsome warrior Rand on his way, but she'd rapidly dismissed that as unworthy speculation.

It failed to matter now. Rand Fullrson wouldn't remember her or the incident. She was a stranger with whom he'd exchanged a few pleasantries once upon a long time ago. And what would she have done if it had developed beyond that? But it remained the last evening before she'd understood how quickly her innocence could be taken and how few would care about what happened to her, beyond her usefulness to the Crown.

'Is that a problem?' she asked, belatedly realising that Sigmund's look had turned speculative, as if he somehow guessed the part she'd played in the events in Agthir. 'This Rand... Randolfr character is coming here at the high King's request, isn't he? Is he trouble or in trouble?'

She winced as her voice took a high-pitched sing-song aspect like it used to in Agthir when she'd been under a lot of stress and feared for her life.

Sigmund's smile turned wintry. 'I doubt he volunteered.'

She swallowed hard and managed to keep control of her voice this time. 'Why is that?'

'The last time we met, I threatened to run him through for making water drip from Maer's eyes. He seemed to take it in good part though, and has left Maer and me strictly alone.'

Svanna tilted her head to one side. It was a coincidence that Lord Sigmund knew the man, nothing more.

'Maer is blissfully happy with her new husband and baby.' She tried to banish the slight sick-to-her-stomach feeling which had become her constant companion when she'd struggled to keep up the façade of being Ingebord. She had thought the usurper's death and their arrival in Islay would make the sick feeling a thing of the past, but she'd been wrong. 'His carelessness enabled her future happiness.'

'He became entangled with one of the high king of Eire's daughters before formally breaking with Maer,' Lord Sigmund said with a cutting motion of his hand. 'She was supposedly betrothed to an elderly king but, after meeting Silver-Tongue, she would only consent to marry him and said as much at a feast. After a furious row, the high King gave in to his favourite daughter. On marriage, the high King gifted a petty kingship with substantial estates, including one of the most substantial ringforts in Eire, Donaghmoyne, to Lord Randolfr, the king's enforcer. Quite the advancement for a sell-sword who left Constantinople with only his sword and the clothes on his back.'

'Should we be expecting the high King's favourite daughter as well?' Svanna shaded her eyes. 'There appear to be only warriors in that boat.'

'She died about the time Maer returned to Agthir, from the story I heard. Childbirth. Lord Randolfr disappeared from court for a time. Last I heard of him until today.'

'What happened to the child?'

Sigmund shrugged. 'End of my interest.'

'For someone you threatened to run through, you know a lot about him and his doings,' she said mildly.

Sigmund tugged at his tunic. 'One hears things. I don't want him here, sniffing around, not when negotiations with the petty kings are at such a delicate stage. Until they swear those oaths, anything could happen.'

'What can he do? The kings will swear on your sword at the feast.'

'He will attempt to charm them and offer excuses for why they must delay while the high King ponders the notion.'

'Maybe the high King will welcome a strong overlord on Islay.'

'His great boots will trample over all the delicate work Astrid and I have done in getting my fellow kings to the table. I want it to be perfect for her sake.' Sigmund tilted his head to one side. 'You've never met Silver-Tongue, Svanna. I have.'

Svanna made sure she swallowed the truth. 'I can't see why the high King would be against it.'

'Our interests are not necessarily the same as the high King's, or indeed Rand Fullrson's. However, some of the kings prefer to think that they can provide an adequate defence, and the greater danger is from their fellows and not the Northmen in Dubh-Linn or indeed further to the North. I don't think the King of Gruinard is that ill, my dear.'

She understood everything Sigmund was saying, but her long period at the Agthir court had taught her that one should look for places where interests coincided rather than risking giving offence and creating an enemy.

Astrid had taken much time and trouble in explaining the art of peace-weaving when she'd thought that Svanna might have to impersonate Ingebord for the rest of her life, a prospect which had filled Svanna with horror, but she'd done her duty and had paid attention to the lessons.

'What are you going to do about him and his band of men? They appear to be peaceable. I thought you always offered hospitality to those who came in peace,' she said, forcing a smile. There had to be a way of making Sigmund see the sense of not alienating the Irish high King's emissary until they understood the situation in greater detail. Particularly as Maer was now happily married to the current king of Agthir.

A faint smile crossed Sigmund's craggy features. 'Me? Nothing. I will leave him to you.'

Svanna took a step backwards. She loathed speaking in such circumstances. Her voice always became sing-song with fear. 'To me?'

'You claimed capability earlier. Leave all the unexpected details to me, you told Astrid this morning. I am leaving this minor point to you. Show me what you are made of. Make your foster-mother proud.'

'What do you want if the fates decide to be kind?'

'I want him gone before the church service ends. That shouldn't be a problem for someone like you.' His gaze raked her form. She wondered if he expected her to use her feminine charm on Rand. She longed to tell him that such a thing was non-existent. Ever since that long ago flirtation with Rand, and the aftermath with the youngest son of the King's advisor, she'd tried to achieve a reputation of calculated coldness, earning her the accolade of being an Ice Princess, something she welcomed in the hope that any harassment would cease. Unfortunately, some, like Turgeis, had looked on it as a challenge, but she'd persisted in developing that shield.

'But he will want to speak to you. Surely a few well-chosen words from you will ensure that he is rapidly on his way.' Svanna held out her hands and willed him to understand. 'We can consider any request he might make. The high king of Eire could be a valuable ally.'

Sigmund frowned. 'Whatever Randolfr Fullrson wants or requires, you deny it. Understand?'

Svanna knew she'd have to draw on her training. Hear him out and then choose the best course of action, even if she had to give a bland answer about not being able to make a decision, something Astrid always advocated. 'Where shall I tell him you are?'

'The church service is about to start. I can hear the good father ringing his blasted bell of St Fillan for all it's worth.'

'You never attend church. You said that the priest was foolish to insist on everyone abandoning their weapons before they entered and you wouldn't be a party to such foolishness. You and my foster-mother argued about it.'

'First time for everything.' The old warrior turned and stomped away before she could object further.

Svanna turned her face towards the oncoming ship and watched the man leap into the surf and start up the shingle towards her. She wished her dog Tippi hadn't remained in Agthir with Maer as, even at her advanced age, Tippi made her feel braver in this sort of situation. However, she refused to fail Sigmund or Astrid. She would not allow the matchmaking scheme she'd agreed with Maer before she'd left to fall at this small stumbling block.

This was now and she was no longer a young girl, thrilled to be noticed by a beautiful boy and half-drunk on the excitement of defying the suffocating strictures of her life. The man in question would not remember the incident in the slightest.

Chapter Two

Lord Randolfr Fullrson, more commonly known as Rand the King's Enforcer at the Tara-based court of King Máel Sechnaill mac Máele Ruanaid, carefully guided his *karfi* on to the sloping shore of Sigmund Sigmundson's steading.

Using the smaller vessel, his crew had made the journey in a short time as they understood the gravity of the situation.

'He left the beach, my lord,' one of his men called out. 'The new high King of Islay seeks to insult Máel Sechnaill's representative.'

Rand frowned slightly at the petite blonde who waited on her own to greet him and his men. Like his man, he'd spotted Sigmund Sigmundson stomp away as they'd entered the harbour but, unlike his sworn warriors, Rand knew of the strife that lay between them, a rift he'd inadvertently caused, and one Máel Sechnaill was well aware of. A deliberate insult from which King?

'Do we know if Sigmund Sigmundson has received a royal helm and spectre yet?' one of his men called out.

'Looks as if it is going to happen today if the sheer number of coracles is anything to go by,' the first warrior said. 'Does this alter your calculations, Lord Randolfr?'

'It fails to alter the charge our King gave me,' Rand said,

absently fingering the vivid scar that ran from his left eye down to the corner of his mouth, a legacy of his sojourn in Agthir. 'We will make them see reason. We will make them see why they need to ally with Eire and not the North, particularly not with the Brothers Drengrson, who now control Dubh-Linn and menace Tara.'

His men gave a ragged cheer. Their belief in him should have made him feel gratified. But he knew what a difficult task it was, particularly as Thorarinn had absconded with one of the high king's illegitimate daughters—the daughter King Máel Sechnaill had intended for Lord Sigmund.

Pushing aside all thoughts of his errant cousin, Rand frowned as he studied the shoreline, trying to figure out what was occurring.

Far too many coracles littered the shore, but there were no Northern ships. Whatever was happening here, at least none of the sons of Drengr had appeared, including the malevolent brains of the family, Turgeis. Small mercies. He'd continue with the scheme he'd worked out when he'd discovered the elopement.

Rand fingered the jagged scar, which still throbbed when he was angry. 'I will prevail because I must.'

The only way to save his cousin's life was to enlist Sigmund Sigmundson to use his newfound influence over the kings of Islay and declare the island for Máel Sechnaill and Eire and not for the sons of Drengr, as disturbing rumours had reached Máel Sechnaill. To demonstrate the peaceful intent, Rand was supposed to offer up his late wife's half-sister Rhiannon to be Sigmund's wife, ensuring the bonds of kinship were strong. He had thought both his cousin and Rhiannon would be travelling with him, but they had eloped instead, a fact which was sure to anger Máel Sechnaill beyond all reason. Rand owed Thorarinn his life after he'd rescued him from Drengr and his heavies, and this was his chance to finally repay that debt.

Perhaps the old man's heart would be moved by the tale of romantic love, but Sigmund had displayed great cynicism when Rand had confessed that he'd fallen for Máel Sechnaill's favourite daughter. Earlier, Sigmund had refused him permission to formally court his niece Maer and had insisted they spend a period apart. A few years later, the niece had married and now reigned as Queen of Agthir a saga-worthy conclusion.

Nothing had happened between them except for a few stolen kisses. Nevertheless, he remained uneasy about how things had ended and, looking back, how callous he must have seemed for forgetting to formally break with her before becoming entranced by the King's daughter.

When he'd met his late wife shortly after the boat had arrived at Dubh-Linn, all other women ceased to matter, and he'd done everything he could to win her. Luckily, it had been her wish to be married to him instead of to the elderly petty king whose suit her father had favoured. They'd had a good life until she'd died from a fever she'd contracted during childbirth nearly four years ago, leaving him with a little girl whom everyone said would swiftly follow her mother. He'd refused to believe them, insisted that she would survive. When his little girl was born, everyone claimed she was dead but he'd cleared out her little mouth and hit her back. His instincts had proved correct. His daughter had gasped and let forth a loud scream. Knowing that she was dying, his wife had smiled and told him to protect their only child. He'd held to that promise ever since.

He pushed all thoughts of his dead wife away. They belonged to his old self, the one who used to smile and joke and had thought life would always be straightforward. How the fates must have laughed at his happiness, particularly as he'd thought how much he deserved it after what had happened back in Agthir.

Now, he had to ensure that his appointed task was completed. His late wife would have expected nothing less of him than to protect Rhiannon as well as serving her father, but then he'd be done. He'd return to his daughter and live quietly at Donaghmoyne, tending his cattle and ploughing his fields.

He waded ashore and walked towards the blonde woman. Despite her finely drawn features and fragile build, an air of authority clung to her. Close up, he could see that she was not in the first flush of youth. He briefly wondered whose wife she was, as he believed Sigmund Sigmundson was unmarried, and why he vaguely recognised her.

'I'm here to see Sigmund Sigmundson. King Máel Sechnaill of Tara has sent me, Lord Randolfr Fullrson of Donaghmoyne, as his emissary.'

Her rosebud mouth curved upwards. 'Unfortunately, impossible. The church service has begun. If you would like to attend, leave your weapons in my care and file in at the back of the church. The good father will seek to accommodate you if you wish to worship alongside the others, but I make no promises about Lord Sigmund speaking with you. There is a strict order to such things today as the other kings notice any and all signs of favour.'

Rand permitted a smile to cross his face and deliberately allowed his gaze to linger on her neat curves. 'You remain on the shore.'

'I'm from the North. I've no wish to cause alarm amongst the worshippers,' she answered in an increasingly lilting voice. 'Lord Sigmund and the priest agreed it would be sensible for me to greet any stragglers. Were you invited, Lord

Randolfr, or do you seek to impose yourself on the assembled throng of warriors?'

The sound pricked his memory. Rand tried to remember where he'd heard the voice before, but he couldn't quite place it. It would come to him in time. He suspected that their paths must have crossed once, even if he had no memory of it.

'The North has many kingdoms. Which one are you from?' he said, inviting her to confide her name.

'Agthir,' she said, as if that ended the matter. 'I doubt you've heard of it. Few have.'

Her tone discouraged any more questions. He kept his face blank, but his brain started to sift through all the women he'd encountered there. It would come to him and he would use the knowledge to further his aims because, whoever she'd been back then, she clearly possessed a trusted position in Sigmund's household. Her clothes were far finer than those of a simple farmer's wife and she carried herself with a dignity possessed by only those who considered themselves powerful.

'More than heard. I visited briefly about a decade ago. Perhaps we encountered each other, but I suspect I'd have remembered one such as you,' he said, forcing a small measure of incredulity into his voice which he hoped would persuade her to confess something about her role in Agthir. 'But the old King kept a good table, from what I can recall.'

'But you failed to remain for any length of time.' The singsong quality was more pronounced in her voice. 'I would have remembered your name if you had, Lord Randolfr.'

'Alas, the east called me and my cousin. Ended up in Constantinople for a time.'

'Constantinople… I believe Sigmund Sigmundson spent some time there. Did you know him then?' The full lips of the woman drew up in an insincere smile. 'Or do you know him from somewhere else?'

A formidable ice princess with no sense of humour. He'd met enough of that type over the years, populating the courts he'd visited—lovely to look at but without any fire or deep conviction beyond artifice and caprice. He pitied the woman's husband, if she had one. He swallowed hard and hoped that her husband was not Sigmund.

'We met in Constantinople but truly got to know each other on the journey to Eire. Aren't you interested in my time in Agthir? Perhaps we had friends in common.'

'I lived in Agthir my entire life until now. I doubt you could inform me of anything I don't already know.'

Obviously, a withering putdown complete with an arched brow was meant to have him stammering and scurrying away.

'I encountered the King, his family, and his advisor, Drengr.' Rand instinctively fingered the scar, which had started throbbing again. 'It was, alas, a short but instructive stay, in particular my acquaintance with Drengr.'

'The King is now dead, and his advisor Drengr, along with his family, were banished as wolf's heads after they tried to usurp the throne.' She tilted her head to one side. 'I presume you were not overly fond of him.'

'Fond of him? You mistake me, lady. I loathed him.'

'That is something, at least.'

Again, that inkling in the back of his mind that he should know the voice. Rand rubbed the back of his neck and hoped that they had not met in his misspent youth. Ever since the attack that had forced him and his cousin to flee, great holes existed in his memory of the time.

'Sigmund Sigmundson will want to speak to me. There are things the high King wishes him to know about Drengr's sons' current whereabouts and the threat they pose to the region's peace. I need to know he understands the precise nature of the threat.'

'He doesn't want to speak to you. Trust me on this. Nothing but strife for you exists here.' She inclined her head. 'Forgive me for being blunt, but it's best *you* understand the precise nature of the situation. I'm simply Lord Sigmund's messenger.'

'And you are?'

'Svanna Guthardottar, the dowager Queen of Agthir's foster-daughter.'

Rand instinctively touched the puckered scar. The dowager Queen of Agthir's foster-daughter. According to rumours, the dowager Queen had taken Maer as her foster-daughter when she'd married the late King's son. The only other daughter he'd ever heard about was the golden-haired beauty whom he'd been unjustly accused of kissing. The ice princess in front of him and the Queen's daughter were probably about the same age. Her name had been...he concentrated and dredged the name up... Ingebord. Were they the same person, or was something else going on? If so, he could use it to his advantage to get this treaty negotiated with terms which would be acceptable to his King and allow Thorarinn to keep his head on his shoulders.

But now he knew where he'd heard Svanna's voice before—during that unlamented sojourn in Agthir. Ingebord calling for her dog. Odd how his brain recalled the sound when he couldn't remember having spoken to her as she was closely guarded and sat at the top table during the feasts, but it showed how little things could become embedded. It bothered him that he should remember that voice but knew his late wife's crystal-clear tones were fading with each day.

'Svanna Guthardottar, I will bear that in mind,' he said,

inclining his head. He would reveal his knowledge of her true identity when it suited him. 'But I must insist on speaking with Sigmund Sigmundson. I am prepared to wait.'

'Lord Sigmund authorised me to speak for him.' Svanna Guthardottar spoke with great finality, as if she expected obedience without question. 'Leave in cordiality. Inform your king that Lord Sigmund has never sought war with Eire or indeed Tara. He looks forward to this peace continuing for a long while.'

'Are you his wife? Is that why you are authorized to speak for him?'

'Married? No, no.' She took a step backwards. 'He instructed me to tell you this. My foster-mother and I are visiting. Lord Sigmund and the Queen have been friends for many years.'

Rand gritted his teeth. As if he would give up that easily. This woman was about to learn a few hard truths about playing games with him. She had no standing. Unmarried? What was wrong with her if she was indeed the Queen's foster-daughter?

'It will be worth his while,' he said, making a bow and attempting to ensure his words were laced with honey. 'The high king of Eire has sent me as his emissary. What I have to say is for his ears alone.'

'I doubt that very much.'

'Why?'

'Because once a message is told, others hear. If he wanted to speak to Lord Sigmund himself, he would have travelled here, rather than sending someone like you.' Having delivered the pronouncement with a slight curl of her lip, she started to turn away. 'If the desire for a strong alliance is the only message, I fear you will be destined for disappointment.'

'What?' Rand tilted his head to one side and stared at her, incredulous at her brazen dismissal. 'You doubt my word? Why do you claim that right? Why do you think you know how the game of high politics is played? A strong alliance is in both Islay's and Tara's interests.'

'Sigmund Sigmundson will parley with the high king when the time is right and not before. They will parley as equals, Lord Sigmund will not be subservient.' She inclined her head. 'You can inform your king of that little fact if you wish, but I believe he already guessed this. He sent you on a fool's errand for reasons of his own, not to better relations between the two countries.'

'Now, having never met my king, you claim privy to his innermost thoughts.'

'I believe we are done here.' She held out her arms in dismissal. 'I wish you a pleasant return journey, Randolfr Fullrson. You are welcome to return but I cannot guarantee that Lord Sigmund will ever receive you.'

She turned on her heel and started to walk away.

He caught her arm. She gave him an ice-cold look and he slowly released his fingers.

'I made promises to the high king of Eire. I intend to keep them.'

'The promises you gave fail to concern me.'

'One of those promises was to speak with Sigmund Sigmundson personally and deliver the message for his ears alone.'

'Why should I grant this request? The high king of Eire's writ does not rule here. Nor is it ever likely to.'

'But Islay does trade with Eire. Islay wants to remain safe and at peace.' He gestured to the coracles and willed her to stop being stubborn. He would speak to Sigmund Sigmundson one way or another. 'Several petty kings in Islay, including the king of Gruinard, claim kinship to my king and would be distressed to hear how his emissary was mistreated, particularly by a member of Northern nobility. Do you wish to cause a rift within Islay, my lady the Queen's daughter? Is your position with Lord Sigmund that secure?'

She worried her bottom lip, turning it the colour of an Irish autumn dawn. She was truly lovely in a marble statue sort of way, which made her unmarried state all the more interesting. Why? What was wrong with her that no man had won her hand? Did she fancy capturing Sigmund herself? Rand was tempted to enlighten her that Sigmund had confided that he intended to remain single for the rest of his days. Apparently, his heart belonged to a woman who had betrayed him. But Rand also knew this Svanna would learn soon enough.

'Islay wishes to remain at peace,' she said at long last. 'Lord Sigmund will ensure that this happens.'

'Good to know, but you are asking the wrong question.'

Her brow knitted. 'The wrong question?'

'Not if Islay is at war with anyone, but does anyone wish to make war with Islay and Tara? And if so, will the kings require a strong commander to lead the men of Islay or will they give up without a fight, seduced by promises of golden treasure from Dubh-Linn?'

'Peaceful trade is beneficial to both Islay and Dubh-Linn,' she said, tilting her nose in the air. 'Why should it be in peril if you do not speak directly with Lord Sigmund?'

He could feel the conversation slipping away from him. Perhaps she truly did not know who was now in charge of Dubh-Linn and why they bore the new nickname the Dark-Foreigners or Dubhghaill. It had nothing to do with their appearance and everything to do with the black-hearted brother Drengrson. Turgeis had been particularly ruthless in his dealings with some of Tara's people, including a suspected poisoning of one of Rand's closest friends at court, a few months back.

He knew he had to give her part of the king's message and hope that she wasn't already aligned with the trio who had given him much trouble in recent months.

'You know about the Dark-Northmen, the ones who have taken over Dubh-Linn? The ones we call the Dubhghaill, or Dark-Foreigners. They have no love for Gaels of any sort.'

'The need for trade remains. The great whirlpool swirls to the North, making passage difficult, particularly in the winter months. Islay controls the safest route.' She sent him a condescending smile, confirming Rand's suspicion that she knew little about what had happened in Dubh-Linn and cared less. She was the sort of woman he generally loathed—ice-cold, complete with an exaggerated sense of self-importance and political acumen.

'A far more serious and ruthless threat to peace than any Northmen before.' He willed the Ice Maiden to comprehend the danger that would descend on them if they ignored this threat.

'You wish to unsettle me.' She gave a firm nod. 'Dark-Foreigners indeed. Who are they, precisely?'

'The Sons of Drengr is what they call themselves.'

She swallowed hard and put her hand to her throat. 'The three sons of Drengr?'

'The very same. Turgeis is reputed to be the brains and the other two the brawn.'

'I…we all…had assumed they had gone east to make their fortune,' she whispered.

'Obviously not.' He paused, allowing her to absorb the news. 'My king considers the news vital for Sigmund Sigmundson's prospects.'

'He does?'

Rand carefully shrugged. 'Máel Sechnaill sent me to warn him. A personal message from me, someone Sigmund once knew intimately.'

'Why don't you trust me?'

He looked her up and down, allowing his gaze to trace her curves. 'Do you expect me to answer that?'

Her cheeks flushed, proving that she was human after all. 'I suppose not, but Halfr—that is to say Sigmund Sigmundson—will be busy for a long while yet.'

The fact that she had nearly called Sigmundson by another name intrigued him. Unsettled, she had made a mistake.

He put his hands behind his back and concentrated on breathing. One mistake often led to another, and he needed an advantage, given the debacle of the elopement. 'We're in no hurry and are prepared to wait.'

'Some of the petty kings have cause to fear the Northmen.'

Rand swallowed the obvious answer, pointing out that Sigmund was from the North and had been elected high king. 'We are not asking to attend whatever feast is planned. We can wait elsewhere.'

'You could always leave. Return in a few days' time.'

He forced a smile enough to make his scar ache. 'What, and miss the chance of seeing Sigmund's grizzled face again? Particularly as you have helpfully confirmed that he has another name. Halfr the Bold, by any chance?'

She wrinkled her nose before examining the ground. 'I have heard the name used before in connection with Lord Sigmund,' she admitted quietly. 'I should not have used it, but the news about the sons of Drengr shocked me.'

'We will stay. We can camp out here or you can accommodate us somewhere suitable.' He paused before going for the jugular. 'Your choice, *Ingebord*.'

She took a step backwards and he knew he had penetrated her disguise. 'I... I... I no longer use that name. I much prefer Svanna.'

He narrowed his gaze and saw the fear she tried to mask. Not quite the impervious Ice Maiden, but a woman with secrets that needed revealing. He instinctively fingered his scar. 'Don't lie to me. We encountered each other in Agthir. Nine years ago.'

Her eyes widened and her hands played with the neckline of her gown. 'You remember me? I mean...did we?'

'You are quite memorable,' he purred, looking at her directly, willing her to believe the exaggeration. He had no memory of what had happened preceding the attack, or if they had ever conversed, but he'd never attacked a woman nor stolen a kiss from an unwilling one.

A frown puckered her forehead. 'I will find you accommodation. Given the sheer number of warriors, it will be in one of the disused buildings.'

She obviously expected him to instantly turn up his nose.

'Luckily, my men and I are remarkably unfussy and will not look upon any accommodation as an insult. Shelter is welcome.'

His men made non-committal noises. He knew they would obey him. And there were many worse places to spend a night. But Sigmund Sigmundson—or Halfr the Bold—would hear him out. He would make him understand the danger their two adopted countries now faced. Their common enemy must be stopped before it was too late.

'And you will stay there until I come for you. Whatever you want from this place, you will not get it if you fail to keep to my instructions.'

Rand made his best courtly bow. He would find a way of getting what he wanted, and save his cousin's life. And Ingebord—or Svanna, as she now called herself—was going to ensure it happened, even if she failed to realise that. He looked forward to the realisation dawning on her.

'To hear is to obey, my fair lady.'

Of all the things Svanna didn't need to happen today, the arrival of Rand Fullrson and his subsequent refusal to leave ranked up there. He required more than a polite conversation with Lord Sigmund about the threat from this new band of warriors. And, unfortunately, he'd guessed her previous identity and, what was worse, appeared to remember something of their brief encounter.

Svanna tried to concentrate on the practical problem at hand rather than allowing her mind to loop round and round. She required a place where Rand and his band would be able to lodge but be out of the way until she could quietly let the Queen know about the problem and its potential to disrupt the proceedings.

Rand, with the jagged scar down the left side of his face, did not resemble the boy who had featured in her girlish dreams all those years ago. She knew if she asked about their encounter, she risked confessing about the night, the stolen kiss on her cheek and then the sweet accidental meeting of their lips.

'This is where you want us to stay?' Rand's gaze narrowed. 'It looks to be a disused pigsty rather than a barn. Anyone would think that you don't want us to remain here, my lady. My king will not look favourably on any who refuse hospitality.'

'Everywhere else is full due to the celebrations,' she said, forcing a smile that dripped with insincerity. 'You are welcome to remain on your ship. Whichever you prefer. I'm sure your king will understand. We had no idea about your arrival.'

She waited and hoped he'd make his excuses.

He watched her with guarded eyes. 'When shall we see Sigmundson?'

'He has gone to the church. I suspect the Queen has gone with him. Arrangements will be made once I can speak with him.'

She'd noticed that the Queen had not come hurrying out of the hall as they'd made their way through the small village to the wide-eyed wonderment of some of the villagers.

It must mean that she'd gone to support Sigmund in the church. Svanna could understand her reasoning, but she'd hoped to offload the burden of accommodating Rand and his men to her.

Rand fingered his scar. 'Does he normally go to church?'

'He seeks to honour the petty kings.'

His lips turned up, making his scar move. 'And not trying to avoid me.'

'Imagination be a cruel mistress. Sigmundson believes in hospitality towards all who come in peace.'

The scar turned his frown into a fierce scowl. 'Please don't take me for a fool, my lady.'

'Why would I want to do that?' She held up the horn of mead. 'You are obviously a warrior with a formidable reputation, but I trust and hope you come in peace as you are the high king's emissary.'

She was quietly proud of her speech and thought it struck the right note, letting him know that his fearsome past as the king's enforcer failed to intimidate her.

He gestured to his men to make themselves comfortable. 'I don't care how long we must wait, my lady, but I will speak with Sigmund before I depart from this place. I will deliver my message.'

'Lord Sigmund makes his own decisions.' Svanna examined him from under her lashes and wished she could ask Maer about what had truly gone on between them. If he considered Svanna to be Ingebord in truth, then they could not have been that close. Maer had held that secret close to her chest.

'I wanted to ensure that we both understood the situation, *Ingebord*.' His voice had lowered to a low purr which slid over her skin. 'Too important for mistakes to happen.'

She ignored the hard clenching of her stomach and permitted a smile to play on her lips. 'I believe we both understand the situation, Lord Randolfr, but I must warn you I only borrowed that name for a time.'

A sudden rustling caused her to turn. The assistant swineherd stood there with an open mouth. 'Northmen everywhere.'

Svanna pinched the bridge of her nose. An excitable youth. Now her day was complete.

'All well,' she said slowly in Gaelic. 'These Northmen are with me.'

The lad's eyes widened as he took in Rand and his warriors. He stumbled back several steps. 'Not them! Northmen surround the church. With flaming torches.'

Svanna's stomach knotted. Halfr and the Queen had dismissed the warning about the additional ships as the product of an overactive imagination. What if they'd been wrong? Were they about to pay for it?

'There shouldn't be,' she said, hating the note of uncertainty which crept into her voice.

'Are they dressed in battle gear?' Rand asked in perfect Gaelic. 'Are their helms down and swords drawn?'

The boy nodded vigorously. 'Shields, helms and weapons. Gleaming axes and torches.'

Bloodcurdling shrieks rent the air. Svanna stiffened, knowing the lad spoke the truth now and had spoken the truth earlier. The wisdom of hindsight. By dismissing the earlier intelligence, disaster had arrived.

Her lungs forgot how to work for several heartbeats.

'This is crazy,' Svanna said eventually, striving for a steady voice and trying to think logically, despite the urge to gasp for air. Despite the all-consuming longing to curl into a small ball and hide like she'd done as a young girl when Agthir had fallen, letting someone else take the lead. There was no one else. 'Who would be so foolish to attack when many warriors are here?'

'Where are they now?' Rand asked. 'These warriors of yours.'

'The service is taking place, the street was quiet. Almost everyone is there or at the hall.' Svanna stuffed her hand against her mouth and tried to swallow the scream welling up inside her. 'The priest insisted they leave their weapons in storage so as not to sully the church. Lord Sigmund set several to guard the weapons, but that was purely for show.'

'Who knew this gathering was going to happen?'

'All the kings on Islay.'

'And they are all here?' Rand's voice was hard and insistent, forcing her to think. 'It is important, *Ingebord*.'

'The name is Svanna.' Svanna tried to concentrate despite the rising panic in her throat. 'All except the king from Gruinard who is ill.'

Rand nodded and put his hand on his sword. 'Your potential culprits. One or both spread rumours. Gruinard is probably how my king heard of the gathering.'

'Did you know about the attack?'

'Do you consider me foolish enough to sail into a planned attack? Or not to seek to warn you about it?' He shook his head. 'I'm many things, my lady, but risking my men in that fashion? Never.'

She stared at the harbour. Rand, irritatingly, had a point.

'Now, what are we going to do about it?' he murmured.

She blinked twice, thinking she'd misheard. 'We?'

'I'm not prepared to allow Sigmund to be slaughtered before I can speak with him, particularly as I suspect we share a common enemy.' He bowed slightly. 'My men and I are at your disposal, my lady.'

The tension in Svanna's neck eased slightly. The gods were being kind, for once. She wasn't entirely alone. She had a band of warriors and, working together, they might be able to tip the balance back in Halfr's favour. She silently prayed that the Queen was all right.

'Go to the church and see if we can free the warriors.'

He tilted his head to one side, his long lashes hiding his eyes. 'We can try, but is there a secret way out? I know the church on my estate in Eire has hidden passages in case of difficulty. Funnily enough, men do not always fear God.'

'A secret way?' Svanna put a hand to her now-pounding head and tried to think. It sounded like something Sigmund would do, or instruct the priest to do. 'I've no idea. The Queen and I haven't been here long. We never go to the church. But I suspect she may be there to support Lord Sigmund, or I hope she is.'

She hated how her voice trembled on the last word.

Rather than replying, Rand hunkered down to look the assistant swineherd in the eye. 'Do you know if the priest can escape?'

The lad's eyes widened at being addressed in Gaelic by a Northern warrior, but he gave a hesitant nod. 'His altar boy is my best mate. He showed me the secret way in a month ago. We used it to play tricks on the priest only last week. The priest doesn't know we know, but we were fooling around and discovered it.'

Rand clapped him on the back. 'What all lads do.'

The knots in her stomach eased. Sigmund and the others were not necessarily caught in a trap, provided the attackers had no idea of where the escape route led.

'Am I going to get in trouble?' the lad asked.

'Not at all.' Svanna forced a bright smile. 'If you help Lord Randolfr, you might get a reward. I'll make sure of it.'

The lad's eyes shone. 'My lady.'

Rand rapidly gave orders to his men. Several of them were to follow the lad to where he thought the priest might emerge, while the rest would help him secure what weapons he could.

Her jaw stopped hurting. He had thought as she did and had acted how she'd hoped. He had divided his force, but she hoped the men would be enough to ensure a successful escape.

'You said the Queen might not be with Sigmund. Where else could she be?'

'Do you think they are looking for her?'

He shrugged. 'It would be embarrassing, and the new King of Agthir might be annoyed if the former Queen became a captive. If I were organising such a raid, I'd look for high status women.'

'My foster-mother was going to the hall. I've no idea if she decided to join Lord Sigmund at the service or not,' she said. 'What should I do? My status is unimportant.'

'I've no idea what you are worth to the invaders, my lady. But any woman captive fetches a price at market.' He lifted a brow. 'I presume you will want to hide.'

Said with a slight curl of his lip as if she was the sort to scurry away and leave everything to the warriors. After the fall of Agthir, she'd vowed never to be defenceless again and had begged Astrid for instruction in the arts of battle.

'I can fight.' She crossed her arms and dared him to say differently. 'Long ago, the Queen ensured that I could play my part in resisting any invasion.'

His gaze raked her up and down and seemed to linger on her curves. 'I welcome all those who can use a weapon, but you don't appear dressed for war.'

She gritted her teeth. 'Greeting guests in battle armour might have been off-putting.'

He laughed, a rusty sort of laugh as if he hadn't had much recent practice in such things, but it was a rich laugh, pleasant to the ear. 'Don't blame me if you encounter trouble.'

'I know where the weapons are stored, particularly the large quantity of arrows,' she said, rolling her eyes. 'Please will you try and rescue my…the Queen first?'

He put a hand on her shoulder. The impersonal touch caused a warm pulse to go through her. 'I would be delighted to have your help in securing more weapons.'

'Delighted to have yours.'

He gave a crooked smile and held out his hand. 'The beginning of a friendship?'

'I prefer friends to enemies,' she said, repeating one of the Queen's favourite sayings.

She grasped his hand and shook it.

'Funnily enough, I do too.' He nodded to the remaining men and gestured to the rising plume of smoke. 'Shall we move before the situation gets any worse?'

She rolled her eyes 'What? If I had taken you straight to Lord Sigmund, then these warriors would not have attacked? I deal with realities, not fantasy.'

'You are the one who said that. I merely suggest that Sigmund might have taken more care. Perhaps posted a few more guards. Who knows? I dwell in the realm of facts, not speculation.'

She wrapped her arms about her middle and willed her voice to sound normal and not become high-pitched. 'As long as we save my foster-mother, then I will be content.'

Chapter Three

When they reached the harbour, Rand surveyed the swiftly burning buildings that were the former hall of Sigmundson and the church and swore under his breath. Flames appeared to be coming out of the church's roof, but the hall was where most of the raiders were concentrated, beating their swords against their shields and taunting the people trapped inside both the church and the hall.

The sole purpose of their mission appeared to be to burn people alive. Rand tightened his jaw. He refused to understand how anyone could wish to do such a thing. It pained him that most were from the North, although he was aware that Gaels could also behave without pity.

The number of the raiders failed to alter his hastily formed plan. In fact, they were fewer than he'd initially feared. Further indication, if he required it, that this was a raid meant to discredit Sigmundson and to serve as a warning, rather than an open declaration of war.

He narrowed his gaze, surveying the scene, particularly the well-blocked doors of the hall and sheer number of warriors poised to capture whoever emerged. Who was the real target? Sigmund or someone else, including Agthir's dowager Queen? Whoever was behind this had calculated Sigmund was unlikely to be in the church.

In his years as the high king's chief enforcer, he'd learned to keep an open mind on how assassins behaved. Caution, rather than jumping to premature conclusions.

He needed to focus on the task at hand, namely vanquishing the raiders or giving them a reason not to remain for any length of time and taking as few prisoners as possible in their departure. He'd done this sort of thing countless times for the high king—ensuring any raiding Northmen died or departed was part of the price the high king had demanded for giving permission for him to marry the king's daughter.

He pulled his heavy leather gloves on, settled his helm more squarely, and unsheathed his sword. He surveyed the battlefield for a final time. The attack obviously had been meticulously planned, but the planning had not accounted for him and his men.

'What happens next?' Svanna asked, putting a hand on his arm.

'What do you mean?'

'I presume you're not just going to stand watching those Northmen with your sword raised. I presume you will act to distract them and allow the people to be rescued. Strategy is all.'

Despite the sing-song quality, her words were sensible. Most women, including his late wife, would be openly weeping. He winced slightly at the disloyal thought and then pushed it away.

'Watch.'

He signalled his men to give their battle cry, which they roared out and allowed to echo. As he'd hoped, his other men heard it where they were trying to free the people trapped in the church and answered in kind. His men joined in, and the air reverberated to the sound.

At the combined roars of the full-throated battle cry, the

raiders glanced at each other and started to run, presumably back towards where their boats were waiting. He motioned for half of his remaining men to follow.

'Impressed, my lady?'

She rolled her eyes and crossed her arms. 'They're running? Forgive me if I doubt your assessment, but nothing is that easy.'

'It was planned,' Rand said, knowing that she needed to understand before they went any further. 'In and out. They're not going to stick around and fight, having delivered their message and wrecked Sigmund's coronation. They came to sow doubt. They want the surviving petty kings to slip away in the night, disillusioned.'

'I hope you're right about the not-sticking-around part.' She tilted her head to one side. 'But all they have done is to make me more determined to resist them. Lord Sigmund will feel the same. We will not cower in fear.'

He could tell from the way her nostrils quivered that she was very frightened, but she kept that fear under control. Most women would be gibbering wrecks when confronted with such chaos, but Svanna seemed to be forged from hard tempered steel. A useful ally at a time like this.

'What would be the point? They must have assumed that some warriors will escape from the burning church. They want to send a message. To do that, they need those kings alive. No, the real test will come in a few weeks, after they have destroyed any show of unity.'

'What sort of message? To whom?'

'That's what we need to find out.' He gestured to the warriors who were now rapidly leaving the scene of their crime. 'Did you recognise any? Any at all?'

She shaded her eyes with a hand, then stiffened and shrank back. Her face drained to whiter than fresh milk.

'Turgeis, Drengr's youngest son leads. I recognise his shield. He is waving at them to hurry. Wait. He's stopped. He's saluted me. Why me? It is almost like he knew Queen Astrid and I were on Islay. How did he know we were on Islay?'

'You're both from Agthir.' He nodded with grim satisfaction. 'He wants his message taken back to the new King and Queen. He wants them to know the sons of Drengr have returned to power and will seek vengeance.'

She put a hand on her throat. 'Returned to power? What is next for Agthir? For this battle?'

'Those men of mine will follow them and hurry them on their way, but there is little point in engaging them in a pitched battle. Máel Sechnaill will deal with them soon enough.'

Genuine fear shone on her face. 'Was the church their true target? Or a feint because Turgeis wanted to harm the Dowager?'

'As you said—how would they know?'

'I'll bear that in mind.' Her lips turned up in a little smile.

A small curl of attraction grew within him at her continued bravery. He dampened it down. It was not the time for such things when he had this delicate mission to complete.

'Now, shall we go rescue your mother?'

'To risk repeating myself—the Queen has been my foster-mother for many years, never my actual mother. The difference and explanation is there, if you care to see it.'

He inwardly rolled his eyes. He'd little time for game-playing, particularly at a time like this. A foster-mother in the North had much the same responsibility as a birth-mother. 'But you will not deny you are normally called Ingebord in Agthir?'

'We can discuss this fantasy of yours later, but right now we must ensure people are safe, including the former Queen of Agthir, a woman who did not give birth to me.' Svanna strode off towards the blazing hall.

Rand stared in confusion at the woman. With his salute, Turgeis had obviously indicated that Svanna was the dowager Queen's daughter, but she swore she was not. He'd normally leave it, except something deep inside told him that the truth was somehow linked to the mysterious beating he'd received at the hands of Turgeis's father back in Agthir. Figure out the mystery and he could finally uncover who had set him up.

She glanced towards him. 'Are you coming? Or must I do this myself?'

'We will find her, Svanna,' he said and internally added that he hoped she was alive, maybe even in the church or escaping through the tunnel, but he doubted anyone could survive that inferno. He hated to think about what they would uncover when it cooled. To even attempt a rescue would require a special sort of madness and disregard for personal safety. But he refused to deny her even the smallest shred of hope.

A smile trembled on her lips. 'I'll hold you to that.'

'You do that, because it is one promise I intend to keep.'

It seemed to take a lifetime for the barriers to be removed from the hall's doors. With every breath Svanna took, she hoped that she'd see the Queen marching alongside Halfr, having escaped from the church, but each time her lungs emptied, the conviction that the Queen was trapped in the hall grew. And that somehow the sons of Drengr were bent on exacting revenge for their father's exile and ignominious death.

A shiver went down Svanna's spine. She'd nearly been sick when she saw Turgeis Drengrson. Where he was, his two brutish brothers lurked. She hated to think what would happen to any woman they captured. Only her dog Tippi and then her nurse's timely appearance in the herb garden had saved her from Turgeis's violent embrace that day after Rand vanished.

Ever after Turgeis had occasionally muttered what he intended to do to her once the world went his way, appearing to enjoy her discomfort.

Svanna tightened her fists until her knuckles turned white, trying to beat the panicked thoughts back down inside her. Collapsing in a heap of fear over his mocking salute would be wrong when she had to find a way to avert a greater disaster. But right now, she had to allow the men to clear the heavy debris from the doors and break them down.

When the doors were freed and finally flung open, several people stumbled out, dishevelled and gasping. But none of them was Astrid.

'Where is she? Where is the Queen?' Svanna asked, grasping the nearest servant's arm. 'At the church?'

The man was coughing too much and shaking his head but managed to raise a trembling arm back towards where he'd come.

'In the hall?'

He nodded, tears coursing down his cheeks.

'No!' Svanna heard the cry and knew it had come from her throat. She also knew that her foster-mother was probably severely injured or dead, or she'd have stumbled out with the rest. A faint hope remained if someone was prepared to search.

She couldn't ask anyone else to do it either. It had to be her. She owed Astrid her life for all the years Astrid had protected her, first taking her under her wing after Svanna's mother died and then doing her best to keep them both safe while the usurper ruled.

Without giving herself time to hesitate, she plunged in.

The fire smouldered on the roof, throwing an eerie orange glow on the walls, but the smoke-filled hall remained relatively intact. Svanna dipped a handkerchief in a jar of ale and put it over her face to give some relief from the searing heat.

She scanned the hall and spotted the Queen's prone figure. A heavy table had been knocked over and the whetstone for saying the oaths had fallen on top of that, pinning Astrid to the ground.

'We must get you out of here.' She tugged at the heavy oaken table, but it refused to budge even a little fraction.

She shook Astrid, willing her to wake up.

Astrid's eyes opened. 'Svanna? Not safe… Go now…'

'You're alive. Thank the gods.'

'Stuck. We tried…everyone. Save yourself. Go.' Astrid pointed with her finger. 'Now.'

'Save your spit.' She tore off her mask. 'Put this over your mouth and breathe. It might help. I'll return. Hang on.'

Out in the cool air, she shaded her eyes, looking for help. Still no Sigmund. She had no idea what she would say to Maer if both had perished. She spotted Rand supervising a bucket brigade while he waited for news.

She rushed over and grabbed his arm. 'You must help me now.'

Rand frowned at the interruption. 'What is going on?'

'My foster-mother is in there. Alive. Her leg is trapped under a table. I can't get it to move.' Her voice gave a little hiccup and she blinked rapidly, stuffing the fear down deep inside her. 'We only have a little time. If we're going to stop this disaster becoming worse, she must be saved. Send someone. Anyone.'

He tilted his head. 'One condition.'

'If I can give it, it is yours. My foster-mother must live.'

'One single kiss.' He gave a crooked smile, captured her chin between his forefinger and thumb and brushed his lips against hers.

A jolt went through her. She was tempted to touch her mouth but she kept her hands firmly away. 'What did you do that for?'

'Made a vow years ago when I escaped Agthir that if the chance ever arose, I'd kiss the Queen's daughter. My mind is at rest. Finally. I'd have remembered something like that. Nothing ever happened between us.' He put a hand on her shoulder. 'Remain here, *Ingebord*.'

She shook her head. After that unexpected meeting of mouths, dogged determination replaced the blind panic which had engulfed her after Turgeis's salute. 'Absolutely not. She requires me. I said I'd return.'

He sighed and signalled to someone behind her before fastening on a mask. 'I won't try to stop you then, but I make no promises about your safety.'

'I'm not asking for any.'

He nodded and plunged through the door. She shook off one of his men's restraining hand and summoned her fiercest glare. The warrior retreated several steps.

Grabbing the closet bucket from a servant, she doused her apron with water and plunged into the building. The fierce intensity of the heat made her face burn and her throat hurt. She lifted the wet apron over her nose and mouth. With each heartbeat, she knew the rescue of Astrid was slipping away from her.

She forced her burning eyes open and breathed through

the apron. The entire room glowed in an eerie light, but nothing else had fallen in the short time that she'd been gone. Rand gave her a brief nod.

Astrid lay still, her lower leg trapped under the table, but her eyes were open. Her lips turned up into a tired smile when Svanna approached.

'If we move this whetstone even a little, we can pull her out,' Rand said, beckoning her over. 'A two-person task.'

'If you lift, I pull,' Svanna replied, dropping the apron from her face. 'We don't have time to get anyone else.'

'Deal.'

He put his shoulder to the heavy stone. 'One, two, three.'

It crashed to the ground with a thump. The entire hall shook. The oak beams started to creak and snap.

A renewed surge of urgency shot through Svanna. 'The roof is going to come crashing down!'

Astrid groaned and turned her head in weary acceptance of the inevitable. 'Svanna… Tell Ingebord that I love her. Go.'

'You will be able to tell her yourself. Now, save your breath. Rand and I will rescue you.'

Rand lifted a brow. 'You are not Ingebord?'

She smiled back at him and indicated that he should move the table. She grasped Astrid's leg. 'One, two three. One last try.'

He lifted the heavy table and this time she was able to pull the leg free.

'Done. Let's go'

Rand let the table drop with a thud. Svanna attempted to raise Astrid to her feet but her leg buckled under her.

'I can't walk, Svanna. Leave me.'

'Never fear.' With one movement, he picked up Astrid and tossed her over his shoulder. 'Let's go. All of us. Now.'

They rushed towards the door, Svanna allowing Rand and Astrid to go before her. Her heart eased slightly when she saw them out. 'All will be well.'

Behind her a beam crashed down, catching her gown. Her scream echoed.

Rand's hand grasped hers. 'Come now.'

She pulled hard and heard the gown tear.

'I liked that gown,' she said, keeping focused on the small things rather than giving into the wave of panic which threatened to overwhelm her.

'Gowns can be replaced.' His fingers held hers. 'Now.'

Together they plunged through the open door. Behind them, further beams crashed down, covering them in a shower of sparks. Rand's men threw water over them.

'Not going to go into any more burning buildings today, are we?' Rand asked.

She dropped his hand. 'All good.'

'Excellent.' He patted her back. 'You recover, and I'll make sure your *mother* gets medical attention.'

Rather than correcting him, Svanna put her hands on her knees and filled her lungs with cooling air. Astrid had a chance, which was all that mattered. She had to hope that Sigmund had also survived, but the wreckage of his dreams was clear in the smouldering buildings.

'Where is Astrid?' Sigmund called, rushing up to the smouldering remains of the hall. 'Where is my darling? Was she in there? Or has she been captured? Is she alive?'

'She is there...safe,' she said in a croaking voice which sounded dimly like her own.

Svanna nodded to where Rand stood over Astrid's prone body. Sigmund went over to her and gathered her in his arms, murmuring over and over that he'd put her in danger and he planned to devote the remainder of his life to her. Astrid weakly smiled and told him not to make promises he'd break, but he needed to thank the warrior who had saved her—Lord Randolfr Fullrson.

Sigmund's eyes bulged. 'Is this true, Svanna?'

'He went into the burning building and rescued her. A table had fallen on her leg.' Svanna kept quiet about her part in the rescue. 'Just as well I disobeyed your direct order and allowed him to stay.'

Sigmund bowed his head. 'I believe I owe you a life debt, Rand the Silver-Tongue. You predicted such a thing would happen when we last parted. I regret I failed to believe you.'

Rand bowed his head. 'The only boon I ask is that you listen to the words from my king in due course. And perhaps find favour with his suggestion. I did come to warn you that an attack is imminent.'

'Why is that?'

'I too owe life debts, Halfr the Bold, and we now share a common enemy—the so-called Sons of Drengr. They seek to destroy you and the former Queen of Agthir.'

Sigmund gave a half-smile. 'How convenient for both of us that you now know my birth-name, but those men are elsewhere.'

'Turgeis Drengrson led the raiding party,' Svanna said in a quiet tone, willing him to listen instead of picking a fight with Rand. 'Rand had nothing to do with this.'

'How do you know this? Because Silver-Tongue told you?'

'No, because I witnessed Turgeis supervising the barricading of the hall. He saluted me as if he wanted me to take a warning back to Agthir. Back to Maer. The sons of Drengr will have vengeance.' She pressed her hands against her ruined gown and bade the trembling of her limbs to go.

'A few more heartbeats and we would not have been able to enter in time to save my foster-mother.'

Svanna was pleased her voice sounded loud and she had not given into the paralysing fear. She knew tonight her recurring dream would have a new twist—being trapped in a burning building while Turgeis gloated. She silently resolved to keep from sleeping for as long as possible.

'Are you sure it was him? Astrid claimed he and his brothers had gone east after their father was rightly convicted of treason.'

She crossed her arms over the wet apron, aware that the wind moulded the dress against her bare legs. 'I'm not bloody likely to forget his face after the torments he inflicted on me.'

Rand raised a brow, but Sigmund nodded. 'Drengr was ever cruel. I suspect his sons are worse.'

'I never liked them.' Svanna wrapped her arms about her middle. 'I tried to stay well away from them and not give them any opportunity.'

'Silver-Tongue came to warn me of this attack? Why did you not run immediately to the church?'

'No one knew it would happen today,' Rand said. 'My king simply had concerns and asked me to parley.'

'When I require your opinion, I will ask for it. If Svanna knew it could be the sons of Drengr, her first duty should have been to alert me, rather than carrying on a conversation with you.'

'You discounted the swineherd's fears. Until I saw him, I too would have discounted Turgeis and his brothers as culprits, but I speak the truth.' She summoned her last ounce of strength and forced her backbone to straighten, refusing to cower even though she wanted to sink to her knees and scream at the unfairness of his words. 'You do me a grave disservice when you fail to trust my word.'

After what seemed a lifetime, Sigmund pressed his lips together and nodded. 'I see. Your enemy is indeed my enemy, Silver-Tongue. The battle is joined. You may inform your king of the fact.'

Rand made an ironic bow. 'May it be the start of a productive friendship, Sigmund Sigmundson. Friendship between Islay and Tara is all I desire.'

'We will talk after things settle. I will listen to what sort of friendship your king desires.' Sigmund bestowed Svanna a look which seemed to ask for forgiveness. 'When I am wrong, I do admit fault, Svanna. You were right to allow the warrior to stay. You averted disaster today.'

Ignoring Rand's curious gaze at the bubble of laughter which emerged as the relief at being believed surged through her, Svanna swallowed hard and forced her voice to remain even. 'I'm pleased you think that way.'

Svanna rested her head against her hand and stared at the embers of the hall as a distinct weariness settled over her bones. She knew she should find some place to curl up and sleep but she couldn't, not yet, not until she knew the Queen had survived the night. She still had much to do, including finding another clean gown as the one she'd changed into had become covered in soot smudges and ash, but she couldn't abandon her place, waiting and watching in case she was needed, in case Astrid called for her.

She'd lost track of time long before the last fire had burned down to embers and ash. All she knew was that Astrid was safely being attended to now and resting. The priest had said that her quick thinking had saved her foster-mother's life. She hung on to that and studiously avoided looking at the smouldering wreck which had been the hall, and which had nearly been her tomb had Rand not pulled her to safety.

She peered at the night-black sky, hoping for the faint streaks of dawn while listening out for the first cockerel crow, anything to tell her that she and Astrid had survived the night.

A cold chill went down her spine and she wrapped her arms around herself. She hated to think how many times she'd waited for the cockerel to crow, telling her that she'd survived another day. She had thought all that had ended after Drengr and his sons were declared wolf heads and exiled, but now, with the return of Turgeis, she knew safety was an illusion. Somehow, she had to figure out a way to ensure Astrid's safety, and indeed that of all Agthir, from whatever the sons of Drengr had planned. Because of Astrid's injuries, and the time it would take to reach Agthir to consult with Maer, all the hard decisions had to be hers. Maer would back her, but she needed to find a solution which worked.

'Drink this.' Rand settled his bulk next to her and held out a steaming goblet. In the dim light from the embers' glow, she saw his eyes crinkling reassuringly at the corners. She hated that her breath came easier knowing he was here and had been willing to rush into a burning building on her say-so. He appeared to believe in her when others like Sigmund discounted her worth.

She tilted her head to one side and deliberately wrinkled her nose. 'What is it?'

'A calming draught. The priest gave it to me when I asked.' He waggled the drink, sending a cloud of steam skyward. 'I thought you might need something to help your throat. Luckily, the priest knew precisely the remedy I sought.'

She touched her neck and was suddenly aware of how it and her face burned. She suspected that she might have even singed her hair. 'My throat? Nothing wrong with it.'

Her voice sounded more like a frog croaking than her usual tones.

'Are you so busy looking after the Queen that you forget to look after yourself?' He tilted his head to one side and watched her under impossibly long lashes. 'Do that often?'

'I… It is more complicated than that,' she mumbled, hating that he'd guessed. Now that she considered it, her throat did ache. 'I will take whatever the priest gave you. His potions work, unlike the soothsayer's back in Agthir.'

'The Queen would want you to ensure your health,' he said in a gentle tone.

Rather than argue with him, Svanna took the cup from him and carefully took a sip. The bitter liquid mixed with some honey did taste good against her fire-parched throat. She swallowed the remainder in one great gulp and then wiped her hand across her mouth. The soothing balm filled her, warming her.

'Do I look so unsettled?' she asked. She hated that she wished she looked fresh and sparkling, instead of smoke-smelling and in need of a good wash.

His fingers caught a strand of her hair, wrapped it and then let it go. 'You've been through much, but you remain outside, awake and alert.'

She hated that his voice made her want to lean into him and draw comfort from him. There must have been something in that potion. 'Other people have been through more. I'm waiting my turn. My main duty is to ensure the Queen's safety.'

He caught her chin between his forefinger and thumb. His eyes loomed large. And she knew her heart beat faster. She could almost taste his mouth. 'I can take the watch now.'

She instinctively wet her lips. 'Take the watch?' Her voice sounded more smoke-infused than before.

His hand released her chin. 'It is what you have been doing, waiting and watching in case you are needed. Go get cleaned up. I will fetch you if there is any news. You deserve that. You did enough today.'

Her eyes pricked from tiredness and relief. He'd noticed that her demeanour of self-reliance was a façade. She hadn't expected that, particularly not from him. Astrid and Maer seemed to think she was indestructible. She tried to appear that way. It was how her mother had been until she fell ill. But she always knew deep inside that she wanted someone to understand without her having to put it into words.

'Why?'

'If not for your quick thinking, catastrophe. You believed that lad. You took a chance on my men. And me. That took raw courage.'

'What?' She tried for a laugh but it came out strangled. A coughing fit racked her frame. 'Asking for your help? Hardly brave.'

'Accepting my help and going in to rescue your...mother the instant the door was unblocked. Such daughterly devotion.'

Svanna put the empty cup down. After what he'd done and the vow he'd supposedly made to kiss the Queen's daughter, he deserved the full truth about what had happened all those years ago in Agthir.

'My foster-mother rescued me once. I owe her a great debt.'

He tilted his head to one side. 'But…you do not deny being called Ingebord, the Queen's daughter, in Agthir?'

'I understand you and Maer were close once,' she said, trying another way.

His brows drew together. 'A shipboard flirtation which fizzled out, in part because of Sigmund's disapproval.'

'Sorry to be the bearer of bad news, but you obviously were not that close. You didn't know the most important thing about her. I suspect you fulfilled that vow of kissing Ingebord years ago without realising it. She prefers the name Maer now, but she was born Ingebord.'

His mouth open and shut several times as the realisation of Maer's true identity washed over him. She felt almost sorry for him as he tried and failed to speak.

'Maer is the Queen's daughter?' he finally spluttered out. 'I heard the saga which tells of how the King stayed his hand because of Ingebord's plea. I saw her—you—at a distance a long time ago. Maer, my Maer, had brown hair, not golden. The girl in the story had golden hair.'

'You finally have it. The usurper had sworn to kill her. I was merely the companion, the chosen friend. The Queen had me impersonate Ingebord because she wanted her daughter to escape. Afterwards, telling the truth would have resulted in my death. I owe her my life many times over.' A huge weight rolled off her shoulders to finally give voice to the truth. 'Luckily, not many people had seen Maer. The *skald* thought the line about the golden hair was the perfect sentimental touch to the usurper's saga.'

He nodded. 'The continued deception meant the Queen kept you both alive.'

'Hard to guess who had the easier part. Maer travelled the wide world while I concentrated on never putting a foot wrong or making an accidental slip which could expose the entire scheme.'

He stared at her for a long time. 'Why are you telling me this?'

'Because it no longer matters, or it shouldn't. But after what you did today, I thought you deserved to know, particularly as we share a common enemy.' Everything swam in front of her and a bone-aching tiredness swept over her. She knew she couldn't get up, even though staying here next to him was a poor idea. 'You can stop feeling any sense of misplaced guilt over the way you treated Maer, if that is what you are feeling. The fact that she never told her heart's secret speaks volumes to me about the nature of your relationship.'

'Are you normally this blunt?'

She put a hand on her forehead. 'I'm not usually this forthright, but you earned the right to know.'

'I've found our conversation most intriguing.'

She struggled to stand but abruptly sat back down. 'My legs feel like they are made of liquid. Whatever the priest gave you must have been strong stuff.'

'Close your eyes.' He put his cloak about her. 'I'll keep watch, Svanna the Steadfast, and will wake you should the situation alter.'

'Kind…' Her eyes fluttered shut as warmth seeped into her bones. He believed her and it seemed to count for something, but she knew she could not confess the true reason for her terror of Turgeis and what he would do to her if he could. Her nurse had implied that she bore much of the blame and if Rand thought so as well, she knew that the faint flickering of hope would die. Some demons she faced on her own.

Rand settled himself down to keep watch. The sleeping draught had worked well on the woman who had once been a princess. All the saints and angels knew she required it after what she had done for Astrid.

In the dim light he watched the smudges her long lashes made against her soot-grimed skin. He shuddered to think what she must have been through, posing as the Queen's true daughter and knowing that it could easily come undone. It also made it far more unlikely that she'd had anything to do with setting Drengr on him all those years ago.

'Maer hid things from me. My arrogance knew no bounds back then,' he murmured. 'Sigmund said she was far wiser than I realised. He was right.'

Svanna said nothing in return. He put another cloak over her. She sighed and settled against him.

In the faint grey light of the early dawn she seemed an odd combination of inner strength and fragile beauty. He'd been wrong before. She was not some Ice Maiden but a woman who guarded secrets well and controlled her emotions.

Looking at her generous mouth, sensations he'd long considered dead stirred within him. Some instinct had made him turn back and witness her difficulty. In that heartbeat he'd known that he wanted to live for himself instead of merely existing for his child, a feeling he'd not had since his wife had died. He briefly wondered what his daughter Birdie would think of Svanna, but then dismissed it. The pair were unlikely ever to meet as Birdie lived with her nurse in his ringfort, the most secure place in the kingdom to his mind, and he'd promised her mother that he'd keep her safe.

Giving in to impulse, he smoothed a tendril of hair from her forehead. 'Who else knows, I wonder? I never heard a rumour, so I suspect it remains a closely guarded secret. But, knowing how Agthir works, I suspect there is some logic to it.'

She mumbled something indistinct.

'Have Turgeis and his brothers guessed?' he asked, fingering his suddenly throbbing scar. 'Doubtful. Are they going to try and attack the soft underbelly of Agthir through you and your foster-mother? It gives me something to work with if they are.'

She murmured a few vague words about a garden which he did not understand.

He thought back to the mission the King had given him about ensuring the two kingdoms were united through kinship, a plan his cousin's elopement with the intended bride had scuppered. But now three kingdoms were involved. Perhaps there was a way through the problem after all—an alliance between the three—but how?

He was grateful that most of the kinder and better part of him had been buried with his wife, with that tiny particle remaining for Birdie. It made it much easier to decide what he needed to do next. Somehow, he had to find a way to use Svanna to ensure Sigmund entered into an alliance acceptable to his high king. He would use any means necessary to ensure his daughter continued to be protected.

'Next time I will succeed. It may be a long time coming but there will be retribution for what Drengr and his sons did before I die,' he vowed, settling his arm about her thin shoulders and gently pulling her head more firmly against his chest.

She raised her hand in her sleep and snuggled closer, instinctively trusting him.

'I made this vow back in Agthir and I mean to see it through. Many times, that vow has been the only thing keeping me alive.'

Chapter Four

When Svanna struggled to consciousness Rand's arm was about her shoulders, her head pressed against his chest and her right hand splayed perilously close to his groin. The steady thump of his heart thrummed in her ears. The intimacy startled her as it closely followed her confused dreams.

It worried her that she had sought out his warmth in that way. She had never been one for such things, not after what happened in the garden that time with Turgeis. Every time she encountered a flirtatious man she froze, remembering how Turgeis had remarked on what he intended to do to any rival. She guessed that her nurse would call it 'boastful young warrior talk' and tell her to avoid him if she complained. But she'd always known that there was more to it than mere boasting.

She immediately drew back her hand and sat up. His arm fell away. She concentrated on straightening her gown and hoping he didn't think she had somehow taken liberties.

'I'm sorry. I didn't mean to…' She swallowed hard and tried again. 'I only planned to rest my eyes for an instant. Now the sun has risen on another day. The servants are beginning to stir.'

She silently prayed to the Norns that no one had noticed her intimate entwining with Rand. Maer had given her a lecture about how strict the priest was before she'd departed from Agthir. She'd not had the heart to explain that after what she'd endured, she doubted anything like that would happen. That attack had taken so much from her, including the ability to trust any man. Although she loved children, she doubted that she'd have any because to do so would involve an intimacy which made her deeply uncomfortable.

She risked a glance upwards into his face.

In the cold light of an Islay dawn, his lips turned up. 'Easier than having you fall backwards. And an honour, truly, after your heroics of yesterday.'

'Heroics? Hardly that. My love for my foster-mother compelled me to go in.'

'Your queen is lucky to have one such as you. I've served in the high king's bodyguard. Very few would have gone into a burning building to search for him.' He dipped his head. 'Your devotion to duty is beyond compare.'

His words flowed over her like honey fresh from the comb. Too often, Astrid and Sigmund seemed to take her devotion as a given, rarely offering her any praise or indeed thanking her for the risks she undertook. Lately, she had started to wonder if Astrid saw her as a tool to be used, rather than as a person she cared for, and she hated feeling that way because, deep down, she wanted to believe Astrid did care for her.

She wet her parched lips and tried to dispel the images from her dream of a warrior enveloping her in his arms to kiss her thoroughly. She needed to think clearly, not dwell on something which wouldn't happen, and the last thing she wanted to bring up was the kiss he'd bestowed. 'A compliment, I think.'

An unexpected twinkle showed in his eye. 'Definitely.'

With nerveless thumbs, she undid the cloak and handed

it to him. 'I thank you for the loan of this. I hope it doesn't stink too much of smoke.'

'No news,' he said, putting the cloak on his knees. 'I'd have woken you if there was.'

'Then my foster-mother lives another day. Good.' She rubbed a hand against her temple. She started to rise and wished she hadn't when the world gently spun. She blinked and it righted itself again. 'I should change, or she will worry.'

'I'll wait until you return and take any message.'

She hurried off before she was tempted to stay, his soft laughter echoing behind her.

Rand watched her backside sway as she went. He shook his head, amazed at the bubble of laughter which had burst from his lips. An inner glow infused her this morning. He'd enjoyed holding a flesh and blood woman in his arms far more than he'd thought he would.

When she'd looked up at him with that sleep-soft mouth, he'd nearly lowered his lips to hers. In full view of everyone. He should feel remorse, but instead felt gloriously alive, as if he'd been asleep for a very long time. Svanna the substitute daughter would provide the key for him to keep both his cousin and Birdie safe. But he was under no illusions of what would happen to his little girl if he lost the King's favour in this manner.

'Do you think you will be able to do what we came for?' one of his men asked, sidling up to him. 'Do you think you can deliver the kinship alliance our King requires? Can you bind Islay to Eire with the fair Rhiannon?'

'Patience.' The high king had been very specific about what he wanted—his illegitimate daughter Rhiannon married to Lord Sigmund to bind Islay. Thorarinn's elopement with the woman had scuppered that, and returning to Máel Sechnaill empty-handed was likely to result in Máel Sechnaill losing his temper and stripping everything from him. He refused to do that to Birdie. 'I am doing what is right.'

'But that woman, is she the one who caused your scar? The golden-haired daughter of the Queen of Agthir.'

'What do you know about that?'

'Your cousin told me the tale one night when we were tossing the dice. He figured she must have been passing her favours about, and you were chosen to be the example.' His helmsman rubbed his jaw. 'Odd, that. She seemed like an Ice Maiden to me, not at all like a woman who readily opened her legs like Thorarinn claimed.'

Rand bit back an unaccustomed surge of anger. The man had no business discussing Svanna in that overly familiar fashion. The anger surprised him. He knew his late wife would have given a tired smile, like the one she'd given before she died and whispered, *'I told you.'*

She'd made him promise that one day he'd find another woman, a promise he'd reluctantly given and had little intention of keeping as *one day* had not happened yet. However, that mythical woman was not Svanna, even if his body had been uncomfortably aware of hers when she'd slept curled up into his side.

'Thorarinn ought to know to keep his mouth shut.'

The man laughed. 'One trick he'll never learn, particularly not when he is gambling.'

'She was the excuse for, but not the cause of my beating. We'd never met before you and I arrived here. I've little idea about the state of her virtue and neither have you,' Rand said, fixing him with a hard stare. Thorarinn had tried many times to give up the gambling. He'd sworn he'd do so after Rand had received his wound, then again when they'd escaped from Constantinople, and Rand had begun to hope that it was true. But he should have known better. Thorarinn struggled against the lure of the dice. 'We share a common enemy in Turgeis.'

The man nodded, accepting Rand's word. 'When we first arrived, I was willing to swear that she must be related to an Ice Giant, such was her control,' the man said, shaking his head. 'But I was wrong. A magnificent passion exists in her. The way she tore away from me when she went into that hall after you. Such bravery.' He sobered. 'But you know what is at stake if you don't give the King what he requires.'

'I will face our king when necessary and not before,' Rand said, and prayed that his gamble about a verbal alliance and exchange of rings would be enough to temper the high king's anger. Not every strong alliance had to be one of kinship. His king was aware of that, even if it was not his preferred method of ensuring loyalty.

'Is there some reason why you are hanging around outside here?' Sigmund said, coming out of the hospital area and glaring at him. 'Our countries are now friends, and we will discuss what that means when the time is ripe and not before.'

'I told Svanna that I'd keep watch until she returns. She worries about the Queen.'

The older man crossed his arms. 'Svanna is under my protection.'

'I will not dishonour her. I buried much with my wife.' Even to his ears, his words sounded feeble. Sigmund must have heard about the kiss he'd given Svanna. Rand didn't regret what had passed between them. The temptation to beg another kiss had threatened to overwhelm him earlier. 'The kiss we shared before I rescued Astrid had to do with a vow I made back in Agthir.'

'You kissed her before you went into the hall?' Sigmund made a rude noise. 'It is a problem with you—you never consider implications. Maer's heartbreak…'

'Tell me, have you thought about the Queen's honour?' Rand asked, before Sigmund launched into another diatribe about Maer. 'Everyone saw you gather her to you.'

'If I didn't owe you a life debt, I'd run you through. Whatever happens between Astrid and me is none of your business.'

'After what happened yesterday, you must surely see that we share a common enemy—Turgeis and his brothers. Ask Svanna who she saw yesterday, who saluted with a smirk and why they concentrated on blocking the hall instead of the church.'

Sigmund stroked his chin for a long time. 'Astrid says I get tetchy when I'm overtired.'

'We will speak when you have rested.'

The wash and another change of clothes helped restore Svanna's equilibrium. She felt better dressed in her favourite blue gown with the box brooches which had belonged to her mother fastened on the front.

'Here I find you,' Rand said, advancing towards her at speed. The sunlight turned his hair to a golden infused cloud. 'I have been searching high and low for you.'

She was pleased that her hair was tightly under her *couvre-chef*, her face clean and the apron correctly pinned to her gown. 'Is something amiss, Lord Randolfr? Has my foster-mother called for me?'

'Rand, please. We are now friends, Svanna, after what we have been through.' He tilted his head to one side. 'Or are you going to deny it?'

She dipped her head slightly, carefully trying to preserve

her hard-won poise, but the warmth of his tone sent ripples down her spine. She silently cursed. There were many good reasons why she should not be attracted to this man, starting with what had happened back in Agthir and ending with the problems currently facing Halfr. 'Rand, then. Is something amiss with my foster-mother?'

'The Queen rests comfortably. The priest asked me to tell you that he wants you to visit this afternoon and not before.'

The muscles in her neck eased. She sent a silent prayer of thanksgiving to any god who might be listening. 'Is there anything else I should know?'

'Any remaining king will swear fidelity to Sigmund later today. Sigmund has set a work party to making a platform.' He frowned. 'But how many will remain is unclear.'

She bowed her head. Rand had given voice to one of her fears—Astrid's scheme was unravelling quickly.

'How many have left?'

'Three that I noticed, but Sigmund believes they'll return in time. Little by little.' He gave a smile. 'Your swineherd does like a good gossip.'

'Has Sigmund properly thanked you for your timely intervention?'

He laughed. 'Sigmund has stopped threatening to run me through. I take progress where I can.'

'What you wanted…' she said carefully, willing him to confide so that she could find a solution to what she considered to be the growing peril. If she could do this, then maybe Astrid would finally acknowledge that she was capable of contributing more than simply her decade of pretence. She hated that disloyal thought, but it lingered in her mind. 'What I think you came here for was his friendship.'

'Yes, I suppose.'

'Only suppose?' She tilted her head. Something was

wrong. She needed to figure out a way to make it right. She knew of the huge debt she and Astrid owed him. What good was mouthing words about life debts if one was not prepared to follow through? 'What else does your king require from you?'

'You were right—Maer and I must not have been as close as I feared,' he said quietly, altering the subject. 'You have given me greater comfort than you can imagine with that simple observation.'

She examined her hands rather than meeting his serious gaze. 'None of my business what passed between you two. It was wrong of me to bring up the past, but I couldn't think of any other way to make my point. Blame it on the smoke and the confusion.'

He shrugged. 'It happened, though. Although I loved my wife dearly from the first instant I spied her, I knew deep down I'd behaved badly towards Maer in allowing her to find out the way she did about my relationship with Bridget. I should have explained before she confronted me, despite Sigmund telling her to stay away.'

Rand in this mood was easy to like. Svanna reminded her heart of the promises she'd made while she washed—that she would not become attached to him, that she would not be attracted to him, and that she would maintain a friendly distance—because if she allowed herself to be attracted, she might start believing that those old dreams might have some basis in fact. Perhaps it was an overreaction due to her girlish fantasies. Or perhaps a reaction to her brush with death in the hall. Rand was a man with the same sort of appetites as Turgeis, but a growing piece of her heart kept screaming that she was wrong, and Rand could offer more.

'If it makes you feel any better, I doubt he'd have approved of any man Maer was attracted to,' she said to keep her errant thoughts under control. 'He is not overly fond of her husband either. Swears Karn can be headstrong and stubborn.'

'Did Maer make a good match?'

She pressed her hands together and concentrated on the waves. Confessing that she envied the relationship Maer shared with Karn would be inappropriate. She had thought him shallow before he'd returned with Maer, but the love and friendship Maer had with Karn was something she doubted she'd ever experience. 'They're well-matched. Agthir prospers under their joint rule.'

'I met my late wife and fell harder than I ever thought possible,' he said, continuing as if she'd kept silent. 'She was unlike anyone I'd ever met. Our souls called out to each other and everyone else faded. I should have broken with Maer straight away, instead of having her discover us in an intimate embrace. I'm pleased she found someone better.'

A tight knot formed in Svanna's stomach. He'd forgotten the girl he'd flirted with that long-ago night. She had been next to nothing to him. She should have allowed the memory to crumble away like the flowers had. And she knew she could never mention it, or why that long-ago encounter meant that even today she found comfort in his company. Ultimately, the love of his life was his late wife, and she meant nothing to him.

'How did your wife perish?' she asked. 'If you don't mind speaking of her.'

She quickly glanced at him and saw that his scar stood out purple on his ruined face.

'The birth was hard. No one thought our little girl would live more than a few days, despite my intervention of clearing her mouth and getting her to breathe. Then Bridget caught a fever and things became much worse.' His voice had a slightly hard edge to it and bleakness filled his eyes. 'As Bridget lay dying, I cried out to the saints and all the angels to take me instead, but they laughed at me and took her.'

'I'm sorry.'

'My life is better for Bridget having been in it.' The way he stood as if he expected to parry a blow tugged at her heartstrings. 'But my world became a truly bleak place without her.'

'What happened to the baby? Did she live?' she said, knowing she shouldn't ask about his daughter. She needed to keep her distance from his life because there was no future for them, but all she could think of was the motherless little girl and how she should have someone to look after her. She dismissed the notion as fanciful.

She should make an excuse and leave, but her feet refused to move. The desire to reach out her hand and touch him in sympathy grew within her, but she suspected that he didn't want that from her.

'She didn't travel with you.'

'Birdie is all I have left of my late wife and the happiness we once shared.'

'Pretty name.'

'Short for Bridget.'

'What's she like?'

'A fighter. My determination to ensure her safety has only grown with time.' He shrugged. 'My daughter lives quietly at Donaghmoyne, rather than being exposed to the rough and tumble of court life, which my late wife grew to hate. I see her when I can. Unfortunately, my king keeps assigning me tasks which take me away from her. She weeps when I go, but I've no choice.'

She stared back at the bay, now bathed in the clear morning light. A light breeze made white crest ripples on the surface. Her heart ached for the little girl who cried when her father had to do the king's business. She knew what it was like to be motherless. She remembered when her father had remarried and her stepmother made it clear that she considered her an unnecessary burden. Only when Astrid required a companion for her daughter did she begin to feel safe, but that feeling of being unwanted and a burden had never truly left her. She always felt one step away from being cast aside if she failed to prove her worth or live up to Astrid's expectations.

'Hopefully, you will get to see her soon.'

'My day is always brighter when I do, but I've promises to keep before I can.'

She watched the small wavelets in the bay. The farmyard was truly awake and full of sound as they started to clear it after the attack, but she and Rand were alone, down by the water's edge.

'Why are you telling me this?' she asked, keeping her gaze firmly on the waves. 'Not to bare your soul to a friendly stranger, surely, or to seek advice about whether you should have your daughter with you.'

'Why do you want to know?'

'Some purpose exists beyond a tale to pass this late summer's morn. I think I deserve an honest answer.'

'Because you must know the full truth about me before we go any further.'

She quickly turned towards him. His eyes had taken on a deep intensity. 'Any further? Why?'

'I wanted to do this.' He cupped her face between his hands. 'To thank you for reminding me that I still live, rather than simply to have kissed the Queen of Agthir's daughter as I once vowed I would before I died.'

'My secret held. You did fulfil your vow,' she whispered,

watching his mouth loom and knowing she should step away, but equally knowing a part of her wanted her to stay and taste his lips again. For some reason, he could break through the defences she'd carefully erected after Turgeis, and that intrigued and horrified her in equal measure. 'I apologise if anything was done to you to avenge my honour. I'd never have asked anyone to do such a thing.'

She clamped her mouth shut before the sorry tale spilled out. His old vow demonstrated that he blamed her in some measure for what had happened to him back on Agthir. She wondered if his jagged scar dated from then. She'd never been able to determine who had told Drengr or his sons that she had consorted with Rand, but she doubted that would bring any consolation to Rand, who had suffered greatly for the forgotten flirtation.

'I know that now,' he said with his lips no more than a breath away. 'It makes you intriguing. What you did for Queen Astrid and her daughter goes beyond simple duty.'

She wet her lips. Her entire being wanted to feel his mouth move on hers. She wanted to see if what she'd experienced earlier was real or if she'd simply imagined her intense reaction to him. 'If you say so. I just wanted to prove my value.'

'I do.' His mouth lowered and captured hers.

Unlike the brief kiss earlier, this one lingered and deepened, moved over her lips and gently persuaded. Warmth entwined itself about her insides. She lifted a hand to his neck and kept his mouth firmly against hers. Far too soon, it ended. He stepped away, watching her with solemn eyes.

She wrapped her arms about her waist rather than exploring her aching mouth. The longing for him to say something grew, because she knew she'd find it difficult to say anything comprehensible.

She concentrated on filling her lungs, and the way a pebble pressed against the tip of her boot. The kiss had been a gentle, seeking not demanding balm. She, unfortunately, knew the difference. But the warning in his earlier words resounded in her head. He was not offering her anything beyond that solitary kiss.

'As long as you breathe, you live,' she said, pleased her voice remained steady rather than lilting up and down like it always did when she was nervous. 'If you have any doubts, simply ask any passer-by, but the fact that you have enough air to ask the question gives the answer, rather than trying to take a kiss off a woman, even one like me.'

He captured her hand and squeezed before letting go. 'Thank you.'

'For what?'

He tilted his head. 'For your matter-of-factness. No stars in your eyes. No maiden blushing and trembling. It's more refreshing than you might realise.'

'Do women often have stars in their eyes around you? Interesting.'

'Some have, but you don't.'

She turned her concentration back to the waves, watching them pound ever harder against the rocky shore as the tide rolled in. Answering that bald statement without confessing about their Agthir flirtation was next to impossible.

'Why did you tell me about your family?' she asked instead.

'It's important for you to know.' His hand pushed the hair back from her forehead. 'I don't want to keep things hidden from you, Svanna. I'm not making promises I can't keep, but you did something I thought impossible—you made me feel alive again.'

'Why should I expect anything from a simple kiss?' A

tight ball of hurt curled inside her. That unnoticed hope withered—that somehow something of the boy she'd once flirted with remained within him and he'd remember the kiss which had so many echoes to this one. He'd kissed other women like that. She wasn't special to him. The sooner she accepted that, the better.

He raised a brow. 'Some women might.'

'A handshake would have done if you had wanted to thank me.' She snapped her fingers. 'Already forgotten.'

His shoulders shook with suppressed laughter. 'Practical to your fingertips.'

She shifted uneasily. She knew she'd turn the kiss over in her memory and bring it out again and again, as she had done a long time ago, but that was a problem for later. Right now, she accepted that the kiss went a long way towards erasing the memory of the intrusive pawing she'd received from the youngest son of Drengr in the garden that day. Spotting him during the battle had brought it all back and contributed to why she'd found it difficult to sleep last night.

'Being practical saves heartache later,' she said with an arch laugh, aware her voice had reverted to sing-song. 'As you are no longer attempting to keep secrets from me, can you explain why you are here? You are not here to renew an old friendship. You are here to forge new alliances, but how, and what hasn't Lord Sigmund given you that you require?'

His scar stood out on his cheek. 'The high king wishes an alliance with Sigmund, particularly now that he will command over-lordship on this island.'

'An odd choice, given your shared history with Sigmund.'

'He sent me because I am one of the trusted few who can speak both Norse and Gaelic.' He drew his brows together. 'He is serious about an alliance. He believes neither Islay nor Tara will prosper as long as Turgeis and his brothers rampage, encouraging the worst excesses.'

Svanna drew on years of practice and ensured that her face betrayed none of her inner thoughts. Most alliances were strengthened through the bonds of marriage. Sigmund was unmarried. The high king knew this. Who was the high king offering and why wasn't she here? Why was Rand seeking to conceal her identity? What was this unknown woman to him? Why was he risking so much to protect her? And what would happen to him and his daughter when the high king inevitably found out?

'You came on your own without a peace-weaver,' she said carefully. 'Knowing that Maer had married and Sigmund has no other female relations, but he himself is resolutely unwed. Why did she fail to travel with you?'

The scar burned again. 'Unfortunate for all concerned.'

'The high king must assume this female relation travelled with you as, from what I know of him, he is not a man to accept soothing words about unfortunate circumstances. He must know Sigmund is unlikely to agree to a marriage without first laying his eyes on the intended bride. It is common knowledge that Sigmund has already refused several offers from various petty kings. The excuse he gives is that he is too old and set in his ways ever to take a bride.'

The silence between them stretched until the morning sun highlighted Rand's unblemished cheek. Svanna forced her tongue to the roof of her mouth to keep silent. Astrid held that filling the air with noise when you wanted to discover something meant you'd discover nothing, but equally a woman should always appear as if the silence did not disconcert her. And this missing peace-weaver was the key to ensuring the current situation did not spin widely out of control. Her entire being tingled. If she could solve this conundrum, she could save the situation and rescue the match between Astrid and Sigmund.

'As far as I know, my king remains in ignorance about where his daughter is,' he admitted with a long sigh.

'His daughter?' Svanna assessed him from under her lashes, trying to remember that scrap of gossip Sigmund had divulged earlier. 'Didn't you marry one of his daughters when she refused to wed the elderly king her father had chosen?'

Another long silence. 'Obviously. We were in love. Bridget convinced her father that I was the better man for her.'

She swallowed hard and tried to make sense of what he was not telling her. 'I take it that the king thinks you travelled with this daughter. Furthermore, you've not secreted her for yourself because your heart is buried with your wife, but you know where she is.'

He rubbed the back of his neck. 'My cousin Thorarinn knows.'

Svanna could not hide her astonishment at the recklessness of the behaviour, which now threatened to endanger many lives including, she suspected, Rand's daughter. 'Your cousin ran away with the woman the king intended in kinship alliance? Was that wise of him? Or indeed her?'

'My cousin possesses a romantic soul. She was way too young for Lord Sigmund. Some might even say she is too young for my cousin, but she preferred him above all others,' he said as if that explained everything.

'A romantic soul? Something you no longer possess but did once, which is why you defied a powerful king and married your late wife,' she continued, despite his scowl. 'Did you encourage this folly?'

'My king might think I did,' he said in a low voice. 'Sometimes what appears to be the truth matters to him.'

'Why didn't you remind her of her duty to her king and country?' Her breath caught as the enormity of his confession washed over her. Rand was attempting to put things right and present the king with a scheme which would be acceptable. If he lost the king's favour, she had no doubt there would be severe consequences for him and his daughter. 'You didn't know. They kept it hidden from you until it was too late. Now you are trying to retrieve the situation.'

He absently fingered his scar. 'I owe my cousin more life debts than I care to count. Whether or not he was wise to do what he did remains to be seen. Sigmund could have refused the offer and all would have been well. Rhiannon was wrong to panic.'

'But she did panic.'

'She and my cousin fell in love.'

'Was your cousin with you in Agthir?' she asked as a faint memory surfaced. Her nurse had indicated that two men had left suddenly when she'd enquired after Rand.

'He tried to halt the beating I received from Drengr and his sons. They would have pummelled me to death. Thanks to his quick thinking about jumping aboard that ship though, I survived. Recovering except the scar.'

Her stomach knotted. Who had observed the fateful encounter between her and Rand and then informed Drengr? Probably immaterial now. However, she knew that confessing any of the past was beyond her because he would surely blame her.

'How do you think you will solve this? Any idea?'

He put his hands behind his back and stared out at the water. 'Sigmund must agree to an alliance. I will provide surety in some fashion. I will make up the rest. No point in borrowing trouble.'

'But your king will only be satisfied if there is a kinship to bind the countries together.'

The instant the words tumbled from her throat, she knew there was a way through this for him, and a way for her to show that her future could have more meaning than simply being the companion who had once served an important purpose but was now no longer truly required. She could even be a mother, like she'd dreamt of. So many possibilities if she dared give voice to what must be the obvious solution. She clenched her fists and tried to hold back the fatal words which could alter her life.

His scar stood out more vividly than ever in the dawn light. 'Aye, my lady, but—'

She felt like she had as a young girl when she'd heard Tippi crying from the other side of her hiding place and knew she couldn't stay hidden, even with Agthir burning all around her. She had to make a move. And she could argue from a position of strength because she suspected he intended something similar.

A marriage of convenience would mean she could avoid the terrors of the marriage bed. She suspected he'd agree to it if she put it in vague terms because his heart belonged to his late wife. It could be why he'd explained about his late wife before kissing her.

Going forward is better than going backwards. A saying from when she was a little girl, and its truth echoed in her brain. And Rand was not like Turgeis. She knew that from the way her body reacted to him, even if that was going to have no part in any marriage. The more she considered it, the more the idea appealed to her.

'I offer myself as a peace-weaver in this unknown's stead.'

Her words hung in the morning stillness.

Rand's mouth dropped open. 'You? A peace-weaver? Between Islay and Tara? Or Lord Sigmund and you?'

'Islay, Tara and Agthir.' She braided her fingers together. 'All woven together with bonds of kinship and a determination to prevent Turgeis and his brothers from succeeding. Your king would desire that, wouldn't he?'

'My king believes in the binding bonds of kinship.'

'I assumed that was what you were angling for with your praise of my practicality.' She forced a smile but her insides knotted tighter than ever. She hated being manipulated, but she also knew she had something to bargain with. She could set terms for any marriage. 'Stealing a kiss which any could view. By Freya, I should have seen the half-hearted seduction for what it was.'

He blinked several times. 'My king has no need of a wife.'

'But you are the king's blood by your former marriage.' She crossed her arms and dared him to say differently. 'Or are you telling me that you have not considered this point? You're many things, Randolfr, but I doubt you're a fool. Don't treat me as one either. You require a mother for your daughter. Two birds, one stone.'

'My late wife even mentioned the possibility as she lay dying but…the time never felt right. Birdie has me.'

'It will solve your conundrum though. Let's not play any undignified games with stolen kisses.' She held out her hand. 'Will you accept my offer of marriage, because I shan't make it a second time? You must see it is the best way to secure your daughter's future.'

His fingers hovered over hers for several long heartbeats

while his eyes appeared to bore into her soul. His smile turned wintry. 'A political alliance only?'

'Your heart remains with your wife. I wouldn't dream of intruding,' she whispered, giving the barest of nods.

His fingers finally curled around hers. 'Shall we inform Sigmund of the scheme and get his verdict?'

'Allow me to do it,' she said, trying to ignore the pounding of her heart. 'My foster-mother needs to hear of the proposal from me first.'

He watched her mouth. She licked her parched lips, but he made no move to take her into his arms. Her heart ached. She'd guessed right. His kiss had been an attempt to manipulate her into a marriage. A lesser woman might have fallen for the honey-sweet words.

'My cousin and his wife will be grateful.'

'And you?'

He bowed his head. 'Marriage to you is one answer to the problem I had not considered, but it makes more sense than any other option.'

'Sometimes the Norns twist our life threads in mysterious ways.'

'You do have a way of putting things, Svanna.'

Her stomach hurt like it had after the usurper declared he was sparing both Astrid and her life because, as her daughter, she had begged prettily. Back then, she hadn't intended to impersonate Ingebord; it had just happened. This time, she was certain she could control events and the marriage would be the sort she wished, one based on practicality and not attraction.

She wrapped her arms about her waist and watched his retreating figure. Only after he disappeared did she realise that he had not actually agreed to her proposal.

Chapter Five

'You are going to do what?' the Queen croaked from where she lay in the makeshift hospital, when Svanna confessed what she had done late that afternoon. 'Have you lost your mind? Svanna, you are taking an unacceptable risk. You barely know the man. Halfr mentioned the way he treated Maer.'

Despite her injuries, her voice had lost none of its intensity. Svanna concentrated on straightening the furs that covered the Queen, rather than answering straight away. The heavy scent of incense combined with the dust from the dried herbs hanging from the rafters clogged Svanna's mouth and nose, making it difficult to think straight, but she knew she had to get this encounter right.

'It makes the most sense for everyone concerned if I marry Lord Randolfr. Something more tangible for him than simply exchanging arm rings with Halfr to demonstrate the alliance will be respected.' She forced her voice to sound matter-of-fact, even though her heart hammered. Her scheme had to work. Once Turgeis realised she belonged to Rand and Tara, they would leave her and, more importantly, Islay alone. That salute that Turgeis had given as he left still sent chills down her spine.

'Where is the wisdom?' The Queen stared up at the rafters rather than fixing her with her gaze. Svanna took it as a hopeful sign. 'What will it accomplish? How will it help Halfr or me?'

'Someone must make the hard decisions, including how to stem the exodus of kings before they swear the oath of allegiance. I refuse to allow all your hard work these past few months to go to waste.' She balled her fists until they ached, trying to control a sudden rush of anger. 'Particularly as Turgeis is involved. I suffered much at their hands. I refuse to allow their power to grow until they threaten Agthir again.'

She stopped her words before she spilled out more of her secret. It was the closest she'd come towards explaining what had happened to her that day and why she feared Turgeis.

The Queen made a clicking noise at the back of her throat and shook her head. 'Svanna, I know they made you uncomfortable back in Agthir, but you can be impulsive. It will be a long time before they can threaten Agthir. Trust Karn and Maer to protect our country.'

'They believe Turgeis and his brothers to be in the east. Agthir will be in peril if I…if we fail to act.'

'What do you know of Lord Randolfr? Lord Sigmund has his reservations about the man. He refused to meet him before the attack.'

'Lord Randolfr rushed into a burning building to save your life.'

Astrid's lips curved upwards. 'There is that.'

Svanna leant forward. 'We must strengthen alliances and quickly or Halfr will lose everything he has worked so hard to build here,' she said, forcing a bright smile. 'Three of the petty kings have slipped away before the morning's tide turned, preferring to return to their halls without swearing obedience to Halfr.'

The Queen put her hand over Svanna's. 'But marriage for you? I promised Maer that I wouldn't allow you to be used as a political counter ever again. You have gone through too much, my dear. Maer is right about that.'

'Not your choice, but mine. Maer will understand the difference.' Svanna sat up and hugged herself. 'Tell her that if she asks, won't you?'

'What are you not telling me? I can hear you trying to hide things from me, Svanna. Did he seduce you? Were you caught in flagrante? At your age and with your status, no one in the North will think less of you, Svanna. Only on Islay are they closed minded about such things. Return to Agthir straight away if you fear gossip.'

'Seduce me?' Svanna's mind skittered around the second lingering kiss they'd shared and how she had wanted it to continue. 'He has done nothing to dishonour me.'

Astrid's gaze seemed to pierce her soul. Svanna forced her head to remain high. Eventually Astrid sighed and closed her eyes. Svanna allowed her body to relax.

'Whose idea was this?' Astrid asked, not opening her eyes. 'Please tell me it was the Northman's and not yours.'

'My idea. I refuse to allow Turgeis to threaten Agthir or Islay ever again. We need to act while there is time.' Svanna tried not to think about seeing Turgeis leading the attack and how he'd saluted her. If he'd had his way, she'd now be one of the Disappeared. She knew that and knew what would have happened to her in the process. There would have been no intervention from Tippi or anyone else. He'd finish what he'd begun all those years ago.

A shiver went down her back as she remembered the way he'd used to whisper about how he was going to use her body once she belonged to him, whenever he thought no one could overhear him. And she'd never complained to

Astrid because she'd suspected Astrid would have endorsed her nurse's view that Svanna bore the blame for going off on her own.

'My dear brave girl. What did your nurse and I create? We wanted to keep you safe from them, but this?'

'Halfr must bind Tara and its high king to him if he wishes to stop these attacks,' she said instead, putting it in terms Astrid would find harder to object to. Marriage to Rand would ensure she finally had some measure of permanent protection from Turgeis. And she could be the right sort of stepmother for that little girl, one who would look after her interests, and not simply treat her as a leftover from an earlier relationship like her own stepmother had done until Astrid had stepped in with her offer. But she doubted that Astrid would see those reasons as valid. 'More than ever. It will strengthen his hand with any reluctant petty king. I know how hard you and Halfr worked.'

Astrid made a cat's paw with her hand. 'Those kings need Halfr, his sword arm and his eye for strategy. They do not want to become vassals of the Northmen.'

'Maybe, maybe not. Someone collaborated. Someone knew when the church service would begin. Two kings failed to attend.'

'Suddenly we need a kinship alliance with Tara to ensure their loyalty? Please, Svanna, it might be so, but Randolfr made Maer unhappy. She discovered him entwined with another woman.'

'The woman who became his wife. Maer and Rand had a flirtation. She laughed about it to me, even if I wasn't aware of his name. She married Karn and they are very happy.'

'How do you have kinship with Islay? Remind me again.'

Svanna returned the sceptical look with a steady one.

'Technically, you are my foster-mother and, under Gaelic law, it makes us kin.'

Colour infused Astrid's cheeks. Her good hand plucked the fur which covered her, sending it slithering to the rush-covered floor. Svanna bent to retrieve it.

'He hasn't formally asked.' The Queen's words were barely a whisper. 'I doubt he ever will. Unlikely to. He may need…a peace-weaver, someone who can give him an heir.'

'You do him a disservice.' Svanna tucked the fur more firmly about Astrid. 'He maintained a vigil beside your bed, shooing me away.'

Astrid's eyes widened. 'He did? I treated him badly when Agthir fell, you must understand. I couldn't make any other decision for my country or my daughter. For both my girls.'

'Marriage between you two is something both Maer and I desire.' She gave Astrid a hard look.

Astrid struggled to sit up. 'Are you proposing this marriage of convenience for my benefit?'

Svanna clasped her hands together until her knuckles shone white. 'Rand is correct—an alliance with Tara will help in the present circumstances and the high king demands a kinship alliance. Only a fool would deny that.'

'But you as a counter again? I thought you wanted to leave that behind.'

'My choice is to be useful instead of merely existing.' And she would be useful. She'd have a chance to have her own household and to raise a child, but she didn't dare admit such dreams aloud when Astrid was so ill.

A single tear trickled down Astrid's cheek. She wiped it away, muttering about potions. Svanna struggled to think of the last time Astrid had openly wept.

'The smoke was stronger yesterday than you might

think,' Svanna said, handing her a clean cloth to wipe her eyes. 'My eyes have been streaming off and on ever since.'

Astrid's lips turned up into a watery smile. 'This Randolfr who saved my life. The one you say you will be marrying. Do you like him rather than tolerating him?'

Svanna carefully rearranged the fur. Astrid was coming around to her way of thinking. 'You live, thanks to him. The life debt needs to be repaid. He requires a kinship alliance to satisfy his king. The calculation is that simple. But yes, I believe we can forge a productive partnership. As you did with the late king Thorfi and the king before that.'

Astrid made a cat's paw again and batted the remark away. 'We are speaking of you, Svanna, not my compromises. You've spent a lifetime doing others' bidding, including mine. Your mother wanted more for you than fetching and carrying for someone like me.'

'Rand understands the necessity of a political marriage. He buried his heart with his wife, but he has a daughter who must need a mother. I can be that mother.'

'I'm fond of you, Svanna. I, too, know what a political marriage entails. The loneliness can eat into your soul. My first marriage could be hard. Harder than my second one.'

'Maer is the rash one. Always I pride myself on being sensible and taking a long view. Feelings of mutual regard can develop with time and effort.' Internally, her heart screamed that she was settling too easily for far too little, but she silenced it. Love was far too expensive a commodity and she'd settled for a friendship of sorts. With Rand's heart buried, he would agree to her suggestion to make the marriage platonic. It would satisfy both their purposes.

Astrid's nearly bloodless lips turned up. 'The stories we tell ourselves when we are afraid to face the truth. Even you—no, especially you, my dear. Remember I didn't raise you to be a coward.'

'We will speak later.' Svanna forced her feet to turn and walk away. The one thing she wasn't was rash. She knew what it was like to live a lie, where every heartbeat offered the possibility of betrayal. She'd learned to dart about like a salmon in a river, seeking to evade the hook, flashing colour here and there but always turning at the final instant. She'd accepted long ago that love and passion happened to other people, people like Maer, not sensible people like her. She considered passion untrustworthy, and she had no expectations of that from Rand. Right now, she'd settle for a purpose, even if the purpose was raising another woman's daughter while assisting in ensuring her own country's security. Lacking in romance maybe, but worthy in its way.

After speaking briefly to the priest, she went out of the hospital and filled her lungs with fresh air. Even in the short time she'd been in with the Queen, things had altered.

The charred remains of the hall were being dismantled. In the square, a small platform for this afternoon's ceremony was rapidly being erected. It was amazing how much could be accomplished in such a short span of time if people were properly directed.

An ever-dwindling number of petty kings and their entourages stood gossiping in small huddles. She suspected that they would stay until after the ceremony, but probably no longer than that. She made a point of lingering briefly near each group.

Their faith in Sigmund's invincibility was badly shaken, or that was what she seemed to make out from the unguarded snippets she overheard.

The kings made the error that she could not understand Gaelic and forgot to guard their tongues while she was in earshot. She might not be able to speak it very well, but she could understand far more than she let on. Keeping her ears pricked for any more gossip, she made her way slowly towards the kitchens to ensure that enough food remained for everyone. All the little tasks that ensured no one had cause to complain about the hospitality on offer and use that as an excuse to depart.

If this chance slipped away from Sigmund, she suspected much would change and there would be no need for a political marriage for her.

'Did you speak to Queen Astrid? Does she approve of your scheme?' Rand asked from where he lounged against the wall in the hazy sunlight when she emerged from the kitchen.

The midday sun caught his forearms, making them dappled in gold. Despite her promises, the warm place in her middle began to curl about her. She hastily averted her eyes and tried not to think how strong they had felt around her when she'd woken up this morning.

Theirs was to be a marriage of political necessity, not one of carnal lust, she reminded that little insistent voice in the back of her mind. Despite their lingering kiss, he wasn't interested in such things, not with her. Her value lay in the kinship alliance she brought, rather than in lust or burgeoning affection. It was the subtext of the discussion they'd had about his late wife. And he did need a mother for his little girl. She knew she could take Astrid's foster-mothering as a guide and improve on it. Ensuring he understood precisely what was on offer was her immediate task.

'The Queen and I conversed at length. Given time, I think she will make a full recovery. That priest's ability to heal almost makes me want to believe in their Christian God.'

'I became a Christian when I married my late wife. Miracles are possible.' His smile tugged at his scar. 'I simply don't believe every single miracle that I hear of.'

'Must I become one as well?'

'Forced conversions are counterproductive.'

'I do what is necessary to protect my country, Rand.'

'Somehow, I think you mean that. Tell me, when was the last time you did something which wasn't your duty, Svanna? Something for Svanna Guthardottar and not Agthir.'

'I washed my hair.'

He threw back his head and laughed. A great booming laugh. Svanna concentrated on keeping her face carefully blank but as the laugh continued, her mouth twitched upwards. Eventually, he wiped tears from his eyes. 'Washed your hair. Very good. But you know what I meant.'

Under the intensity of his gaze, Svanna immediately became aware of the imperfections in her dress and the way her hair escaped from its *couvre-chef.* She tried to keep her hands from automatically adjusting it. It should make no difference what he thought of her appearance, but somehow it did. She could not confess that kissing him in the way she had earlier had nothing to do with her duty.

'My foster-mother understands the necessity of repaying a life debt.' She fought to keep her voice steady and not lapse into a nervous sing-song lilt. 'She allows me to use my judgement on marriage. I can be of value to you personally as well. Your little girl must long for a mother and I know how to run a household.'

Rand's mouth turned down. 'Leave Birdie out of this. I will protect my daughter my own way.'

Svanna lifted her chin and refused to crumple. She would find a way to assist that little girl. 'Agthir can't risk Turgeis becoming powerful. He bears a significant grudge. A kinship alliance makes political sense.'

'I can't fault your logic of why a marriage is required. I hate that it solves many of my problems.' His smile again tugged at his scar. 'In my experience, women are seldom logical, particularly where matters of the heart might be involved.'

'Romantic notions belong to women like your missing peace-weaver.' She put her tongue to the roof of her mouth to prevent the words *and your late wife* from slipping out.

He inclined his head and his expression turned inscrutable. 'We must keep my cousin and his bride out of the tale. One day, they will face the high king and explain themselves, but until then they should play no further part.'

She fluttered her lashes. 'You intend to tell the high king some pretty tale about you and me? How else will you explain the woman's absence from court?'

A muscle jumped in his jaw. 'Unfortunately, I know the reasoning, but I dislike women being manipulated.'

'I made the offer. My choice—or should I be denied that right?' She tilted her head to one side. 'Maybe you doubt that your king will believe you. Is there some reason why he thinks you will never marry and will suspect you have tried to trick him?'

He watched her with hard eyes. 'He knows I loved his daughter.'

'And therefore, you would never fall for me?' She forced the words from her throat.

'I believe I can spin a tale with the best of them.' His gaze travelled slowly down her form. 'The high king is not so old that he fails to understand basic instincts, even from a battered warrior like me.'

Svanna hoped he'd think the burning on her cheeks was merely from the late afternoon summer sun beating down her, rather than from her inexperience with the physical side of marriage. She'd taken her nurse's words to her heart and shied away from such things after the garden incident. After Maer had returned, she hadn't encountered anyone who made her pulse race sufficiently to even think about joining with them. *Until now*, a little voice in the back of her mind reminded her. She silenced it. Her attraction to Rand was a holdover from a girlish fantasy. She had to think with precise logic and not give into romantic fluttering. First the agreement to wed and then she'd explain about her scheme to ensure that the marriage bed remained cold.

'Battered?'

'Battered, hard-bitten and cynical. But even one such as I know when to accept help to avoid losing everything.' He inclined his head. 'I will speak to Lord Sigmund and obtain his permission.'

'Lord Sigmund is not my guardian and has no say in the matter,' she said in a rush. 'I make my own decisions.'

'A particular order to things exists. Lord Sigmund must agree to the marriage, or what value do you hold for my king and adopted country, as the alliance must be with Islay?'

She gritted her teeth. Value existed, if only he'd see it. And she intended to be an equal in the proposed marriage.

'If you return without an agreement, will you have betrayed your king's trust more than you have already done by allowing the elopement? You may know why it happened, but will your king blame you?'

Rand's mouth became a tight white line.

'Quarrelling?' Sigmund asked in his heartiest voice. 'Here, you two had such a blossoming friendship after your heroics. What to do about a quarrel between two such as you? Peace must blossom between Tara and Agthir, or else how will little Islay survive?'

Svanna smoothed the creases in her gown. Maer had

warned her before she'd left to be extra wary when Sigmund was in an overly jovial mood, as it often changed faster than a summer thunderstorm could blow in.

'We've formed a friendship after a fashion, true,' she said carefully and gave Rand a significant look, hoping he'd play along. She hoped he understood that she was giving him the opportunity to speak with Sigmund about the proposed marriage. 'How could we not after the adventure we inadvertently shared?'

Rand's voice lowered to a rich purr. 'Indeed. Most enlightening how quickly our *friendship* has developed. Deepening it has caught my interest.'

Sigmund rocked back on his heels, rubbing his hands together as if he was at a marketplace. She had the distinct impression that he was laying traps and hoping for explosions. 'Good, good. Is this a new friendship or a renewal?'

'What do you mean?' Svanna asked, hating the way the sick feeling returned to her stomach.

'I seemed to recall that Rand here spent some time in Agthir. Part of Maer's attraction to him centred around that. I wonder if your paths crossed then.' Sigmund shrugged. 'Merely a fancy of mine.'

'The world has altered much since that time,' Svanna said. 'After what happened yesterday, I would have to say the world has become a more dangerous place for Islay and Agthir. We ignore it at our peril.'

'Putting thumbs in one's ears to ignore the music is always folly,' Sigmund replied. 'The approach to the problem must be carefully considered. No one, not even I, anticipated it.'

'Svanna has agreed to serve as Agthir's peace-weaver to Eire,' Rand said, putting a firm hand on her arm and drawing her back against his hard body. 'A wise and prudent move, don't you agree?'

Sigmund sucked in his cheeks as if he had encountered a particularly sour plum. 'A peace-weaver to Eire? Svanna?'

'Yes, a peace-weaver to Tara and thus to all of Eire as the high king does command real power and is opposed to the sons of Drengr obtaining more,' Svanna said, keeping her body still.

'Most unexpected. At your age, Svanna…' He coughed. 'I must admit to wondering if marriage had passed you by. Not trying to be rude, but most peace-weavers are younger.'

He made it sound as if she was a withered crone. She stepped away from Rand's protective grasp and turned to face the pair of them.

'My peace-weaving will strengthen your hand with the kings on this island. I know how hard you worked to get the kings to this point. I will not have Turgeis dash this cup from your hand.' She pressed her hands together and willed him to stop being difficult.

Sigmund rolled his eyes. 'Once I bested his father. Fair fights hold no fear.'

'Turgeis struck when you least expected it. Fighting fair is alien to him,' Svanna said, keeping her voice steady. 'I refuse to allow their foul odour to seep back into Agthir. The threat must be contained before it grows. A blood alliance with Eire will do that. Will you allow me to serve Islay in this way as well?'

She drew back her shoulders, tilted her chin upwards and dared Sigmund to say differently.

'The new and increasing threat from Turgeis and his brothers is why my king sent me here,' Rand said. 'I suspect their ultimate target is Agthir, but I don't claim to know their precise mind. My king seeks an alliance with Islay. He knows little of Agthir.'

Sigmund's mouth dropped open as if he were trying to puzzle out this new development. 'And you are willing to do this, Svanna? For Islay as well as for Agthir?'

'You did much for me during the dark period, and I know how dear Maer holds Islay.' She held out her hands, palms upward, and willed him to understand. 'What is there for me in Agthir? I'd make a very poor soothsayer.'

Sigmund chuckled at that. 'You have me there. You've never shown any aptitude for soothsaying.'

Svanna's back brushed Rand's chest again. Her entire being tingled with unexpected awareness and the sense that someone finally had her back. She instantly straightened. If she started believing in such things, she'd be lost before her peace-weaving could begin.

'Will Islay support this?' Rand asked.

'Are you to be the other half, Silver-Tongue?' Sigmund's eyes narrowed. 'What is in it for you?'

Rand moved his hands, skimming Svanna's arms, and tried to come up with a plausible reason, anything to avoid mentioning the elopement. Defying a direct order from the high king generally resulted in swift and severe punishment. He couldn't risk Birdie being put into danger as Máel Sechnaill was unlikely to think him innocent, given the way the elopement had occurred. He hated that Svanna offered the only viable solution to ensuring his daughter survived and that he had no option but to take it.

'Máel Sechnaill does prefer kin alliances,' he said, choosing his words with great care. 'Svanna was correct in that respect. I have been sent to figure out a way forward and Svanna provided one.'

Svanna made an irritated noise in the back of her throat, a bit like a baby owl that Rand had once briefly kept as a pet. His admiration for her grew. She was the sort of person who he wanted to have on Birdie's side as she grew.

'Máel Sechnaill wanted me to supply the bride?' Sigmund said. 'Unusual.'

Rand inclined his head. 'I would be proud to have Svanna Guthardottar as my wife. I understand you and Astrid enjoy a growing bond. It would weave the alliance together.'

Sigmund muttered something about people keeping their long noses out of his private business.

'He agrees with my scheme.' Svanna's smile shone out, but he glimpsed a wariness return to her eyes. It bothered him that he'd noticed the way her eyes reflected her moods and the desire to banish the storm clouds from them had grown. 'Shall we announce the proposed alliance to the kings today? I overheard the mutterings earlier and was trying to find you when I encountered Rand. Suddenly, the way forward became clear, rather than littered with boulders.'

Sigmund lifted a brow. 'Mutterings? To be expected. Yesterday would not have happened if I'd not allowed that fool priest to sway my judgement. But it did and we can only go forward, rather than wringing our hands and lamenting like some wish to do.'

'The lamenters do not worry me. The leavers do.' She nodded towards where a petty king stood. 'An alliance will alter everything, Sigmund.'

'Do you think a mere betrothal will stem the tide?' Rand asked.

Svanna's neat white teeth turned her lower lip the colour of a stormy sunset over Tara. 'What do you propose?'

'Only an actual marriage will do,' Rand said. 'The kings will most likely discount a betrothal.'

Svanna swayed. 'An actual marriage? When?'

He watched her from under his lashes. A small part of him twisted. Was she playing games for some frolic of her own? Dangling a sweetmeat and then pulling it away? He'd endured that with Bridget just after they were married. It had begun to sour the marriage until he'd started to pull her up on her tall tales.

'As soon as it can be arranged. It's to both our countries' advantage to conclude this as swiftly as possible. My king would wish it so.'

Sigmund threw up his hands. 'Such impatience. What is it with young people and their hurried lives? In my day, we slaked our lust and allowed matters of state to take their course.'

Rand permitted a low growl but held on to the remaining shreds of his temper. 'Your observation was deliberately rude. Do you want to provoke a quarrel? What will that prove? That I intend not to dishonour Svanna and will not permit her to be dishonoured in the way you suggest?'

'First time for everything.'

'People are allowed to grow and alter. I give you that courtesy. Why do you refuse to extend it to me, Lord Sigmund?' Rand bit out between clenched teeth.

'I dislike being rushed. Makes me wonder what else is going on.'

'Forgive me, but alliances of this nature are best settled swiftly,' Svanna said with a low curtsey. 'There is little need to draw this one out as there are no obstacles to the union and many benefits to all. You know what Maer would say on the matter and how she will defer to my judgement. A marriage can be arranged in short order if all are willing.'

Sigmund's face became mulish. 'Bah. Bullies me like Astrid.'

'There I couldn't comment,' Rand said as his insides twisted. 'Makes me wonder why you are insistent on it, Svanna. Why such concern for Lord Sigmund?'

'I gave my word to Maer that I'd do all in my power to ensure an alliance between Islay and Agthir. We now have that.' The small upturn of her lips made him realise that she thought ahead instead of acting on impulse but was also willing to seize opportunities when they were presented to her. 'Have you considered what might happen to your daughter if you fail?'

'My daughter is always uppermost in my considerations.'

She raised her brow. 'Most people think it important for a little girl to have a mother. An insurance if something untoward should befall the father. I can understand your reasoning on why you want this completed swiftly so that you can return to your young daughter.'

Sigmund's face cleared. 'My dear, of course, I understand now. Thank you for explaining.'

Svanna gave him a nod and he knew she'd used Birdie as an excuse to avoid speaking about the missing lovers. Clever, but he hated that she knew he required it to be kept secret for Birdie's sake.

'Tell me something I don't know.'

'It surprises me that you feel women can't be practical.'

In his experience, women were rarely practical in matters of marriage or the heart. Whatever bargain they were making, he would ensure that he obtained the better portion. But sometimes he had to go through an open door and worry about the precise details later.

'Don't put words in my mouth.' He reached for her hand and raised it to his lips. 'I'm wary when life answers prayers, but I know enough to seize the answer with both hands.'

'There you have it, Lord Sigmund. An actual marriage

as soon as is practical,' she said, turning to him. 'Will you accept the gift in the spirit given or will you continue to cut your nose off to spite your face?'

'Attention, attention!' Sigmund called, before she could say anything more. 'Come and hear!'

The various kings, including the one who had been standing waiting for the right moment, frowned and came closer with curious expressions. Svanna gave a little sigh and sagged against him. He instinctively put an arm about her waist. The faint scent of wildflowers rose to envelop him. Somehow it felt right to hold her in this way. She wriggled slightly, putting a distance between them.

'On second thoughts seemlier this way,' she murmured.

'Why have you called us here?' the king who'd looked ready to depart asked with a faint sneer. 'Is there some new menace we need to know about? Something you should have warned us of weeks ago?'

The other kings began to mutter.

Sigmund put a hand on Rand's shoulder and then Svanna's. He dramatically cleared his throat.

'I am delighted to announce an alliance between Tara and Agthir,' Sigmund proclaimed. 'I had wanted to save the announcement for after the ceremony, but it appears you are in a great hurry, and I will not have gossip about my prospective foster-daughter.'

'With Islay acting as the intermediary,' Rand said, fixing the slippery man with an eye. He had come this far. 'An alliance between all three. Held together with the bonds of kinship.'

'I'd hardly like to presume without consulting my fellow kings.' Sigmund held out his hands. 'What say you? Shall we stand up to the blackguards, these so-called Sons of Drengr?

Or shall Islay burn under their sword and weakly give up our women to a servitude too terrible to contemplate?'

The kings stomped their feet on the ground, even the one who'd looked as if he planned to leave, and shouted that Islay would never surrender.

'It appears that Islay does wish to enter into this alliance,' Rand said, ignoring Svanna's smug expression.

Sigmund gave a nod. 'One more thing, Svanna. I do my own courting. I mean to have your foster-mother as my bride, but allow me to ask.'

She inclined her head, and her lips turned up even more. 'Did I ever say differently?'

'Incorrigible.' Sigmund's eyes twinkled. 'Maer would never have dared manipulate me like this.'

She smiled back at him. 'Who do you think gave me this task? On this, my foster-sister and I are one.'

Rand kept his face impassive. His king would be satisfied. All he had to do was to acquire a wife, something he'd sworn on Bridget's grave that he'd never do. But the compromise meant he had ensured his daughter's future safety by providing the blood-kinship alliance his king desired. And it was just possible that he could discover the missing pair before anyone else was any the wiser.

'Done.' Sigmund bowed his head. 'If you can truly peace-weave, then some good will come of this debacle.'

Rand held out his hand. 'On behalf of Eire and its king, I swear friendship to both Islay and Agthir.'

'And I swear on behalf of Agthir, friendship to Eire and Islay,' Svanna said, clasping his fingers with a firm grip.

'Islay makes the only choice it can.' Sigmund enclosed both their hands in his grip. 'Svanna will serve as our peace-weaver with Eire.'

Chapter Six

Svanna stood down beside the bay, watching the waves lap the shore. Behind her, the feast to celebrate Sigmund becoming high king echoed. She'd done it, but her safe life was going to alter. She simply needed to figure out a way to get Rand to agree to a platonic marriage. In theory, it should be easy as his heart lay with his dead wife, but she wondered what she'd do if he refused and how she'd explain that the marriage bed frightened her.

'Amazing how something like that turns the tide,' Rand said, coming to stand beside her. 'Quick thinking on your part.'

'Once one started to leave, the rest would have rapidly followed. Trickles become floods if not dealt with promptly,' Svanna said, trying to keep her gaze on the bay and not on the frowning man she was now betrothed to, with a marriage looming. Several kings had openly stated their intention to stay until it happened. 'One must always act decisively to ensure the best possible outcome. Something the Queen taught me years ago.'

'There is more to peace-weaving hospitality than I considered.' Said in such a way that it could mean absolutely anything. 'But there again, my sword ensures my point is understood. Too many years serving as Máel Sechnaill's enforcer now to make a change.'

She glanced up at him and saw that his face was carefully blank. He was the high king's brute enforcer, but he'd been chosen for this delicate mission even though the woman in question had appeared reluctant in the extreme and the chosen bridegroom unlikely to immediately agree. Why? The high king must have had a reason.

'Peace-weaving may seem like working in the shadows, but well-presented hospitality is vital if alliances are to be maintained. Ties of friendship are stronger than drums of war to my mind.' Svanna knew she needed to explain the basic principles to make Rand understand what she'd bring to their marriage. It wasn't simply the act of union, but a dedication to ensuring the alliance was strong and benefited both sides against Turgeis and his followers. 'A well-run household enables harmony.'

'I will admit to not having thought much about it.' He picked up a stone and tossed it far out into the bay. 'Something women do instead of making their point with their sword arm.'

'Understanding how diplomacy works is important for men as well. And once you do, you are less inclined to dismiss it or the way peace-weavers work. When alliances turn tricky, they often lose everything.' She shrugged. 'However, I also insisted the late usurper teach me about strategy and the arts of war. He thought me to have a level head.'

'The late King thought that? Have you ever fought in a proper battle?'

'Besides the one we endured and the fall of Agthir?'

'You did well then.'

She put her hand on her stomach and bade the tight knots to ease. She'd trained for many years for her level of diplomacy, not to serve simply as the Queen's handmaiden. At long last she was going to do something positive with all her training, all the late-night conversations she'd had with the Queen, and indeed sometimes with the usurper, about how one woman could change a country's destiny. And she'd have a little girl to look after and mould, just as Astrid had done with her, except she would ensure Birdie knew she had value.

'We need to speak about the marriage and our expectations.'

He picked up another stone and tossed it into the bay, making it skip. 'What are you saying?'

She swallowed hard. This was far harder than when she had practiced it. 'Ours will be a strategic marriage, Rand, not a runaway love match like your cousin's. I wanted to let you know that I am not looking for more than to be useful. I will run the household and serve as a foster-mother for your daughter.'

'Birdie's mother is dead. Her nurse looked after my late wife and her sisters.'

'A difference exists between a nurse and a mother.'

He raised a brow. 'And you know all about it?'

'Before Astrid, I suffered with a stepmother. I endured my nurse, who had once been Astrid's. I would see your daughter right.' Svanna shrugged. 'All I require in return is respect in public.'

A small part of her willed him to take her in his arms, kiss her senseless and tell her that he wanted her. That even the smallest part of her remained enthralled by the romance of him, despite everything she'd witnessed and endured, disconcerted her. He was never going to care for her. He'd made that quite plain, and that bit of her kept hoping, even though she didn't want to.

He reached out and lifted her chin. In the starlit darkness, he examined her face. His thumb traced the outline of her mouth, sending warm pulses coursing through her. 'A platonic strategic marriage is what you envisage. Or are you trying to put words in my mouth again?'

'The union was forced on you. We should discuss this sensibly before we go further.' She was pleased that her voice did not become high-pitched, even though her stomach knotted.

'Sensibly?' His thumb traced the outline of her mouth again. More slowly this time. Her entire being tingled in anticipation. 'You are the one who behaved in a rash fashion. You appear to do that quite a lot, Svanna. Rushing into burning buildings, heedless of the consequences to your life.'

'Ask anyone,' she whispered. 'Those who know me say that I am cautious—too cautious.'

'A platonic marriage is truly what you want? You don't want this?'

His thumb traced the outline of her mouth a third time. Her tongue darted out to wet her lips and encountered the edge of his thumb. She rapidly retreated, taking two steps backwards and nearly stumbling over. She put out a hand to steady herself and encountered his tunic. What did it say about her that the thought didn't repel her as much as she'd imagined it would? That rebelliously hopeful part of her kept whispering that the possibilities were there. 'Unnecessary in the circumstances.'

He hauled her against his hard chest. 'We can't have you twisting your ankle before the marriage.'

'I've no intention of twisting my ankle.'

'If people had the intention they would never get hurt, but, my fair lady, to put your mind at ease, I've little intention of having a platonic marriage with you.' A hearty laugh made his frame shake. She wished she could interpret the expression in his eyes.

'Why are you doing this?'

'Because, Ice Maiden, our marriage mustn't be in name only. Alliances are always strengthened with blood and that means children—our children. I assume you know how children are made.'

She wrapped her arms about her waist. Ice Maiden was what he thought she was. She had heard the term before and embraced it. But since encountering him again, he'd penetrated that hard shell which had kept her feelings and her desire at bay since Turgeis's assault in the garden all those years ago. That fact terrified and intrigued her in equal measure. What was it about him that made her long for his touch?

'I'm unafraid of the physical,' she said, choosing her words with care. Confessing now what Turgeis had tried to do to her and how she'd kept herself apart from such things ever after solved nothing. She had to put the past fear behind her. With Rand, she'd never felt frightened, but she also didn't want to ask for more than he was prepared to give. 'I wanted to give you the option.'

'Know that all my women have been willing. I've no intention of changing. Where would the pleasure be taken from an unwilling one?'

'You want your women to enjoy you,' she said slowly. 'Men say that and then things get out of hand. I have seen much of that in Agthir. The usurper's feasts were notorious in the end. Astrid always made certain that we left early.'

'You would know more about that than I.' His voice held a note of hesitancy, as if he had not intended to put it that way.

She waved her hand. 'We proceed at my pace. Good.

I'll let you know when our marriage may alter from the platonic.'

His thumb and forefinger captured her chin. Her lips parted, giving a lie to her words. Her body protested that she wanted his mouth on hers now. She wanted him to erase all memory of the pawing she'd received from Turgeis, but she feared he wouldn't and that would make things harder to bear. What if Turgeis had spoilt her for ever and her reaction to Rand was merely wishful thinking?

'Are you trying to get me to wager? I'll admit the chase adds spice.'

'I explained the necessity of a quick marriage, but we need time to get to know each other. We will have a working partnership for many years. As my foster-mother had with both her husbands. Trust builds over time,' she said, her words tripping over each other.

'I pulled you from a burning building.'

'I'm willing to learn to trust. Are you used to women falling into your bed simply because you crook your little finger? Lord Sigmund's assessment.'

He stepped away from her and ran a hand through his hair. 'Yes… I mean no. I haven't thought that women will simply fall into my arms. Life doesn't work like that.'

'Somehow, I doubt that.'

'Has Sigmund been telling tall tales? I apologise once again for the behaviour of my younger and unwise self, but my memory differs to his.'

'Don't worry. Maer never really mentioned you either.' She waited a beat and knew she was treading a very fine line, bantering with him in this way. 'I simply know the type from what little I've gleaned. I've encountered men like you before and resisted them all.'

His smile warmed her all the way down to her toes. 'And

here I like to think of myself as unique. Consider me told. Will you be able to resist me when the time comes for our wedding night?'

She made a brief curtsey. 'We both know the why behind the marriage. Best to be honest about such things.'

'But will you be honest about your attraction to me?'

'Best that we keep this as pleasant as possible.' She was vaguely proud of the answer.

A smile tugged at the corner of his mouth. 'As pleasant as possible? What exactly are you offering?'

'A marriage without expectations,' she said quickly. 'We will forge a working partnership. I've seen it happen. Against the odds, Astrid and her second husband made it work.'

He grasped her hand and brought her knuckles to his mouth. The light touch sent a fresh tremor coursing through her. She knew her body wanted far more than simply platonic, but she also knew she'd require more than two bodies meeting in the night. And she wasn't entirely certain she wanted to give any man, particularly Rand, whose heart belonged to his late wife, that sort of power over her.

'Here I leave you, lovely lady,' Rand said, turning her palm over and brushing it with his lips. 'Until our wedding day tomorrow. I await with anticipation all that follows. You're right. It can be pleasant for both of us, provided we take the time to enjoy it.'

He let her hand go and strode away. She pressed her hand to her mouth, hating that suddenly she was looking forward to the wedding night.

'Do you think this will be enough to keep the high king's anger at bay—' Rand's helmsman asked '—you marrying Lady Svanna? She isn't even from Islay proper.'

'Máel Sechnaill must accept it. The possibilities are far beyond what he hoped for. Agthir has power in the North.' Rand concentrated on polishing his sword and the other little tasks he needed to have done before the ceremony later that day.

He kept telling himself that it was the obvious solution, not only to save his cousin but also to provide security for Birdie.

With each task complete, his thoughts circled anew to Svanna and his unexpected attraction towards her. After nearly four years of denying his physical needs, his body screamed for the release her body would bring, but he also wanted to make sure she participated with enthusiasm and didn't fear him. Someone somewhere had made her nervous about the physical act. He silently cursed that unknown lover for what he'd done to her. And even though his seduction skills were rusty, he suspected that, given time, he could show her how pleasant joining with him could be.

'The lady in question is easy on the eye.'

'Keep a civil tongue in your head,' Rand said, dropping the sword with a loud clang. He hated how a surge of jealousy went through him. 'Some things are best kept private.'

From the assembled multitude's catcalls, he knew they expected him to perform his duty, possibly in public or at least providing physical proof such as bloodstains on the sheets. He intended to enjoy his pursuit of Svanna, but he needed to ensure they all had the impression that the marriage had been consummated, vigorously and completely. Stabbing his thigh for the sheets, something his late wife had done as they had anticipated the marriage night before they were married, was a possibility. Máel Sechnaill had seemed none the wiser, and it would be the same thing here.

'No need to bite my head off. We are happy for you.'

'Funny way of showing it.'

His helmsman gulped hard. 'We all know what you were like in the first days and weeks after your wife's death. Máel Sechnaill remarked on it. I wondered if he'd sent his daughter to tempt you. She resembles Bridget.'

Rand scrunched up his nose. It did sound like something Máel Sechnaill would do—he knew Rand objected to forced marriages, particularly of young brides to men old enough to be their grandfathers. 'Rhiannon never tempted me to do anything. Only brotherly affection exists between us. Svanna made the offer. Because of political necessity, I accepted.'

The man's mouth dropped open. 'You rushed into a hall to save her.'

Rand shook his head. The rumour mill typically had it backwards. 'Lady Svanna and I agreed a strategic marriage, forced by necessity to benefit our countries. Nothing more.'

'If you say so, my lord.'

'A difference exists between the sudden all-consuming passion Bridget and I experienced and the strategic blood alliance the Lady Svanna and I must share.'

He didn't want to think about their fights over the smallest things, Bridget's sulks at the time he'd spent away on her father's business, or how they'd grown apart during her pregnancy. The guilt at his staying away because it had been easier occasionally clogged his throat and made it hard for him to sleep, even after all this time. As a reminder of his failings, he kept a *tafl* board set to the last game they had played beside his bed at Donaghmoyne. He'd been called away to attend some minor matter for her father, much to her disgust. She'd overturned the board in her fury but must have set it back to where they were as he'd found the game in their special place after her death.

'*Keep your face forward, my love. You will require another woman in your life. Promise you will take one. If not for my sake, then for our child's,*' she'd whispered with life ebbing from her eyes. He'd agreed but then he'd discovered that game in progress and knew he wasn't ready, and never would be.

'You keep saying that and maybe you will start believing it,' his helmsman said, bringing him back to the present with a start.

Rand sheathed the sword and stood. 'You speak boldly to your lord.'

The man rolled his eyes. 'When did you last pluck the strings of your harp?'

Rand picked up a brooch and started polishing it. He'd learned to play an Irish harp at Bridget's request, but it had gathered dust since her death. 'When I need advice, I ask for it.'

'You were wrong about Lady Svanna. That one is not carved from ice. Not from the way she rushed into the burning building.'

Rand tried not to think about how Svanna's lips had softly parted in the pale moonlight, how he'd nearly drawn her to him, and kissed her until they were both overcome with desire. He knew deep down that his late wife would have found another, possibly with indecent haste. He'd always known that. She had told him as much. Not a betrayal but a moving on, she had called it.

'You know nothing.'

The man laughed. 'You know even less. That brooch could hardly be any brighter. What are you trying to be—a shining example?'

'A political marriage suits both of us.' He winced, knowing that once he'd argued against such things, convincing

Bridget to take a chance on him, rather than being locked in a loveless marriage to an elderly man who had already buried three wives. 'I've learned not to question the minds of ladies, particularly when their desires chime with my needs.'

'Will you not wait until I've recovered?' Astrid said from her bed. Earlier she'd moved back into the chamber that Svanna and she had shared, stating that others required that sort of care more, not her. To Svanna's relief, her cheeks had regained some colour, and she had managed to walk a few steps.

Svanna captured Astrid's hand. 'If I am to be of any use, I must go to Tara as quickly as possible and prevent Turgeis from gaining more power and threatening Agthir.'

Astrid tightened her cool hand about Svanna's. 'You do Agthir proud.'

Svanna brushed Astrid's cheek. 'The timing was deliberate. They knew you'd most likely be in the hall and not in the church. Lord Randolfr was right—it was too easy to chase them from these lands. No hostages taken—unprecedented.'

Astrid plucked restlessly at the furs. 'I'd feel safer if I understood what Turgeis wants. You're good at solving riddles. Can you guess?'

'Beyond power? It makes little sense,' she said, closing her mind firmly on Turgeis's assault and subsequent torments. They were in the past and had no bearing on her future with Rand. Astrid had never known the true extent of what had happened and there was no need for her to know now. 'The salute unnerved me. He seeks revenge on Agthir for the banishment was my interpretation.'

Svanna sat back on her haunches and waited, completely still. She'd always found waiting the hardest part, but it was necessary.

Finally, when Svanna's nerves were stretched to breaking-point, Astrid sighed and closed her eyes in resignation. 'You may be headstrong and inclined to recklessness, but you are also politically astute. You will uncover what Turgeis plots and stop him. Remember, if you are truly unhappy, divorce is permissible in Agthir.'

'High praise indeed from you.'

Astrid laughed. 'Our way of marriage or a Christian one?'

'I believe ours will be preferable in the interests of time. If a Christian form is required, it can be done at Tara. After I convert. I am not naïve enough to think the high king will countenance someone like me within his inner circle unless I do.' Svanna silently prayed she was right, because otherwise there would be a lengthy delay while she took instruction. The priest had been quite clear that it could take months. 'I wish to go to my wedding a Northern bride.'

Astrid's lips turned up. 'Then we must make you the appropriate bride.'

Astrid sent one of the servants for her iron-bound chest which Halfr had stored with the other valuables.

'There is no need for anything fancy.'

'What sort of foster-mother would I be if I allowed my daughter to marry in the clothes she stands up in?' Her eyes crinkled at the corners. 'I brought your mother's wedding finery with me, my dear.'

Svanna's insides twisted. Had Astrid guessed the secret offering to Freya, asking not to return to Agthir, she'd made before they'd departed? As much as she liked Maer, she'd known her place was not there. She served as a reminder of what had been and not as a beacon for the future. She knew in her heart of hearts that she wanted to make a difference to the future. She wanted to be more than an obligation.

She could well remember how bitterly her stepmother had complained about having to feed and clothe her before Astrid had stepped in with her offer.

Not wishing to betray her thoughts, she carefully widened her eyes. 'You did? Why?'

'Because I didn't care to have it inadvertently lost. What did you think the reason was?'

'I don't know. We simply have not discussed this before,' Svanna said to avoid asking the direct question.

The servants came back with the trunk, ending the conversation. Astrid sat up and fiddled with the complicated lock and withdrew a small whale-boned casket. Svanna spotted her mother's name carved in runes on the top.

'Here, let me put this on your head. I would see you married properly, like your mother was.'

Astrid withdrew the simple but elegant twisted strands of gold and semi-precious stones from the casket. 'It will shimmer on your head like it did on hers. The Norns knew she deserved that little piece of happiness.'

When the weight hit her head, the import of what she was doing washed over her. She was going to marry a man who'd despise her if he learned the full truth about how she'd inadvertently been the cause of his scarring.

'Oh, help,' she whispered.

'You will be fine,' Astrid said, squeezing her hand. 'I am grateful for your many years of service, but it is time you fulfilled your next role—a role you were born for. I sometimes wonder if I had Helga guard you too well. You never seemed to have flirtations with warriors, or maybe I'm not remembering properly.'

Svanna nodded, struggling to maintain her composure. 'I had best see to the rest.'

'If I can, I will be there. Inge… Maer would expect that

of me.' Astrid hesitated. 'I promise, Svanna. For her sake and my own.'

Stumbling from the chamber, Svanna leant against the wall and allowed the trembling to overtake her. Another obstacle surmounted. Astrid would back her and would in time claim the idea of the quick marriage as her own. A future where she would no longer be required to walk on eggshells beckoned.

It took Svanna a little time to discover Rand in what appeared to be his favourite thinking spot—looking out over the bay. An unanticipated warm curl started at the base of her spine when she examined his jawline. She willed it go.

'Is all well with you?'

'Good news.' She forced a bright smile. 'Astrid has given permission for the ceremony to take place as soon as possible. Turns out that she brought my mother's wedding finery with her. Amazing foresight.'

A smile lit his face from within, making it come alive, and she glimpsed the youth she'd once dreamt about. She tried to gather the remnants of her protective shell about her heart. That youth was long gone and would never return, if indeed he'd ever truly existed. 'Did you anticipate a marriage?'

'A knack exists to ensure the right outcome with my foster-mother. Years of close observation have taught me how to move the seemingly immovable,' she said, pointedly ignoring the question.

'A skill which will undoubtably prove useful in Eire.'

She forced a broad smile. 'A Northern ceremony to save time was her sole suggestion.'

His scar appeared to relax. 'And you will agree to that?'

'If necessary, we can go through another form in Tara, but everyone should accept our marriage,' she said, giving the same answer she'd given Astrid and willing him to see the necessity without her having to explain the ease with which a Northern marriage could be dissolved.

'It has been a long time since I heard the words. My beliefs altered considerably after I left Agthir.'

She smiled back at him. 'The words will return to you.'

'Such confidence in my ability.'

'Someone must believe.' She gave a half-shrug. 'It might as well be me.'

He tilted his head to one side. 'Are you certain we never spoke in Agthir? Your words…' He stopped. 'The memory has slipped away. Forget I said anything.'

She blinked rapidly and ignored the sick feeling in her stomach. She had said something like that to him when they'd flirted all those years ago, complimenting him on his sword skill.

'You say we didn't, but I've had conversations with many people.' He frowned. 'An inkling I once had a similar conversation with a woman in Agthir.'

'Were you planning to marry her?'

He gave his head a quick shake. 'Marriage never entered my head back then. A scrap of conversation. A glimmer. No bearing on today.'

Svanna knew then she would have to confess, but not now when the stakes were so high.

Rand struggled to recall the words of the Northern marriage ceremony as he stood beside Svanna in the open air, listening to Sigmund intone his part.

Svanna looked the picture of the golden-haired princess, the sort that had inspired a thousand songs and sagas from *skalds*. But she wasn't one. She'd been quite clear on that.

'You appear to remember the words quite well,' Svanna said after he gave his vow according to Var.

'Some things never leave you,' he replied. 'Even if they cease to have much meaning.'

Her mouth tightened at that. 'But I take such matters seriously and intend to hold true to my vows.'

She lisped the vows in the curious sing-song voice that she sometimes used. He wondered why she adopted it and what it meant. He resolved to ask her in private. Máel Sechnaill might take her less seriously, but he suspected it was a symptom of her feeling anxious in some way.

He allowed the rest of the ceremony to flow over him.

When Sigmund suggested that they seal the marriage with a kiss, he jumped with a start. At her startled expression, he lifted her chin. Her blue eyes were unfathomable pools.

'Expected,' he murmured, bringing his arms about her and pulling her gentle curves against his body.

'I know.' Her voice was barely above the faintest whisper.

He brought his mouth down on hers, intending the kiss to be merely symbolic, but her lips trembled and parted slightly.

He found it impossible not to drink deeper and further, bringing his arms tighter about her until her entire body moulded against his. Her hands laced about his neck as if she were clinging to him because her legs had melted. Her tongue touched his before entangling. Not entirely indifferent to him then.

The noise from the crowd stamping their feet jolted him back to reality.

He loosened his arms and lifted his head.

'A small taste of what the wedding night will be like,' he

said loudly for their consumption. A loud chorus of cheers filled the hall.

'That should hold them,' he murmured to Svanna. 'I stand by my earlier oath to you.'

Her thumb explored her kiss-swollen mouth. 'I wondered.'

'No pleasure in it any other way.'

Her cheeks flamed to a bright scarlet, making him wonder if her reputation as an Ice Maiden meant her experience was limited.

'We go at your pace.'

She dipped her head so all he could see was her twisted crown. 'I do appreciate the thought.'

He knew he should say something more, perhaps about them making a good team, but words failed him. Instead, he raised her hand and kissed the palm. 'To newfound friendship.'

Chapter Seven

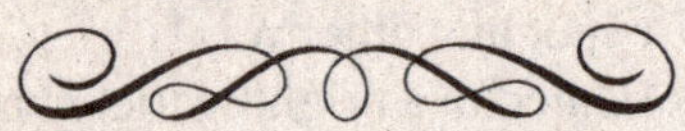

The torches threw shifting shadows on the walls of Halfr's bedchamber, which he'd decreed must be used for the happy couple's wedding night. The women, including Astrid, had all gathered there to ensure that Svanna was given a proper send-off. Her hair had been brushed until it hung about her shoulders like a golden cloud, and she was now dressed in her finest under-gown, rather than her much more serviceable everyday one.

Fighting against a rising tide of nausea, Svanna tried to remain still and allow the women to do their gossipy best, but the nerves she'd experienced during the ceremony had returned with a vengeance. Her insistence on a quick marriage was ill-thought-out, she knew that now. But it was too late for all the fears, doubts and worries which crowded her mind.

She wondered why she had chosen the riskier path. Had her past dreams of the youth she'd fashioned in her mind influenced her? When would she stop being like a sighing maiden? She firmed her mouth. A maiden, that was what she was—just.

'Look at you,' Astrid said, leaning heavily on a servant's arm but upright and able to slowly shuffle about the room, even if she had not felt capable of attending the actual ceremony. 'One could not ask for a prettier bride.'

'Lord Randolfr is very lucky. Beauty combined with brains,' a woman added.

'That kiss they shared at the altar,' another added, touching her forefinger to her mouth before raising it. 'Such passion. Obviously, love at first sight. No wonder neither was willing to wait.'

All the women sighed and giggled. Several made lewd comments about what Svanna would be looking forward to and taking bets on the state of the sheets in the morning.

Svanna concentrated on the rushes and struggled not to explain that Lord Randolfr's heart was buried with his first wife and he therefore welcomed their arrangement of a platonic marriage. A little voice in her head protested that his kiss at the wedding demonstrated that he was not averse to her, even if he had agreed to her terms for waiting until she was ready.

'Being pretty is something you always say,' she said, pushing all thoughts of the passionate kiss to one side.

'It doesn't make it any less true.' Astrid reached out her hand and caught hers. 'I'm proud of you, Svanna. Always. Remember that.'

A lump came into Svanna's throat. Astrid always doled out praise sparingly, which made her words even more precious because Svanna knew they weren't meaningless utterings but came from her heart.

'I've no intention of forgetting such a thing.'

Astrid waved her hand. 'I wish to see you properly settled on your wedding night. Women like us have such a brief opportunity to tie their husbands to them. Oftentimes, a single night. Use it well. Do not waste it on trivialities.'

'I'll not squander it,' Svanna promised, trying not to

think about how Astrid would disagree with the bargain she'd made.

'My lady, your daughter is perfection. No man could resist her,' a servant murmured. 'Lord Sigmund made me promise that I would keep you from over-exerting yourself. He requires you in his life.'

'Thank you,' Astrid mumbled, her body crumpling. Svanna discreetly signalled to several women to support her. One put an arm about her. 'You are a thoughtful person. Better than I deserve.'

Helped by the women, Astrid departed.

'Won't be long now,' Svanna said into the silence which had fallen. The remaining women gave indulgent smiles and burst into another round of telling ribald stories about various wedding nights. Svanna wondered how she'd ever considered any of them prudish. The noise from the men grew louder, and the women's eyes danced. One darted forward and rearranged Svanna's hair and gown, making sure that the shadowy vee between her breasts was exposed. 'Now you are ready to be eaten all up.'

With the sound of swords hitting shields, drums banging and shouts of 'Here comes the groom!', Rand stumbled into the room. The women clapped their hands.

'Ladies,' he said, swaying slightly. 'I have arrived.'

His mouth seemed slack. A vagueness entered his eyes. Svanna's heart sank. He must have drunk quite a lot. She remembered Astrid confiding how insensible the usurper had been when they'd wed, and how he'd forgotten his promises. She had to hope that Rand remembered his.

'Lord Randolfr,' Svanna said, trying to ignore the butterflies which had taken up residence in her belly. 'We've been expecting you.'

Coarse laughter from the assembled crowd rang out.

'Will you leave me and my bride?' Rand made a flourishing bow and appeared to stumble halfway through. He spun around and managed to fall on the bed with his arms open wide.

The crowd shouted encouragement.

He patted the bed. 'Wife? Will you join me? Far more comfortable here than standing in the centre of the room.'

The crowd lapped it up, hooting with laughter and egging him on.

Wrapping the last shreds of her dignity about her, Svanna gingerly walked over and carefully sat beside him, keeping her body as still as possible, despite her hands trembling uncontrollably. However, the fur-draped mattress dipped and she slid into his body. Her entire being was immediately aware of his hard muscle.

She edged away from him and gripped the top fur until her knuckles turned white. 'I'm here.'

She winced at how high-pitched her voice sounded.

He lifted his head slightly at her words. His brow knit. He ostentatiously cleared his throat and waited for the room to grow quiet. 'What is about to pass between us doesn't require an audience, does it, ladies?'

Much renewed tittering and giggling before the women slowly exited the chamber, whispering and nudging each other. One briefly put her hand on top of Svanna's ice-cold one, saying that she hoped Svanna would pass a comfortable night. She winked at Rand, whose smile increased.

Svanna dug her fingernails into the fur and her face grew hot. Rand gave her a concerned glance and she prayed to the Norns he'd consider the burn on her cheeks was due to the torches.

After the last woman had departed, he rose and closed

the door firmly, setting a heavy trunk against it. 'To prevent anyone from accidentally barging in.'

'Do you think they will?' Wild and uncontrollable laughter escaped her throat. She found it impossible to stop until all air had vanished from her lungs. She lay, gasping for breath, staring at the tapestries.

'I lack the ability to foretell the future. I hope for the former and wish to prevent the latter.' His voice had lost its slur.

She turned her head, the better to study him. His eyes appeared alert, his mouth was no longer slack and he'd adjusted his tunic.

'No great display of passion on either of our parts required,' he continued. 'The kiss at the wedding was enough.'

'That was purely for public consumption?' Her heart thudded. She'd allowed those old dreams of hers to get the better of her common sense. She should have expected it, and she hated that she'd wanted to believe that he might be attracted to her in some way.

'I dislike providing public sport. I presume you are not overly fond of it either, if your looks of sheer terror are anything to go by.'

Svanna sat up and put a hand to her head, trying to collect her thoughts. 'The whole experience is new to me.'

He walked over to where a jug and two goblets stood on a table. 'Sigmund thoughtfully provided us with some mead. Do you require any?'

She nodded.

He poured the golden mead with a steady hand before holding a goblet out to her. 'Possibly some of his finest, but guessing is beyond my powers.'

'You were shamming,' she said, shaking her head at her gullibility. She picked up a pillow and threw it at him. 'You utter wretch. You could have warned me.'

'Careful of the mead.' He easily sidestepped the pillow. 'If you'd known, would it have changed the result?'

'Yes…' She tucked her head into her neck. 'Probably not, but the principle of the thing remains.'

'How good are you at playacting?'

Svanna crossed her arms. 'I did it for over a decade without discovery.'

He set the mead down. 'True enough. I hadn't considered the problem in that light.'

'How good do you think you are?'

'Managed to fool you, did I?' A pleased smile split his face. 'Good to know that I can. The tossed pillow shows the truth in my statement.'

'I…' she started and was tempted to give a non-committal answer but then decided to admit the truth. 'I was utterly fooled. And I was deeply worried for a few heartbeats.'

He tilted his head to one side. His face sobered. 'Worried, why?'

Svanna hugged her waist tighter. The feeling of being out of her depth swamped her. Even though, in her head, she'd had many conversations with him—or, to be more accurate, her idea of him—she didn't really know him or how he'd react. All she knew about men was from her time in Agthir.

'Drunken men sometimes ignore their promises. Reasons exist why I kept my dog close and avoid feasts.'

The desire to explain what had happened to her on the morning he'd disappeared rose within her, but she forced it back down her throat. It was unimportant. She had survived and as Helga, her old nurse, had pointed out, she bore a large part of the blame for wandering around without an escort. For many years she'd thought this assessment was correct, but now she had to wonder why Turgeis felt entitled to behave the way he did, particularly against a member of the

King's family. She had not really done anything wrong. No, it was better to leave it, she decided. It was in her past and behind her. Unalterable, like his wife's death.

'The feasts could be raucous affairs, particularly when the King or my foster-mother was absent. I rapidly learned how to ensure I kept my honour.'

He rolled his eyes. 'Not to drink yourself stupid when the company is unfamiliar is a lesson my cousin taught me early on. It suited my purpose to allow others to consider I remain ignorant of such a lesson.'

'Why did you decide to do that?'

'Because I don't require an audience tonight, or any night.' He shrugged and returned the mead to the jug. 'I assumed you didn't either.'

'That goes without saying.' She slid off the bed. The rushes were cool against her bare feet. 'Some things are best kept private.'

'It is good to know you are level-headed.' He ran a hand through his hair, making the curls wilder than ever.

'Did you think I wasn't?'

'Sometimes you use a sing-song voice like you are trying to be a very little girl.'

'When I get nervous, my voice goes too high.' She swallowed hard, knowing that she didn't want it to be a problem between them. 'A habit I dislike immensely, but one I don't seem able to alter.'

'And the laughter?'

'Sometimes it works, particularly when one understands the fate one has avoided.'

'I will remember that about you. It may come in useful.'

'What, me speaking in a sing-song? I hate it when it happens. My old nurse used to tell me to concentrate hard and it would vanish like snow under the summer sun. It only seemed to make matters worse.'

'No, me knowing when you are nervous.' His eyes became deep pools. 'You are my wife now. Part of my responsibility is to ensure you are protected, particularly when you are nervous. And your old nurse sounds like a difficult woman.'

'I can stand on my own two feet,' she said before the temptation to like him too much overpowered her. 'One benefit of having a nurse like Helga. My failures belonged to me even if my successes came from her.'

'Everyone, even me, can use help at times. Try to remember to allow people to help you.'

His voice slid over her like soft fur, making her want to believe in him.

'When the time comes, I'll try to accept help graciously, but wait until I ask for it.'

He inclined his head. 'Understood, but my vow before Var and the other gods was to be your husband.'

She tucked a tendril of hair behind her ear and ignored the way her hand trembled. 'Now, what are we going to do about the sleeping arrangements? Should I make up a bed on the floor?'

The butterflies in her stomach had subsided. She had quietly let him know that she anticipated that this would start out as a platonic marriage. She had little intention of melting into his arms simply because they were now married.

He gave a half-smile. 'We share the bed tonight. I have no wish for any early surprises or accidental entering. Even with the trunk against the door, it could happen.'

'Does that happen?'

'It has been known at Tara. Some people take a great

deal of pride in doing it. Appeals to their sense of humour, I guess.'

He stretched, pulling his tunic taut across his broad chest. She glanced away. She had no business noticing the state of his chest or the fine down covering his muscular forearms. 'I see.'

'But you can take the floor if you wish,' he continued in an ultra-reasonable voice. 'I know the value of a soft bed, even if you seem not to. And I am happy to cut my thigh to provide the blood on the sheets.'

'Blood on the sheets?'

'They are sure to be examined. In the eyes of this community, you are unmarried and therefore a maiden.'

'I hadn't considered you'd think of something like that.'

'Lucky that I have.'

Svanna concentrated on a spot in the centre of the room rather than looking at him any longer. She hated how warmth coiled about her insides at the thought of sharing a bed with him.

'I trust your words from last night. You will keep your promises. I accept your judgement about the sheets as well, but I am willing to be the one who bleeds on them.' She held out her hand. 'Give me your dagger.'

He inclined his head. 'Progress of a sort. One day we will make a fine team, my lady fair.'

Svanna lifted her chin up. 'I consider trust an important part of any marriage, but it needs to be earned.'

'Indeed.' He bowed and handed her the dagger.

She threw back the sheets, made a shallow cut and watched the blood pool. When she started to feel ill, she wiped the sheets. 'That should be enough.'

He took a cloth, dipped it into the water and wiped the remaining traces of blood from her hand. He carefully placed the towel by the basin.

'Won't they know?'

'They will think I washed you clean.' His eyes crinkled. 'It happens more often than you might think. No one questions.'

She put her hands over her mouth. It was all becoming clear. He knew about this because his first wife had done something similar. That had been a love match by all accounts, but she found she didn't want to pry.

'I hadn't thought. You've done this before.'

He raised a brow. 'You may get in first. Try to sleep. Don't mind me. Sleep and I are strangers.'

Svanna needed no second urging and dived under the pile of furs. She wrapped her arms about her legs and curled up into a ball. She screwed her eyes tightly shut and struggled to breathe normally, but every particle of her was aware of him and the way he moved about the room, dousing all the torches until one faint tallow light remained. He settled down on the stool, staring at the flickering light.

'Easier to sleep if you relax,' he said when she eased her legs straight. 'You are safe here. No one is going to mock you. No one is going to harm you while I keep watch.'

Svanna propped herself up on her elbows. 'Sleep brings uneasy dreams.'

The bed sagged slightly when he sat down. He blew out the final light. The soft thump of clothes hitting the rush-covered floor resounded in her ears. She turned her head and vaguely made out that he'd undressed. One fur now covered him while he lay on top of the other furs. 'A compromise.'

'Is that what you call it?'

He lay back and closed his eyes. 'In truth, I find the last few days have been much more tiring than I had anticipated.'

He turned his back to her.

In the darkness she listened to his breath, which slowly but surely became more rhythmic. Her eyes grew heavy, and she realised that he was correct—the last few days had been exhausting. In the morning, this unsettledness would go. She'd return to being the dependable person she'd been for the last few years, instead of this one who was willing to challenge warriors or who wanted to be loved for herself instead of tolerated for what she brought to a marriage. She hated that the thought made her unaccountably depressed.

Chapter Eight

Svanna struggled to waking, uncertain of where she was, but a heaviness pressed on her limbs.

Her dreams were filled with running away from Turgeis in the herb garden and frantically trying to find somewhere to hide. She kept searching for Tippi to save her, but there was no answer. Eventually she discovered a safe place, a haven where she knew she would be safe.

She fumbled about for a few heartbeats, trying to get her bearings, frightened suddenly that she was back in Agthir before Maer's return, and everything was about to crash down about her ears with Turgeis trapping her again. She gave a little cry of distress and thrashed about with her arms, beating with her fists.

'Rest now,' a voice murmured in her ear and the fear vanished from her. 'All is well. It remains far too early in the morning to emerge. Nothing happens without your consent.'

A heavy arm came across her and pulled her back against him. She knew she should make a token protest, but the feeling of being truly safe swamped her senses and she drifted off to sleep again.

She next woke with a start to the grey dimness of early morning. One hand was tangled in his hair, while the other one was splayed over his naked chest. Somehow, during the night, their bodies had become intertwined with the furs. Rather than having several furs between them, as had been the case when she'd drifted off, now the only thing separating her body from his naked one was her under-gown, a garment which was now rucked up about her hips.

The truth hit her—rather than maintaining her distance as she'd thought she would, when caught in her world of dreams she'd decided that snuggling close was the best option. His arms had been the ones she'd sought during her bad dream. She stared at the dark shapes of the tapestries on the walls and tried to make a memory to store away, but she also knew it was not what they had agreed. How hollow her declaration of having only a platonic marriage sounded now.

He remained still and seemingly unaware that her movements had entangled their limbs. Perhaps the Norns had listened to her prayers after all.

She might exit this embrace without him ever being aware of the intimacy they had shared. The thought caused a small bubble of hope to rise within her. Perhaps everything was not as dire as she'd first assumed.

She started to ease away, removing her hand from his warm chest, but he captured it.

'I was enjoying that.'

'What do you mean?' She was aware of how high-pitched her voice had become. She swallowed hard and tried again. 'Dawn is breaking. Jobs must be attended to. You mentioned to Lord Sigmund that sailing back to Eire as soon as possible was desirable.'

'Stay,' he whispered next to her ear. His breath fanned her earlobe, making a warm curl start in her nether regions. 'Like this. There is no need to stir. Yet. Rest awhile longer.'

'Stay?' Her voice was definitely at the top of her squeak range and hysterical laughter was about to explode, but she didn't want to move. She wanted the warm curl thrumming inside to grow into an inferno. 'I'm not sure that is wise. I didn't mean to and can only apologise. We had an agreement.'

His breath traced her jawline and the need to go vanished, driven out by the insistent warm languor. 'Apologise? For what?'

'For disturbing your sleep.'

He smoothed a tendril of hair from her forehead. 'I can't remember when I last rested this easy.'

'Blame it on Sigmund's mead.'

His finger playfully stroked her nose. 'Most of that ended up on the rushes when people were distracted.'

She jerked back. 'You poured it out? Lord Sigmund takes great pride in the mead he serves.'

'I will try to remember the next time and drink with proper appreciation, but last night was my wedding night and I had other concerns.'

His mouth returned to her earlobe, making her nipples tighten to hard points. She knew she didn't want to move, even though it was probably the most prudent thing to do.

She forced her head to turn. 'If you insist…we can lie like this for a short time. No harm in resting.'

He slowly relaxed his hold on her fingers. 'There, you see. Nothing spoiling. Everything to be gained.'

The warm muscle and sinew beneath her fingertips enticed her to explore further. Her hands slipped lower towards his belly.

He caught her forefinger and raised it to his lips. 'Don't start anything that you don't intend to finish, my lady fair. A friendly warning.'

Immediately, she drew her hand back. 'A warning? How am I starting anything?'

He lifted her chin. She glimpsed the fierce light in his eyes. 'A promise. We both know where this sort of play leads, Svanna.'

Her tongue moistened her suddenly parched lips. He thought her experienced—he must, from his words about her knowing where this would lead—but she was a maid. If she explained, would he believe her? She knew the horrible rumours that Turgeis had caused to swirl. She'd heard the doggerels, even though her nurse told her to ignore them because reacting would only give them credence.

'Do we?'

'Yes, lots of time. The tides turn and then turn again.'

'Why are you waiting for the tide?'

'Because one day soon you and I will go to Eire as man and wife.' He wrapped a tendril of hair about his forefinger. 'But I'd be lying if I said I wasn't deeply attracted to you. You were in my dreams and now you are in my arms. I wanted to do this.'

She wet her lips. 'Do what?'

'This.' He cupped his hand about her jaw and brought her mouth to his. His lips descended, seeking rather than demanding, taking their time to explore and gently persuade.

The warm curl within her grew to an insistent white heat. Every particle of her appeared to be gloriously awake and alive.

'Shall I continue?' he asked, moving his lips to her ear. 'We have time.'

She knew that saying no was the last thing she wanted.

'Yes.'

'Good.' His mouth returned to hers and his tongue traced the outline of her lips before penetrating her.

Her body arched forward and collided with the length of his much harder one. She ran her hand down his flank, feeling the indents of the scarring which marked his body. Giving in to impulse, she pressed her lips against the smooth scar on his face.

'I'm sorry you received this,' she murmured.

'Once I blamed you,' he admitted, tangling her hair about his hand. 'But that was wrong of me.'

'Wrong of you?'

'You'd no idea of my existence. You are not the sort of person to lie about something that never happened. It was an unfortunate accident.'

'I… I know who you are now,' she said, her voice faltering. She knew she should tell him about the innocent flirtation and the chaste kiss they'd shared, but she worried about breaking this fragile truce which had sprung up between them. She wanted this white heat to continue. She wanted to feel his hands on her body, making her feel precious and unsullied. She simply wanted to be. Time enough for confessions later.

'The time for talking has ended.' She turned her mouth towards his and parted his lips with her tongue.

His hand slid down her back, urging her closer still, while their tongues touched, tangled, retreated and returned to tangle again.

The apex of her thighs encountered his rampant erection.

'You see, I do want you, in case you had any doubt,' he breathed against her ear. 'But it remains your choice.'

Svanna knew she should be prudent and retreat from the bed, get dressed and make some transparent excuse, but somehow, she didn't want to. Another wave of heat washed over her, leaving her body aching for the relief she instinctively knew only he could give her.

'I'll stay,' she said, not giving herself time to allow reason and prudence to reassert themselves. 'At least until the turning of the tide.'

His chest shook with barely suppressed laughter. 'Your choice. Until the turning of the tide it shall be.'

She longed to ask what the turning of the tide actually meant to him, but decided on balance she didn't want to appear naïve. She simply touched his cheek in response. He turned his face to her palm.

His mouth slowly moved across her jawline before travelling down to where the neck of her gown met the beginnings of the shadowy place between her breasts. There he paused.

His hand brushed against her nipples, tracing small circles while his tongue tasted her skin, drawing ever-increasing circles.

Her nipples became hardened points under his ministrations and the white-hot heat increased until she felt the apex of her thighs grow slick with longing.

Her back arched, seeking relief in the shadowy place between her thighs which she knew his touch would bring. But he ignored her arching and the faint mewling in the back of her throat. Instead, he slowly took one nipple then the other one into his mouth and suckled, while his fingers drew patterns on her belly. All about her, the room exploded in stars.

Slowly, the world righted itself. She found him still and staring at her.

'Shall I continue?' he rasped in her ear. 'Say it, Svanna.'

'Please.' She nodded, knowing more words were beyond her. She tugged at his arms, and her body bucked upwards once again. He traced the line of her jaw.

'I believe I know the solution.'

His knee wedged her thighs open. His hands travelled lower and played in her nest of curls. Round and round until she grew slick.

She moaned in the back of her throat and clawed at his shoulders.

He placed a moist finger against her lips. 'Impatient?'

His finger traced the outline of her mouth before delving in. She drew it into her mouth and jammed her hips upwards.

Her middle encountered his groin, and she instinctively adjusted her position, spreading her knees wide so that he could impale himself deep within her.

He firmly drove in. His eyes widened slightly as he encountered her maidenhead, but she bucked her hips upwards until he fully sheathed himself. He gave a great sigh and collapsed down on her.

She wrapped her arms about him and held him while he lay there, unmoving. Giving in to her instinct, she rocked back and forth, enjoying the feel of him within her. He then joined her, each time driving deeper.

And she knew all her imaginings, both good and bad, had not prepared her for the sheer intensity of sensations which coursed through her and swept her into their maelstrom.

When it reached its height she clung to him, wrapping her legs firmly about him, and heard her voice cry out, then she shuddered and lay still, utterly spent and replete.

A good while later, when the chamber was bathed in golden morning light, Rand lay back against the pillows and stroked Svanna's hair while she appeared to sleep, curled into his side with her head on his chest.

What had passed between had been entirely unexpected in its sheer intensity. He felt as if he'd been sleepwalking through life for a long time and had finally woken to a bright new day.

He'd forgotten what sex could be like, but he had not been prepared for her to be a maiden. In his desire, he'd not taken the time to prepare her properly and when he'd realised, it had been far too late to stop. But he knew he wanted her to enjoy the act as much he did. And he hated himself for believing the lies his cousin had told him back on the boat about how Ingebord must have taken some lover. He'd experienced the proof that she never had. She'd been an innocent. The entire scheme which had led to his beating had been some twisted fantasy of Drengr and his sons.

'Did I hurt you?' he whispered, holding her like precious glass but not expecting her to answer.

She touched his face. 'No more than I expected, and a lot less than I feared.'

'I took your maidenhead. Too late when I realised.'

She withdrew her hand and propped herself up on one elbow. 'Is that surprising? You knew my reputation as an Ice Maiden. I spent many years cultivating it. It became my shield. That and Tippi. Even Turgeis worried about her bite after he'd experienced it.'

Her voice quavered on the last word as if it was supposed to be a joke.

'I'd always considered that I was attacked to protect another. I guess it didn't go as far as I figured it must have done, given my beating.' He put his finger against her lips. 'No need to tell me his name.'

'No other exists.'

His mouth flopped open. He must have heard wrong.

'What do you mean? Drengr decided to invent something?' he asked, genuinely puzzled. 'My cousin Thorarinn assured me that he had heard multiple rumours. I can just about recall some of the jokes.'

'Rumours which had no basis in fact, as you now know. Ugly rumours intended to discredit me. Turgeis was obsessed with spreading them. '*Having his little joke*' was how my nurse put it. I was supposed to keep myself above such things and float like an unperturbed swan.'

She moved out of his arms. She reached for her discarded undergarments and dressed. While she was doing so, she kept her face turned away from him. The silence grew oppressive and he internally winced. His words must have sounded far harsher than he'd intended.

'Svanna? I'm trying to apologise,' he said. 'I would have taken more time to prepare you properly. I didn't consider and I'm sorry. But you should have said something.'

'How was I supposed to know what you thought about my previous love life? We never discussed it.' Her entire being radiated righteous indignation. 'Would you have believed me if I had mentioned it? Or would you have believed those rumours your cousin, whom I have never met, repeated?'

'I don't know. I thought someone must have made you wary about physical contact,' he said, because only the truth would do when each word from her stabbed him. 'I should have thought about the alternative, and I'm so sorry. I am sorry for everything.'

She finished dressing and turned to face him. Her body was hunched and her arms wrapped about her waist as if to ward off a blow.

'I think you deserve to know the full truth,' she said in a toneless voice. 'Try not to hate me too much. I should have told you before we married, but I thought maybe it was unimportant. The past was the past and unalterable, and it could remain there. I see now it was hugely important, and I was wrong. My excuse is that I assumed our encounter was unimportant.'

Rand's throat tightened. 'Why would I hate you, Svanna? Whatever happened was in the past. I accept you had nothing to do with it. I've wronged you.'

'The night you were attacked, I was pretending to be a servant—or, rather, to be myself. Reckless, I know, but I was fed up with being Ingebord. My foster-mother had retired with a bad head and my nurse was attending her. It was what the real Ingebord would have done—snuck off to have some fun. The King had been making his usual prediction of me marrying his son, a boy I considered about as appealing as a three-day-old trout.'

'You were under tremendous pressure,' he said carefully, trying to think. Dim memories of laughing with a young girl, one who blushed and who was called... He groaned, hating what must come next, fearing he was wrong. He had to be wrong.

'I thought no one realised who I was. Such fun.' Her eyes briefly shone with the memory. 'I had a brief flirtation with a young warrior, which ended with a chaste kiss and a promise to meet in my foster-mother's herb garden. I heard my nurse calling, hurried away to my bed, and pulled the furs over my head without seeing anyone. My dreams that night, and many nights afterwards, were filled with the young warrior, but I learned from my nurse that he'd departed for the east to make his fortune. No reason given, other than that.'

A warrior who had suddenly left. His blood ran cold. How many ships had left that morning? Which warrior? Him or Thorarinn? A sickening realisation swept over him. What had happened to her had occurred after he'd escaped, after he'd received that beating where he would have said anything to make them stop.

'Later, I suspected that somehow we must have been betrayed.'

'Why did you think that?' he asked, forcing the words from his throat. In all the intervening years, he'd never once considered whether anything had happened to her.

He couldn't even remember what he'd said when the blows were raining down, urging him to confess and tell the secret place where they met. Maybe he had said something, anything to stop them. And what then? He'd never considered that something might happen to the young woman if she was discovered.

The only slender hope he had to hang on to was that it had not been him and they had already known, but it was a forlorn hope.

'After learning that the warrior had departed on the morning tide, I was unable to resist going to the herb garden to see if any token was there. I was about to leave when Turgeis entered and attempted to rape me… Would have done if Tippi had not intervened.'

Rand put a hand to his scar, trying to make sense of Svanna's confession. She'd suffered dreadfully, but she was blameless. He tried one last time to keep that flickering hope alive. 'You had a flirtation with my cousin?'

She shook her head. 'With you. I'd no idea that you were attacked because of it. You must believe that.'

Rand searched his memory. He had the vaguest memory of Thorarinn apologising, but that was all. Thorarinn couldn't have been the one to betray them? His mind recoiled from the idea. His cousin would never do anything intentionally to harm him.

'I have little memory of that night. I had forgotten our flirtation entirely. And the blows kept coming until the world went black.' He put a hand over his eyes. 'I've no idea what I confessed to. All I knew was that I never did anything to dishonour the Queen's daughter. I want to think I kept saying that, no matter how hard they beat me, but I don't know.'

He waited, hoping for any sign of redemption, any sign that she understood what he was trying to say.

'I believe you. I never blamed you for any of it. If anything, our brief time together stood out as a glorious time before the awfulness. Turgeis was, and remains, at fault, no one else.'

Rand released his breath. She held no anger towards him. She had probably never considered it, but it showed him her depth of character, that she couldn't even contemplate him having betrayed her. 'I don't deserve that, but thank you from the depths of my soul.'

She watched him from under her lashes for a long heartbeat. He wanted to put his arms about her and hold her tight, but he knew he had to let her come to him. Patience had never been harder.

'Because of what Turgeis did, I cultivated my reputation as an Ice Maiden. He used…used to enjoy tormenting me, whispering about what he intended to do to me once he'd secured me. After Maer returned and Drengr was vanquished with his sons banished, I dared to hope the memory would fade to nothing.' Her voice faltered, but she pressed her hands together and after a long heartbeat continued. 'But Turgeis saluted me during the raid. His way of saying that he remembers that awful promise he uttered after Tippi bit him—*he looked forward to enjoying my favours like Randolfr Fullrson had*.'

'He mentioned me?'

She nodded.

Rand's stomach twisted. The reason for insisting on marriage hit him—despite everything, she looked to him for protection from the man who had abused her and still sought to do more.

She trusted him to ensure that their joining was pleasurable, and he'd failed. Why hadn't he considered the possibility that she might have been attacked? By the end, he knew he could have said anything to stop the blows raining down. He was unworthy. Once he'd failed her, and he refused to fail again.

'I am sorry.'

'It's not your fault. I should have told you earlier, but I hoped the explanation would not be needed.' She bowed her head. 'An error on my part. But please, can we move beyond this?'

'And on mine. I offer no excuses, Svanna, but a promise to do better.'

'I can understand if you wish to annul the marriage...' She held up her cut hand and gave a brave smile. 'We can say that we proved incompatible, and the marriage was never consummated.'

His stomach ached more than ever. Annulling the marriage was the last thing he required. He only knew that returning to that walking dead state with its twilight world was not what he needed.

'The strategic reasons for the marriage remain, Svanna,' he said as gently as he could. His instinct was to go and kiss her until she surrendered, but he knew that would be a mistake. He had to work on rebuilding trust. 'What you told me alters nothing.'

She reluctantly nodded as she retreated three steps and glanced towards the door as if measuring the distance she'd have to sprint. 'The sun has risen...my foster-mother will be looking for me.'

Despite his instincts telling him to haul her into his arms, he knew he would take the patient man's way, a way that felt awkward and unnatural, but he suspected was the right course, and would allow her a brief time to recalibrate and collect her thoughts. He put his hands behind his head and gripped the mattress. 'By all means, go to her.'

She needed no further urging and practically ran out of the door, demonstrating what she must have felt in truth about their joining.

He slammed his hand against the bed. He'd managed to destroy his marriage before it had properly begun, and that fact hurt far more than he'd thought it would. He should have thought about the possibility of her being a virgin, but he hadn't. The unvarnished truth was that the sex which had made him feel alive after being one of the walking dead had not been as good for her. And he knew he wanted to make it as good for her as it was for him. He needed to make it right and ensure she understood how pleasurable joining could be. The last thing he wanted was for her to fear the physical side. After what they'd shared, he knew, if she'd permit it, he'd ensure they experienced it again and again.

'Another chance for us must be possible. I will make it happen. I will figure out a way. We can't end like this.'

Chapter Nine

'What are you doing here, Svanna?' Astrid asked when Svanna entered the room that they had previously shared. Svanna narrowed her gaze and concentrated on Astrid, pushing aside all thoughts of her uncomfortable conversation with Rand.

She should have told him before they'd shared that second kiss. Was it any wonder that he'd looked at her in such an appalled fashion? She curled her fists and tried to concentrate on what was important, namely, Astrid's health.

Astrid appeared to have passed a comfortable night, and her face was less pinched. She had to take that as a good sign.

'I wanted to ensure you were resting properly.' Svanna bobbed a curtsey. 'What other purpose can I have?'

'The Norns have yet to cut my life-thread. Far stronger than many think. But it must hang by the tiniest thread,' Astrid said, mentioning the three arbiters of fate which the people of the North believed controlled a person's life and indeed when that life would be cut short. Astrid turned her head. 'Why are you alone?'

'Last night tired Rand.' Svanna silently prayed some small part of that was true. Confessing to Astrid what had passed between them would make her toes curl. 'What sort of foster-daughter would I be if I failed to come and see you?'

Astrid's eyes crinkled at the corners. 'Be with your husband and ensure our interests are well looked after. Your instincts were correct on this marriage.'

Svanna shifted uncomfortably. But going back meant facing Rand after confessing her small part in his scarring. He needed time to properly digest what she'd said.

She busied herself plumping the pillows and straightening the furs. 'Much needs to be done here. You remain injured. I wasn't thinking straight. Now I am.'

'Fear talking, Svanna. Something I never expected to hear from you of all people.'

Svanna bent and retrieved a fur from the floor and held it in front of her like a shield. 'I was headstrong and overconfident.'

Astrid shook her head. 'A limited time remains to make a difference, my dear. Everyone witnessed the way he devoured you at the wedding. You must use his desire while it lasts to advance our cause. Bind him to you. Or Agthir will suffer.'

Svanna forced her lashes to flutter and her voice to be sweet. 'You were the one who cautioned delay. Make desire grow through absence.'

Astrid stared up at the rafters for a long time without replying. 'Last night, it came to me. There was more to this attack than meets the eye. I should have seen that earlier. I was wrong to laugh at that assistant swineherd.'

'What do you mean? We know the Sons of Drengr wish to counteract any threat from Islay. They thought Lord Sigmund was in the hall.'

Astrid's hand plucked restlessly at the furs. 'They could have attacked earlier at any time before the service. Drengr would have done, knowing that the coalition was unstable. Turgeis is no fool, even if I have my doubts about the other two.'

'You are speaking in riddles.'

'There must be more to the timing. Something to do with Rand's arrival. Turgeis wanted to send a message to Eire as well as Islay.'

'No one expected Rand and his men.'

'Turgeis did. Why else did he wait? Why did he risk discovery, anchored in that bay? Your new husband is the key to solving this mystery. Stick close to him, Svanna. Find the answer, prevent Turgeis from gaining power in Eire and Agthir will be that much safer.'

'Drengr beat Rand until he could barely see. Somehow, his cousin managed to get them to stop, and they took the first ship away from Agthir.'

Astrid gave her a level look. 'Drengr rarely did anything without a reason.'

'Someone told him that Rand and I were having a flirtation—or perhaps more than a flirtation.' Svanna tensed. 'Rand only remembers a few details, but he remembered the reason given. It was why he kissed me before he went in to save you. He vowed that one day he'd kiss your daughter in truth. Rumours apparently swirled about me being easy meat for men.'

'How did Drengr obtain that idea? Your nurse and I watched you very closely. The rumours were young men's fantasies. How did Helga put it—*"Young warriors speak with something other than their mouths and should not be listened to"*. I then told her *"but young women should be protected from them"*. She agreed to keep her eyes on you. I know you found it hard to be watched closely, but I didn't want you put in an impossible situation with one of those warriors.'

'I've no idea.' Svanna looked at her hands. Helga had kept a close watch out afterwards, but she never explained why. Perhaps if she had confessed what had happened to her all those years ago, things would have been different. But it was too late for regrets.

Astrid's face showed sudden concern. 'Did you know about the beating Rand received from Drengr before you married?'

'I learned about it when he arrived here.' She took a deep breath and knew for the second time that day she'd have to confess. 'He remembers very little of what happened immediately prior to the beating, but he accepts that I played no part. But I'd spoken with him. Alone, without you or my nurse present. I don't how Drengr and his sons learned of it.'

Astrid made a temple of her fingers. 'Have you told him about your unwitting part?'

'This morning.'

'Did you tell him voluntarily?'

'It slipped out. After...well, I knew I had to say the words.'

Astrid sighed. 'Sometimes, Svanna, I'm amazed at your honesty, but at least that shadow is no longer between you.'

She closed her eyes and Rand's appalled expression rose before her. 'I fear the marriage might be over before it has properly begun. I doubt I will ever gain his trust. And without that, how can I be an effective voice for Agthir in Eire?'

'It alters things in some ways and yet not in others.' Astrid held out her hand. Svanna grasped it. 'I shan't blame you for that, but your marriage isn't over. Solid reasons for its existence remain. Face the future and not the past.'

'I thought that I could remain here, looking after you.

Not for ever, but until you are better. Then I can travel to Eire. Or even back to Agthir.'

Astrid's grip tightened. 'Your mother wasn't a coward. I didn't raise you to be one either. Why are you giving in to your fear instead of fighting for your marriage—a marriage you made because you swore it was vital for your country?'

Svanna widened her eyes. Cowardice? She had done the prudent thing, escaping before Rand turned from her in disgust. Why had she allowed the ice shield to fall even the slightest fraction? 'Someone needs to look after you.'

'That someone is not you. Your place is with your husband, whom you insisted on marrying. I refuse to be used as a shield.'

Svanna pressed her hands against her eyes. 'Why? What do you know that I have overlooked?'

'He needs this marriage as much as you do. Maybe more so. But everyone witnessed that kiss you shared during the marriage ceremony. And you've little idea if you have lost his regard.'

Svanna hated that a small tendril of hope sprang in her breast. Inwardly, she resolved to think logically instead of sighing after him. Perhaps becoming friends with his daughter would be a way to earn his regard. She knew she wanted to be a good mother to the little girl.

'I'm unafraid of hard work. I will go.'

'Keep to the path you have chosen. You may yet avert disaster.'

'Do you want the ship ready to go on the next tide?' his helmsman asked.

Rand frowned. He wasn't certain of anything right now, but he knew he needed to be doing something. He also knew staying here was not going to solve any problem. Too many people like the dowager Queen about. Giving Svanna a choice was necessary. Time apart might allow them both to decide what they wanted next, even if he hoped she'd choose to travel with them. 'What I asked for last night.'

The helmsman shrugged. 'Men ask for a lot of things before their wedding night. You'd be surprised.'

'The sooner we return to Eire, the sooner we get to the bottom of the mystery.'

'Will our new lady be joining us?' The helmsman scratched his head. 'I mean, her mother was quite injured.'

'Up to Svanna. I would hardly like to prejudge,' he said around the ash-taste in his mouth. 'We have the alliance now.'

'What will be up to me?' Svanna asked, slipping her arm through his and smiling up at him while his helmsman suddenly discovered he was required elsewhere. 'Surely you can't be thinking of leaving the peace-weaver behind.'

He inwardly thanked the saints and angels. For some reason, she'd returned to his side. He suspected Astrid had sent her, but right now, he didn't care. The tight place in his chest had eased.

'My men and I need to return to Tara and explain about the unprovoked attack, but your foster-mother remains unwell. I've no wish to cause you distress.'

She gave him a hooded look. 'How would it look to the high king if you claim a marriage to a princess of Agthir but fail to produce the bride? Particularly as you were supposed to be ensuring a different marriage altogether.'

'Máel Sechnaill would understand…if it was explained properly. In the end, he cares for the result, not the means for that result. Pragmatic to his toes.' Rand winced at his words. He had no idea what Máel Sechnaill would do or what game he was playing, but he had to give Svanna the option. She had to make her choice freely. He silently prayed she would choose him. 'He would understand your devotion to your foster-mother.'

'He might say that he does, but I wish to discuss aspects of the raid with him.' Svanna peeked up at him from under her lashes. 'I must assume Turgeis knew Astrid was involved in the preparations. We extended our stay. He sought to strike at Agthir. Agthir needs this alliance, Rand, as much as Tara does.'

'I've no idea,' Rand confessed. 'I was unaware of the possibility. I didn't know until I arrived that anyone from Agthir was here.'

'Would you have travelled here if you had?'

He hated that the answer was complicated and one he didn't want to fully examine right now. 'Speculation serves no good purpose as I am here now. What came to pass cannot be altered. We go forward.'

She tapped the side of her nose. 'Possibly best if we leave the conversation until we reach Tara and have spoken to King Máel Sechnaill. It remains of vital interest to me and my foster-mother. That knowledge must form part of any fight back.'

The heaviness vanished from his chest. His clumsiness had not destroyed everything. She wanted the marriage to continue for strategic reasons.

'Then you intend to travel with me?'

Her face became inscrutable. 'Impossible to peace-weave if I remain on Islay. I doubt my words will carry very far over the water.'

He tightened his hold on her arm and resolved that he would find a way to seduce her properly. To demonstrate to her how delightful sex could truly be. 'You make a fair observation.'

She inclined her head. 'Astrid pointed out that the reasons for the marriage had not altered for either of us. I intend to hold that thought in the forefront of my mind.'

'Does Astrid call the tune?'

'She made suggestions.' She made a curtsey. 'Apparently, the sheets have been examined and found to be satisfactory.'

'I'm aware of Gaelic custom. But I intend our consummation to last longer than one night. Provided the bride is willing.'

A light breeze pushed tendrils of her hair across her face, obscuring her expression. Her face suddenly became heart-stoppingly beautiful. He wanted to capture a tendril and twine it about his fingers, but he kept his hands rigidly down at his sides and waited.

Eventually, she nodded. 'When shall we depart? I look forward to meeting my new daughter. I plan to be a good mother, Rand.'

Rand hated the sudden lump in his throat at the thought of Birdie having a gentle hand to guide her. 'When the tide turns, if the terms are acceptable.'

'They will have to be. I'll arrange for my trunks to be delivered.' She paused. 'I've served Agthir's interests for most of my life and I intend to keep serving with our marriage.'

Svanna watched her trunks disappear into Rand's longship. Her brave words to Rand earlier seemed to have little substance and signified less. She wanted to curl up small and hide somewhere until it was safe to come out.

Her few trunks seemed such a small sum of a life. Absurdly, she wished she could take her small loom, the one she'd used to create the intricate braids that adorned hers and Astrid's gowns, but she'd left it back in Agthir. Her idea that she wouldn't need weaving to calm her mind was laughable now. She always found that weaving allowed her to concentrate on what was important. Maybe she could teach Birdie how to weave and calm her mind that way.

Given the way the summer sun beat down, she was also pleased that she'd opted for her thin wool gown, the one that set off her eyes.

'I'll miss you,' she said, brushing Astrid's cheek with her lips. 'But my instinct is to go with my new husband.'

She hadn't expected Astrid to come down to the ship but, leaning heavily on Sigmund's arm, she had. To her surprise, Rand allowed her a little time to make her private goodbyes.

'A mark of good faith, my dear. You're well placed to explain about the perfidy of the Brothers Drengrson, particularly Turgeis,' Sigmund said. 'Astrid explained how uncomfortable Turgeis made you in Agthir.'

Astrid pressed her hand. 'I know you have been wary of that man for a long time, but I think Lord Randolfr will do his best to protect you.'

An ice-cold splinter went down Svanna's back. Astrid believed Turgeis would attack her.

'We need to go, my lady wife, or we will miss the tide,' Rand shouted where he stood at the helm of his boat. 'I'm not minded to forego this particular tide.'

The words were friendly enough, but there was an underlying warning. She went now or she lost the chance. 'I should go.'

'Sooner you go, the quicker we will see each other again.' Astrid gave a tired smile. 'Long goodbyes are wearisome.'

'I will ensure Astrid is well looked after and that she recovers her strength. Never fear that,' Sigmund said, putting his arm about Astrid's waist.

In response, Astrid leant against him and gave a cat-that-got-the-cream sort of smile, before stepping out of the circle of his arm.

Svanna enveloped Astrid in one final hug. Astrid stood stiffly for a long heartbeat before giving her a fierce hug in return.

'I will return for your wedding,' she said into Astrid's ear. 'Halfr put his arm about you in public. He will not have you mistaken for a concubine. Say yes when he asks, please.'

Astrid's cheeks flamed. 'Nothing is settled between Halfr and me.'

'Nevertheless, you have my word about wishing to attend.'

Astrid brushed Svanna's cheek. 'You have a good heart, Svanna, but no more of this matchmaking. Your future is elsewhere.'

'I know that.'

'And, Svanna, seduce him as soon as possible. It will help bind him to you. Stop being afraid. You can do this. I have seen how he looks at you.'

Svanna gulped hard and was pleased Rand was too far away to hear the words. Seduce him at the earliest opportunity? How? She'd spent years being an Ice Maiden. When and where? Her body still faintly ached from what had passed between them, but she suspected she'd been a disappointment to him, a novelty and nothing more.

'I will try.'

'That is the Svanna I know and love. Now, go. Make your mother proud. Make me proud.'

Without a reply, Svanna hurried to the boat and Rand's helmsman helped her aboard. She stood beside Rand, but looked back towards the shore until Astrid and Sigmund became no more than faint dots.

The warmth suddenly appeared to have gone from the

sun. She wrapped her arms around her and tried not to think on Astrid's last injunction. All she knew was that it would be very awkward if Rand guessed. All she could cling to was how much the usurper had liked her and how that had assisted Astrid in the early days of the occupation. Maybe she could bond with the little girl and demonstrate to Rand how useful she could be.

'How long to Tara?'

'Before the sun sets in the West, we will make landfall,' Rand said, handing the helm to one of his men. 'I want to go to Donaghmoyne. Land in the North, rather than making our way from near Dubh-Linn. Less chance of encountering Turgeis and his men.'

Svanna shivered despite the heat of the day. She was voluntarily going to the same country as that man. Was she walking into a web he'd woven or would she be able to cut the strands and finally destroy him for ever? 'You think that is a risk?'

'After what happened, I consider it a distinct possibility. But under Máel Sechnaill, the men of Eire have managed to keep the Northmen contained to the area around Dubh-Linn. We will be safe landing in the North and travelling by land.'

A tremor passed through her. 'We will be safe there?'

'Turgeis requires power, not certain defeat. His ships might occasionally patrol the coastline but they don't land.'

'You sound like Lord Sigmund before Turgeis attacked. What Turgeis will dare depends on what he intends to achieve.'

'Venturing deep within Tara's territory would be an act of war—a war which he'd lose.'

'What do I know of strategy?'

'Precisely.' He nodded and gave the signal to increase the rowing speed and to unfurl the sail. The boat lurched into the open ocean with spray hitting her face. Svanna retreated to the small covered area and sat down on her largest trunk. Safe in the North. She wanted to believe it true. She knew how often safety had been an illusion. Silently, she offered up a prayer that this time she would be able to find a secure harbour for the rest of her life, but experience had taught her not to put too much faith in prayers. Instead, she had to figure out a way to make it happen without relying on anyone else. Seduction perhaps, or ensuring that he saw how useful she could be with his daughter.

Svanna shaded her eyes and tried to pick out any line of green on the horizon. She'd spent most of the voyage daydreaming about what she'd do when she finally met Rand's little girl and how she'd ensure Birdie would begin to look up to her and trust her. To her astonishment, she kept coming up with new ideas like teaching her how to weave, sew and even garden with herbs. With each new idea, a quiver went down her spine; she found the thought of being a proper mother to that little girl excited her more than she'd considered possible.

The waves developed white caps and the spray positively soaked her. She braced her feet and tried not to shiver. The day which had started in brilliant sunshine now had dark clouds obscuring the horizon. And a stiff breeze had sprung up.

An omen? Svanna swallowed hard and tried to rid herself of the sense of foreboding. Her mind circled back to that salute Turgeis had given. Had it been a goodbye or something much worse?

'Is that green I see?' she asked, not expecting an answer.

'Light on the water,' Rand said, coming to sit beside her. 'We will reach the coast soon enough, and then travel up the coast to reach the inlet which leads to the road to Donaghmoyne. If the weather holds, we'll sup in my hall.' He gave a smile that warmed her down to her toes. 'And you will meet my daughter.'

'I'm looking forward to meeting Birdie. Do you see her often?'

'She provides what little sunshine there has been in my life since her mother died. I always take any excuse to see her, but Máel Sechnaill works me hard. I refuse to put her in danger. Donaghmoyne is the safest place for her.'

'Will she be going to court with us? That is such a wonderful idea, Rand.' Svanna forced a smile and her mind eagerly raced ahead to how she and Birdie could become friends while they travelled. A covered cart might take longer, but it would give her an excellent opportunity to truly get to know the little girl before they arrived at court. 'We won't be able to stay at Donaghmoyne long and taking her with us makes sense. A friendly face at court and a travelling companion for me.'

His eyes slid away from her. 'Unadvisable.'

Svanna plucked at the edge of the braid which ran around her right cuff and tried to keep her composure. 'I mean your daughter no harm. I'm eager to play my role. I've always enjoyed the company of children. I can teach her some of the riddles I know from Agthir.'

His smile turned tighter. 'It's not you or your riddles I worry about.'

Svanna rocked back on her heels, studying him. Her grand scheme of showing how useful she could be by smoothing his daughter's way seemed to be over before it had properly begun.

'Would the court be dangerous for her? I wanted to get to know her better. I used to love travelling when I was little.'

'Birdie stays away from court. She will grow up into a chirping little girl who wears sunshine in her copper curls, just like I promised her mother.'

'I don't see the connection.'

'Court ritual wears adults down. I refuse to have my daughter become a shadow of herself.'

Svanna frowned, trying to puzzle out the undercurrents. Rand's face had hardened to glacial planes. Was he going to keep her and Birdie separate? How could that help anyone, least of all her quest to ensure Máel Sechnaill understood the threat Turgeis posed? 'But she is the high king's grandchild. Surely, he must want to see her. Does he often visit Donaghmoyne?'

'The high king has other concerns on his mind. He does not often speak of her.' Rand's scar twitched. 'He did express a wish to meet Birdie once, but he was in his cups and feeling melancholy, missing his favourite daughter. I suspect he forgot the wish by the next morning. He has never mentioned it again.'

'Your late wife was his favourite child.'

'That is the problem.' His words seemed to end the matter.

Svanna stared out to sea. The cold spray positively soaked her but her internal misery bothered her more. She hadn't realised how much she'd been looking forward to making a difference in the child's life.

'You expect him to be upset with your cousin,' she said in a soft voice, urging him to confide more so that she could understand and figure out a new scheme, something which didn't involve seduction. 'I would think seeing his granddaughter, the sole remnant of his most beloved daughter, would soften his heart. A young child can do that.'

'A prudent man seeks as many advantages as possible,

but Máel Sechnaill could not bear to gaze upon his granddaughter at the baptism.' Rand's voice had become flat and toneless. Svanna instinctively covered his hand with hers for a long heartbeat before he moved it.

'Did he say what he wanted to happen with the little girl?' she asked quietly. She needed to know her options and how she could ensure Birdie was going to thrive. Not just now when she was young, but as she grew.

'He said that I was free to bring Birdie up as I chose, but his grief was too great for her ever to command a place at court.'

She examined her hands. Grief could change and alter. She'd have to go slow, but it would help everyone if Birdie could travel with them, just in case. 'Do you think your cousin and his new wife are at Donaghmoyne?'

He gave a bark of laughter. 'Why would they be there?'

'Because you would be unlikely to look there until after you finished the King's business? Because the King refuses to go there?'

'Have you met my cousin?'

'Not knowingly,' she admitted with a shrug. 'But it makes logical sense. And it will be the first place you'd return to after you finish your mission. Your cousin knows you will forgive him, even if you yell at him.'

He put a warm hand on her upper arm. 'You are wiser than I thought. What a combination—brains as well as beauty. It makes me wonder why you remained unmarried until now. It seems incredible that Queen Astrid or Maer did not employ one of their best counters. The need for strong allies never ceases.'

'I was dangled countless times. In truth, the late King had hopes of me marrying his son, which would never have worked.' She kept her face turned from his. 'Drengr wanted me. Initially for one of his sons. After his wife died, there was even talk of him being my groom. I don't know how true that is or if it was to spook me into seeking the illusion of safety with one of his sons. All that man cared about was power.'

He captured her chin. 'Look at me, Svanna. The past. I won't allow them to hurt you.'

'One of the reasons I know about the arts of war is to never feel defenceless again.' Svanna shrugged and pushed the memory back into the recesses of her mind where it belonged. 'Maer decreed that any marriage must be my own decision. There was never a strong enough reason to marry until I was faced with this. Agthir's safety means everything to me.'

She hoped the answer would suffice and he would stop his probing.

'Surely she married for the sake of her country. She married the usurper's son, didn't she? The one you said had the personality of a wet fish.'

'She married because she wanted to. They were, and remain, deeply in love. I'll admit that Karn has improved considerably since he and Maer became acquainted.'

'I am pleased she found the other half of her soul, but you decided that wasn't worth waiting for.'

Svanna looked at the horizon. She knew she wasn't the other half of Rand's soul. That honour belonged to his late wife. It bothered her that in her daydreaming about acting as Birdie's mother, she'd also dreamt about seeing regard in his eyes. Her heart had to stop hoping for miracles. She was being useful to Agthir and that should be enough.

'Something like that. Maer did emphasise that it must always be my choice,' she said, keeping her gaze on the horizon. 'This marriage was my choice. My duty to Agthir. My way of contributing to its defence.'

He nodded. 'Your directness is something I admire about you.'

'Directness?'

'You are my wife and not pretending to be anything else. You're unafraid to explain your reasoning. It makes a change.'

'A refreshing one, I hope.' She forced a laugh but his eyes turned serious. Her heart knocked against her chest. She'd made a muddle of things this morning, completely misreading his mood. If she did so again, it didn't bode well for the future.

'You want to ensure that the high king is in a good mood though,' she said, trying for the brightest voice possible and hoping he would not comment on the slight alteration of the subject when he failed to reply to her comment.

Rand bestowed a smile, but this one failed to reach his eyes. 'It will help keep Thorarinn's head attached to his torso.'

'I understand why that would be advantageous to all, particularly to your cousin, who I would think has grown quite attached to his head.'

The ghost smile faded from his face. 'I owe him my life, Svanna. If he'd not rescued me from Drengr, I'd have breathed my last.'

She wrapped her arms about her middle and wished she had worn thicker clothes as the ice-cold wind whistled through her. She, too, did not know why Rand had been singled out. She sincerely doubted now that they had been seen together. Some other game was afoot, but she couldn't think what it was and what part Thorarinn had played.

'Our past is behind us, but it casts a long shadow. Hopefully, its shadow will ebb.' She knew then she couldn't do what Astrid wanted her to do and manipulate him through seduction, not if he admired her directness. 'My foster-mother—'

'What did your foster-mother suggest?'

'That I seduce you for the good of Agthir.' The words tripped off her tongue in a great rush and, despite the coldness of the spray, her cheeks burned.

He raised her hand to his lips. 'When we next join, it'll be your choice. Yours and not Agthir's. You are the only one I want in my bed.'

She peeped up at him, saw the dancing light in his eyes and knew her ice shield was no more. It would be easy to care for this man, even though he'd warned her that he was unlikely to ever return any finer feelings. She must keep to their agreement, or she'd be doomed to a disappointment her heart would never recover from. 'I never cared for crowds.'

He raised her hand to his mouth. 'You are good, my lady.'

She hated that she wanted to cradle her tingling palm to her cheek.

The first hard drops of rain hit her. She reached for her cloak and wished again that she had thought to wear more layers than the thin summer gown, but the weather had seemed perfect back on Islay, the sort of day which started warm and became blistering. 'I think we might be in for a storm. Luckily, I have my leather cloak.'

'Make sure you keep warm. The cold can creep into your bones.'

'Don't worry, I will.' She hoped she would. She'd never done very well in the cold since she was a young girl and had fallen through the ice when out skating with Karn. It had been partly his fault as he'd dared her to go further and, channelling Ingebord, she had. Her nurse had wrapped her in fur and plied her with hot drinks, all the while berating Karn, but Svanna had known she'd borne part of the blame. Later, after the incident with Turgeis, she'd decided to stop trying to behave like the true Ingebord had because every time she did, catastrophe happened.

'But that is the problem—it is now part of my job to worry. I have seen how little regard you have for your personal safety.'

She concentrated on ensuring the hood was over her head and keeping out most of the bone-chilling rain. 'I won't mention your penchant for rushing into burning buildings then.'

'That might be wise. It could spoil the mood.' His eyes danced again and she knew that her heart had slipped a little closer towards that perilous slope of falling for him.

Chapter Ten

Rand banged his fist against the monastery's heavy oaken door and tried to ignore the pounding rain now pooling about his collar. Normally, he would collect the horses he'd had stabled here and press on to his hall at Donaghmoyne, but the strength of rain made him pause. The fords were notorious for sweeping unwary travellers to their doom. He might be a strong rider, but he had no idea about Svanna.

Thus far, she'd managed the rough crossing with nary a murmur, but he didn't want to push things. He knew exactly how much women could complain if they were soaked to the skin and forced to travel.

He pushed away the faintly disloyal thought about his late wife. Bridget might have been a poor traveller, but she'd had many other wonderful qualities. He wanted to remember all of them to be able explain to Birdie about her special mother when the time came. It bothered him how her good qualities slipped away, and he kept thinking about what had irritated him. Theirs had not been the most peaceful of relationships. He'd always known that she'd only married him because her father had threatened to marry her to an elderly petty king in the far north of Eire, a man who had already buried four wives. Her little rebellion of love was what she sometimes called him; sometimes, far more often towards the end, merely her rebellion.

Rand banged his fist harder than strictly necessary. Their union had worked after a fashion, and he had no desire to recreate that marriage. Svanna would be a very different sort of wife, one married solely for duty.

'Open up. Lord Randolfr on the King's business.' He shook his fist at the still closed door, giving vent to his anger at his own behaviour. 'Do I have to kick this door in?'

'Lord Randolfr as I live and breathe!' The elderly monk peeped out and then threw the door open. 'Back far sooner than any of us here anticipated. On a night such as this! I thought your knocking was the tapping of the oak against the outer wall. Please forgive me.'

Rand allowed the obvious lie to pass. 'Have my horses been well fed? Or will I be having words with the stable master again?'

'Our lay brothers have done what you asked. Everyone regrets the previous mix-up.' The monk inclined his head and Rand could see beads of sweat appearing on the top of his tonsure. 'The horses can be made ready in a short time, of course they can, but the going will be rough if you wish to travel to Donaghmoyne tonight. I fear flooding further up the valley.'

Rand gave a brief nod. Going up and through the valley would be the quickest way to get to Donaghmoyne and Birdie, but if the fords were flooded then they would have to take the longer way around, adding another day and a half onto their journey.

'The morning will be soon enough to make an assessment. I've no wish to brave dangerous floodwaters in the dark, but they can rapidly recede.'

'Our prayers at compline will include ones for the flooding to recede.'

'Prayers on my behalf are always welcome.'

The monk bowed his head. 'We always pray for our main benefactors, including you.'

'Glad to hear it.' Rand gestured towards where a sodden Svanna stood. She appeared to have ducked her head in a bucket of water, but she stood straighter than a newly forged sword. 'My lady wife and I require accommodation for the night.'

'Your lady wife?' The monk's eyes bulged. Rand knew the gossip would spread like wildfire from holy house to holy house, reaching Tara in double time, more than likely, before he had time to put his nose through the gates.

It could not be helped as he needed to discover Thorarinn and his bride, but at least he would control the substance of the rumour as much as possible.

'My bride has accompanied me. The alliance with Lord Sigmund of Islay is complete.'

'King Máel Sechnaill will be pleased as he greatly desired to have such an alliance.' The monk bowed his head, his fat cheeks becoming tinged with pink. 'Rumours have reached us at this lonely outpost.'

Rand schooled his features. He had allowed that rumour to circulate when he'd departed. 'A kinship alliance with Agthir in the North Country now exists.'

'I thought it was to be with Islay and the new high king.'

'That will come in time,' Svanna said in a heavily accented Gaelic. She obviously understood the language far better than he'd previously thought. 'My foster-mother and King Sigmund intend to marry.'

The monk started in surprise. He'd obviously dismissed her as ignorant of his language. 'Your foster-mother?'

'The dowager Queen of Agthir. She and King Sigmund have long been allied,' Svanna added. 'Agthir is wealthy. Their new queen does follow a Christian path.'

The monk licked his lips. 'I can recall hearing something about it, now that I think on it.'

The corners of Svanna's mouth twitched, but Rand noticed she allowed the monk's tall tale.

'I must ask for your best chamber.'

'My abbot is away in Tara with the high king.' The monk started to close the door. 'The private chamber? Lord Randolfr, you must understand that I hesitate because the abbot normally only allows people that the King Máel Sechnaill has specified.'

'We are on the King's business. Send your abbot to me if he squeaks.' Rand gently urged Svanna forward into the vestibule of the monastery before the monk could slam the door in their faces. Svanna, though Rand knew she'd deny the suggestion, was chilled to the bone. Her lips had taken on a bluish tinge and her teeth were chattering.

'I require hot pottage, mulled mead and furs,' Rand said. 'I've no wish for my bride to catch a chill.'

'I'm fine,' Svanna mumbled as a pool of water collected about her boots.

'Your bride appears to be damp.'

'The rain was heavier than I considered it would be,' Svanna said, answering his unspoken question about how much she understood. She glanced up at him, her blue-tinged lips turning up into a brave smile. 'The accommodation will be suitable wherever this monk can find us room. A dry corner to sleep and a fire to warm my hands.'

The monk licked his fleshy lips. A sudden and unexpected surge of protectiveness ricocheted through Rand. He simultaneously knew a man of God had no business looking at his wife in that way and that he needed to get her warm and dry as quickly as possible.

'Excellent news,' the monk said, rubbing his hands together. 'The stables where you last stayed…'

'Your abbot enjoys my benefice. Take us to your best chamber. Now. I require a private chamber and food and I am unaccustomed to having to ask twice. That portable brazier your abbot is fond of will also be required.'

'I know the one you speak of, but…it is in the abbot's private room.'

'The abbot is away and unlikely to return before we leave.'

'Yes, my lord Randolfr.' The monk gulped twice and rushed off as if an imp from hell was snapping at his heels.

'The stables would have been fine. I've no wish to put anyone out or store up resentment.'

'I'll not have anyone disrespecting you, Svanna. When they do, they disrespect me. We will get you warm because you appear incapable of considering your own needs.'

'Unfair.'

'We either argue about nothing, or you can get warm.' He put his hand in the middle of her back and propelled her forward. Someone needed to look after her when she refused to, and that job fell to him.

After taking off her sodden leather cloak, which seemed to keep in the cold, and carefully hanging it up, Svanna stood in the small chamber and tried to keep her teeth from chattering. Several of the lay brothers had ensured that the iron brazier was lit, and a mountain of furs were put on the bed. Finally, a trencher of steaming pottage was brought in. The lay brothers then hurried out of the chamber, leaving her alone with the glowering Rand.

'The food smells good,' she said into the silence which followed. She refused to address his remark about not looking after herself properly. She'd been looking after herself very well ever since her real mother had died. And she didn't need any interference from Rand. 'I can't remember the last time pottage smelt so delicious.'

'Please fill your belly.'

Svanna sank down on a stool in front of the brazier and began to eat.

She waited for the warmth from the food to seep into her, but nothing. If anything, the coldness increased. She gave another violent shiver, nearly knocking the pottage to the ground.

'Clothes off,' Rand said, fastening the door. 'You are sodden.'

She wrapped her arms about her middle. A wave of tiredness passed over her, but if she slept now, she worried she'd never wake. 'My trunks have not arrived yet. I'm warm, far warmer than I was before. My gown is only damp.'

'They will arrive soon enough. I will bring them in when they do.'

'What? I am supposed to stand shivering naked in front of that brazier? No, thank you very much.' She snapped her fingers. A surge of anger rushed through her, providing her with some much-needed warmth. But she also knew her arguments lacked the force of logic. 'Just like that and at your say-so? I doubt that very much.'

'You are far too cold and not thinking straight. I've encountered this before. The cold makes a person do foolish things.'

'Not me. I know what I am doing. I fell through the ice once,' she said, unable to prevent her teeth chattering. 'All I need is some more warm food. Maybe a fur about my body.'

She crossed quickly to the bed, grabbed a fur and tossed it around her shoulders. 'Look to your own needs.'

His scar puckered. 'You require more than that fur.'

She hated his reasonable tone. She hated that deep down she knew he was right. Mostly she hated that she wanted to believe his concern was more than mere words.

She took a step forward and squelched. 'Plenty of time to change once my trunks arrive. No need for sleep yet.'

She crossed to the small iron brazier, which was beginning to give out some heat. She put out her hands and the fur slithered to the floor. She cursed.

'Your words miss the solid good sense I've come to expect.'

He spoke as if being sensible was a compliment. She hated that she wanted to think it was, but she also knew from her nurse's teaching that sensible meant dull.

'Do you even know what that sense is? That sense tells me I need to remain upright and not go to sleep.'

'I've seen the deep cold in action a number of times.' He handed her a cloth. 'I don't want to fight you. Dry your hair.'

'That is good to know.' She wrapped the linen cloth about her hair, but her hands seemed very numb. She whispered a small plea for help.

He picked up the fur, put it about her and briskly towelled her hair. 'Better?'

'I would win any argument,' she muttered, but her mind had become thicker than day-old pottage. 'But thank you.'

'Strip and get into bed. I won't allow you to sleep. Promise.'

She put a hand to her throat. 'Strip? In front of you? Without the torches being doused?'

'I can turn my back, but the bed with the furs should help. Without clothes, you won't be trapping in any cold. I should have considered the possibility back on the boat. All that leather cloak did was to allow the cold to seep into your bones. And then, on our journey here, you became wetter and more vulnerable. We should have stopped at one of the fishermen's huts instead of pressing on here.'

'I agreed with your suggestion. We require horses.'

Rand gave a half-smile. 'Proof that you were not thinking straight.'

She walked quickly to the bed, stripped and dived under the furs and hugged her knees to her chest. The simplest action suddenly appeared far more complicated. 'Are you going to leave me here?'

'Why would I do that? My men are capable of looking after themselves.' His voice came from the other side of the room. 'I promised that I'd keep you awake.'

Svanna stared up at the shifting shadows. 'Someone once told me that human contact, skin to skin, is the quickest way to warm up.'

She internally winced. The words sounded pathetic and pleading. Not seductive at all. She should have kept to being an Ice Maiden, something she'd excelled at, instead of this needy woman who secretly longed for his touch. She knew Astrid had counselled her to seduce him, but Astrid had little idea of how truly inexperienced she was.

'Whoever said that was right. Skin to skin is the quickest way to warm you up.' His warm voice washed over her. A faint curl of heat began in her belly. 'I hesitated to mention it as a remedy because of what passed between us. I know where that could end, Svanna, but I want to give you time.'

The tight place at the base of her spine loosened. 'You're chilled as well.'

'I'm not minded to ask anyone else to warm up my wife.'

She unclenched her hands. A small curl of heat tried to

wind its way about her insides at the word 'wife' said with such possessive assurance, but the cold appeared intent on beating it back. It was her status he cared about, not her per se. If she ever forgot, her heart would surely break.

'Right now, given the chill I've had, I am willing to try anything.' She forced a laugh, even though the deep cold had grown distinctly less because of their conversation. 'Please, Rand, don't make me beg.'

'What can a man do but comply with his wife's wishes?'

She kept her head firmly turned away, but the sound of clothing dropping to the floor made her skin tingle with anticipation.

He slid in behind her and pulled her firmly into his arms. Her back collided with his bare chest. His naked body cupped hers, and his warmth slowly seeped into her. He did not do anything except hold her like precious glass. She touched his hand, which immediately engulfed her fingers. She clung to him, attempting to work up the courage to turn around. A large part of her hoped he'd take the hint, but his hold continued to be considerate rather than lover-like.

Shivering racked her, but still he held her and allowed her to cling to his hand.

'I was far colder than I thought,' she whispered as the shivering decreased.

He stroked her hair. 'It creeps up on a person. You will have to be more careful. Sleep would not be a good idea.'

'What shall we talk about?' She tried to make her voice sound bright. 'Court gossip that I will need to know when we reach Tara? Or something else?'

'Anything you want.'

'Anything?' She winced. Her sing-song voice was back. If she was a stronger person she'd turn and capture his mouth.

'I am fresh out of topics, but this method does seem to be working where others failed. Incredible.'

The soft rumble of his chest with barely suppressed laughter reverberated against her back. 'I am pleased it meets with your approval.'

His breath touched her sensitive earlobe. The small flame of desire had become a raging inferno, but Svanna didn't want to jeopardise their newfound closeness. There was something satisfying about being wrapped in his arms and held as if she were more precious than any jewel—an illusion, but Svanna found she wanted it, something to hang onto in the coming months and years. She waited until her body screamed to take a chance.

She flipped over. His mouth was no more than a breath away. She raised her hand and traced the scar. 'Thank you.'

He caught her hand and brought their joined hands to his lips. 'My pleasure, but your skin remains chilled.'

She released him. 'I'm much warmer. Honestly.'

'It's important that Agthir's representative remains safe from such things.'

'Should I check if you are warm?' She allowed her hand to trail down his chest. Her thumb brushed his nipples. She pretended to consider. 'Further investigations are required.'

She traced round and round the nipples, first one and then the other, and felt them harden beneath her ministrations.

'Svanna…' His voice rasped in her ear, sending fresh waves of heat through her.

Her body pressed closer to his. And where once he'd been the warmer one, he was now the cooler.

'What? I am trying to ensure that we are both warm. A wife's duty, I'd say.' Internally, she hoped that he would not reject her as she was fresh out of ideas.

He gave a rasping laugh. 'Is that what you are doing? Warming us up because of duty?'

'I can't think of any other reason. Can you?' She bent her head to his strong neck and ran her tongue up from where his neck met his shoulder to his jawline, tasting him while the heat inside her grew white-hot. 'Definitely warmer.'

'Two can play this game, wife.'

His arm came around her and pulled her tighter, making her breasts encounter the hardness of his nipples. Using one arm, he held her firmly against him while his lips traced downward from her jaw to her shoulder. Her body bucked towards him. She realised with a flush of heat that his nipples were not the only part of him which had grown hard. His hand stroked downward and cupped her bottom, holding her against his erect member.

A moan escaped from her throat.

His mouth continued its downward trail and caught each of her breasts in turn. His tongue circled her nipples until heat exploded within her.

Her body bucked forward, encountering his ever-hardening groin. She clawed at his upper arms, asking for more, but he continued his ministrations of her breasts.

Before she could question herself, she plunged her hand further down and touched his member. Silky hardness greeted her. She closed her hand around him and felt him grow harder still.

He caught her hand. 'Not yet. I went far too quickly the last time.'

'Did you?'

He stroked her hair. 'I want to make this good for you, better than the last time. Allow me to look after you. Please.'

She withdrew her hand, knowing that if it was any better

than the last time she might expire with pleasure, but finding it difficult to explain.

He eased her onto her back and held her wrists above her head. His mouth moved lower still, pausing to lap and penetrate her bellybutton before continuing its journey towards her nest of curls. There, his tongue drew circles as if he was gently searching for something. Her body bucked upwards again. She twisted back and forth, writhing as wave after wave of white-hot pleasure hit her. He released her. Her hands clawed at his shoulders. She wasn't sure if she wanted his tongue to continue or if she wanted him fully inside.

His fingers replaced his tongue, once again going round and round where she'd become very slick. Her muscles clenched about him, trying to entice him to go deeper.

'Put me where you want me,' he rasped against her ear. 'Now.'

She opened her thighs and placed him near the apex, knowing that she required him inside her. She lifted her hips, tugged at his shoulders and drove her hips upwards, seeking the relief she knew their joining would bring. 'Here. Now. Please.'

'Your wish is my command, my lady fair,' he said against her hair.

He bucked forward and her body opened up to him. He filled her and then they rocked back and forth until her body became drenched with sweat. All the while the heat inside her kept growing until she trembled on a precipice.

'I believe you were right,' she gasped out.

'Right about what?'

'The perfect way to become warm is skin to skin with my husband.'

He laughed and nipped her chin. 'Enough talking.'

His tongue entered her mouth, mimicking what was happening where they were joined.

He moved in her again and she gave herself up to the swirling maelstrom.

Much later, when the brazier had cooled, Rand looked up at the rafters. Svanna was snuggled into his chest.

Her skin was no longer clammy to the touch and a peacefulness had entered her sleep. He dared to hope that his overeager lovemaking on their wedding night had not ruined her after all. Her enthusiastic response gave him hope for the future.

He'd planned to take his time, make her beg for each new intimacy, but when she was ready and willing in his arms he'd found her impossible to resist, despite his earlier promises.

He stroked her hair and knew it would take a long time for his body to tire of her. But his protective feelings towards her alarmed him.

What the episode confirmed was what he had suspected after she'd helped to rescue Astrid from the burning building. Svanna had little regard for her own personal safety. She put duty before her own wishes. Despite her adorable confession that she intended to seduce him, he wanted to believe that their joining had more to it than simple duty.

'I promised to protect you,' he murmured against her hair. 'My heart may be buried, but it doesn't mean I want to see you harmed or to take crazy risks. As you appear unable or unwilling to, I promise to do all in my power to stop you in the future.'

She murmured something and snuggled closer to him. He chose to take that as agreement. He'd protect her from herself if necessary.

'Our joining was more than duty for me.' He tightened his arms about her. 'I'll work to ensure it means more to you.'

The sun sparkled on the puddle-strewn yard when Svanna emerged with Rand from the monastery. She knew they were later than Rand had planned, but he'd kept stealing kisses as she'd tried to dress. In the end, they'd returned to the tangled furs because Rand had proclaimed that the floodwaters needed to drop.

She might have succeeded at seduction and ensuring the blood alliance remained, but she was no closer to discovering why Turgeis had targeted them. Had he known she would be there or was it something else entirely? Until she knew that Agthir was in fact safe from Turgeis she had to press forward with trying to find answers. Once she knew why, then she'd begin subtly weaving the binding ties between Eire, Agthir and Islay. She would have to use all means at her disposal, and that meant ensuring Birdie was there to soften hearts.

'Remaining still, despite how pleasant it may be, accomplishes nothing. To progress, one must move.'

Rand nipped her chin and said that he would defer to her wisdom on the matter.

'I believe this will serve your lady well,' the monk said, bowing to Rand and indicating a covered cart. 'The abbot is currently using our best one.'

Svanna stared at the covered cart with its heavy wheels and knew it would not make it through any deep puddle, let alone thick mud. 'Alas, I must decline. A horse will suit our purpose better.'

'We've no horses suitable for a lady.'

'I ride well,' she said, daring Rand to gainsay her. 'My lord Randolfr is anxious to return to his hall.'

'From what I can recall, you were considered an excellent horsewoman in Agthir.' Rand nodded. 'My lady rides.'

The lay brothers brought out a dappled pony who appeared fairly placid. She held out her hand and the pony immediately nuzzled it. She caught a mischievous glint in the pony's eye and knew that it would try to get the better of her.

'This one shall suit me fine.'

The monk frowned. 'That one…'

'Plays tricks? I like a pony with a bit of spirit.'

'My lady has spoken.'

Svanna breathed out. After what had passed between them, she dared to hope that he would finally start listening to her and allow her to make decisions. Somehow, she'd figure out a way to demonstrate to him that she could be a good mother to his little girl and that they should take her with them to Tara. Despite Rand's concerns, how could a grandfather's heart stay hard when confronted with a young child?

Astrid had been right—she had to take advantage of this time. Instead of remaining hidden, waiting for a rescue which would never come, like she'd done that long-ago day in Agthir, she needed to take risks to prove her worth. Hopefully, she would be able to do this quickly with Birdie and, if necessary, with the running of Rand's household. But the one thing she refused to risk was her heart.

Chapter Eleven

From its well-tended fields outside the large circular earthworks to the bustling centre with its hall and round tower, Rand's ringfort was larger and better presented than Svanna had envisioned. The healthy cattle and sheer number of chickens showed Rand clearly ran a prosperous estate, even if he was not there as often as he'd like. As they neared the fort, the butterflies in her stomach had turned into rampaging cattle. She was going to meet her new daughter and much depended on her getting the first meeting with Birdie right.

'This has become one of my favourite places in the whole world,' Rand said, gesturing about him. 'If I could, I'd never leave.'

'When you said ringfort, I didn't think it would be this large.'

'You look surprised,' he said, handing his reins to a servant and dismounting.

He strode over to her and held out his hand.

'I had no expectations,' Svanna confessed as she clutched his hand and dismounted from the pony she'd christened Star because of the white blaze on her forehead. 'Unlike Agthir or Islay, but it exudes prosperity.'

'I have worked to ensure it, but thankfully I have many

servants who do the jobs assigned to them without too much grumbling. Not bad for a sell-sword who had to flee Agthir.'

His words sounded slightly pompous, but Svanna could hear the real pride underneath. He cared deeply for this land and its inhabitants. She'd half-hoped that she could quickly demonstrate her prowess at running a household, but she would struggle to improve on what was there. All she could hope was that Birdie needed her guidance.

A little girl with shining copper curls ran out of the stone round tower which stood at one side of the main hall and threw her arms around Rand's middle.

'Oh, my papa, my papa! My papa is home!'

'My daughter comes to greet me! All is right with the world.' Rand gathered the little girl in his arms and swung her around and around.

The mirrored happiness on their faces made Svanna's heart ache. It was as if suddenly Rand had become truly alive and she was intruding. She winced slightly and knew that he had told her the truth back on Islay about only living for his daughter, and her heart had chosen to ignore it. But she was used to being considered second-best.

It was how Astrid had always treated her. Not unkindly, but she'd been aware that Astrid would have preferred her real daughter to be at her side. Was it wrong of her to want to be the focus of someone's life? She allowed the self-pity for another heartbeat and then stuffed it down deep inside her. Wishing failed to alter reality and watching the father and daughter's joy was beautiful to behold. Svanna quietly resolved to become Birdie's friend. It would be good to think that one day the little girl might greet her with half that much affection.

'You should have sent a messenger,' the little girl said with a frown, stroking his cheek. 'Nurse would have prepared a meal. All we have is hard cheese, hard bread or pottage. Ugh.'

'Did you think I would stay away, Birdie? From my best girl?' Rand asked with a light-hearted laugh. Svanna caught a glimpse of the boy she'd shared that long-ago flirtation with, the one she had considered must be confined to a fading memory. He'd spoken the truth about his daughter being the only person who could bring him to life. That secret place inside her had been wrong in hoping for anything more than the faint consideration a man owed his lawful wife. But now she knew and could adjust, thankfully before Rand realised her growing feelings for him. She could put that shield back in place.

The girl's face puckered in thought and Svanna could see the resemblance to Rand. Birdie would break many hearts one day. 'I didn't know. Auntie Rhiannon said you were bound to. Because my grandfather takes you away.'

At the woman's name Rand's face became thunderous. He put the little girl down abruptly. She looked up at him with a confused expression.

'Your auntie has been here? Tell the truth, Bridget. Is she still here?'

Birdie slowly shook her head. 'I wasn't supposed to say anything. I gave my promise and everything.' She put her hands over her mouth. 'Oh, my saints and angels.'

Rand glanced towards where the round tower loomed. 'Where is your auntie? Perhaps in the tower, waiting like a spider? Playing a game of hide and seek with me?'

Birdie vigorously shook her copper curls. 'Rhiannon and Uncle Thorarinn were here, but they left early this morning because the rain had stopped.'

'Do you know why?'

'Uncle Thorarinn has serious business to attend, because

things might be getting dicey soon.' She said the words as if she had learned them by rote, rather than words which came naturally. Perhaps the errant pair had expected Rand to question his daughter.

He cursed under his breath. 'Before I left, I gave orders that if, by some minor miracle, the pair appeared here, they were to be detained. Who decided to disobey me?'

The nurse hurried forward and scooped Birdie up. 'My lord, a messenger arrived yesterday. We thought he might have come from you, but he only stayed a brief while and spoke to Lord Thorarinn. He refused to stay and threatened to slit men's throats. I wanted them to spend the night in hopes of Thorarinn reconsidering.'

'But he refused?'

'His temper became even worse, and he upset Birdie.' The old woman curtseyed. 'I thought it best that they depart.'

Rand swore under his breath until Birdie covered her mouth, saying she didn't think his words were nice. Rand mumbled an apology.

'They left directly after the messenger, didn't they, Nurse,' Svanna said, 'if the messenger arrived yesterday?'

The nurse regarded her as if she'd grown two heads. 'Aye, you are right about that one, and Birdie was wrong. The rain was starting, not ending.'

'It can't be helped,' Svanna said, forcing the sense of regret back down her throat. There was little she could do now. She had to keep going forward rather than trying to alter the past. 'No doubt I will get to meet both of them soon.' She added for Birdie's benefit, 'I was looking forward to it. You made them both sound interesting, Rand.'

Wriggling out of her nurse's arms, Birdie gave Svanna a quizzical look and then stuck her nose in the air as if she was determined to ignore this stranger who had arrived with her beloved father.

'Auntie said that she was going to take me to court to finally meet my grandpapa,' Birdie said. Her brow knitted. 'She made it sound exciting. Lots of things happen at court. She said that I'd be at the centre and that was a good thing. Is it a good thing, Papa? To be at the centre?'

'I'm sure I don't know,' Rand answered as if he were thinking of something else.

'It will be when it happens,' Svanna said, hunkering down to bring her face level with Birdie's. She wanted to make things right with the little girl, not simply because it would make her peace-weaving easier but because she wanted to be the right sort of mother for Birdie. 'Sometimes things are even better when you are a little older, even if you don't think so at the time.'

'I am older than I was yesterday but not as old as I will be tomorrow. When my nurse says it, I laugh.'

Svanna glanced towards the older woman. 'Your nurse sounds like a very wise woman.'

Birdie took two steps backwards. 'Who is this lady, Papa? She talks funny.'

'This lady is my new wife, Svanna Guthardottar. And she is from the North, but I think you will like her just the same. She fights for what she believes in and she is kind.' Rand touched his daughter's nose with a light tap. 'I dare say you sound funny to someone from the North.'

Birdie's eyes went big and she stuck her thumb in her mouth. Her jaw took on a stubborn aspect, one that reminded Rand of his late wife when she took a notion to be unreasonable in her head. He hoped that Birdie would not prove difficult with Svanna. He knew all too well how important first impressions were and how he'd failed miserably in the past. And he suspected that his ire at Thorarinn and Rhiannon would not have helped, but it was too late.

'The child is tired. She wouldn't settle for her nap, kept insisting exciting things were going to happen,' her nurse murmured as if that explained everything.

'They have,' Birdie said with a huge smile. 'I'm normally right about exciting things.'

'Shall we get the lady Svanna inside? I'd hardly like her to think our hospitality was lax.'

Rand scooped his daughter up again and balanced her on his hip. Coming home meant having her in his arms once again. As always, she appeared to have grown considerably in the time he'd been away. He wished he could remain with her always, but he'd promised Máel Sechnaill when he'd married Bridget that he would serve as his eyes and ears where required. It had not mattered as much when Bridget was alive and at court, but now there was a gaping hole whenever he was gone.

Little point in wishing for things to change, he'd made that bargain long ago. He simply had to go forward and be content, even if being content was getting harder and harder.

'Will she be my new mother?' Birdie whispered in his ear. 'I don't remember my real mother. But you need a mother to be a real family. I prayed for one, but one who is kind.'

'Svanna is my wife,' he said, trying to keep his footsteps steady as he carried the little girl into the hall. He wished he knew who had filled his child's ears with such nonsense about real families or why the little girl had taken it to heart. But maybe he'd done one thing right in marrying Svanna and giving Birdie hope. 'We will sort everything out later, but she is exceptionally kind.'

Birdie nodded as if she accepted his verdict. 'Auntie said that maybe I could have a real family with her, but I can stay with you now, can't I? I like it when you are with me.'

Rand tightened his hold on the little girl and tried to keep the sense of foreboding from bubbling up. He'd not anticipated Rhiannon making noises about fostering Birdie. It was most likely a passing fancy. Like her sister, Rhiannon blithely made promises which later she found impossible to keep.

'Did your aunt say where she was headed?' Rand asked his daughter. 'Any little scrap that would help your old papa?'

Birdie shook her copper curls. 'Uncle Thorarinn refused to tell. They had an argument. Auntie wanted to take more trunks, but he called her an unreasonable spoilt brat.' She put her hands over her ears. 'Lots of screaming. I'm not a brat, am I?'

'How could you be if you're your father's daughter?' Svanna said with a smile that lit up her whole face.

The muscles in Rand's neck eased. He'd worried that Birdie had made a bad first impression and Svanna might react against the little girl, but she appeared to take everything in her stride.

Birdie narrowed her gaze and concentrated on her thumb. 'Uncle Thorarinn said I was just like my aunt.'

Rand kept his face still. That there was trouble in paradise was no surprise to him. The pair had the combined attention span of a gnat.

'Quarrels happen when people are first married,' Svanna said in a low voice.

Birdie tugged at his sleeve to get his attention. 'I want to be part of a family with a mother. And I wanted to go with Auntie. You might be sad for a while, but we could still see each other.'

'I brought you a mother, Birdie.' Rand clung onto his temper. Birdie sometimes found it difficult to let a notion go and the whole situation could spiral out of control.

'Some boys tease me and say you found me under a cabbage leaf. How can I ever have a mother, if she is dead? If she died just after I was born?'

Rand set the child down and tried to think of a logical answer for her. When Birdie was in this sort of mood, he always deferred to others. 'Maybe your nurse is right. You're too tired. You are a very important part of my family, Birdie.'

'I can't replace your mother, but I am willing to be the mother you tell the boys about,' Svanna said slowly. She hunkered down until her face was level with Birdie's again. 'My own mother died when I was young, a little older than you. Now I have a foster-mother.' She held up two fingers. 'Two mothers…'

Rand's scar stopped pulling. Svanna appeared able to handle the situation. He dreaded to think how Bridget would have coped. She'd hated rejection of any sort.

Birdie considered Svanna afresh. 'A foster-mother? What's that?'

'Like a real mother, but different. I can teach you things like spinning and weaving. I bet you are nearly old enough to learn.'

Birdie's eyes grew as big as the brooches Svanna wore on her apron. 'Truly? Auntie left her loom for me to practice on. She was teaching me. Back and forth, forth and back.'

'Was she indeed?' Svanna said with a frown. 'How do your hands manage with the shuttle?'

'Easy—it is little, little.' Birdie demonstrated with her

hands. 'For making braid. Auntie left some for me to practice because she doesn't want it any more.'

Svanna tapped the side of her nose. 'Ah, I understand. I like doing that sort of weaving. Maybe I can help you.'

Birdie gave a drawn-out sigh. 'I doubt you will be staying that long. Papa never does. But maybe.'

'Time for your nap,' Birdie's nurse called and patted her side.

'Not tired!' Birdie gave Rand an appealing glance.

Rand shook his head. 'You know the rules. No gainsaying your nurse. We will spend time together later, I promise.'

Birdie sighed and gave him a tight hug before she allowed her nurse to lead her off. Rand watched his daughter go, again inwardly marvelling at how much she'd grown in the few short weeks since he'd seen her last. But Birdie was here because it was the safest place for her. Keeping her safe had to be his priority, as it now had to be with Svanna.

'My daughter…' he said, trying to smooth things over. 'My daughter can be a handful.'

Svanna's face became wreathed in a genuine smile. 'Your daughter is lovely. I am sure we will become friends in time.'

'Her reaction didn't annoy you?'

'She is little still.' She shook her head. 'I was about her age when I first learned to weave. I was all thumbs, but in time I became decent. Now, I find it helps me to think. Hopefully, as we do things together, we will find a bond. Trying to rush things will frustrate us both.'

'I would like that,' Rand said, capturing her hand, bringing it to his lips and knowing within his heart that the angels had smiled on him when he'd taken Svanna for his wife.

Her cheeks flushed.

The temptation to haul her off to his chamber nearly overwhelmed him. He knew precisely why they'd had a late start this morning, but he also knew that he had enjoyed every heartbeat of it.

'But more importantly, what are we going to do about your cousin and his bride?' Svanna said, putting her hands behind her back. 'We can't remain here, waiting for word.'

'What do you mean, we?' Rand tilted his head to one side. One thing which he was going to stop was Svanna taking unacceptable risks. There was no need for her to participate in any search. She could easily remain here and build this bond with Birdie. 'I must find them. The first thing Máel Sechnaill will want to know is that his daughter is safe.'

'I would have thought it was more important to get to Tara and meet with the high king. He needs to know that you successfully negotiated the alliance with Lord Sigmund,' she said, lifting her chin and clearly not taking the hint. 'Why I travelled with you, rather than remaining on Islay until my foster-mother healed. I want to know if Agthir is in danger and what, if anything, Eire can do about it.'

He inclined his head, acknowledging the truth of her words, even if they hurt. He knew she would have to go to Tara and would refuse to be left behind. He'd simply hoped she'd travelled with him because of the intimacy they'd shared as well.

'I want Thorarinn to be there when I inform Máel Sechnaill of the change in our plans,' he said. 'It would be best for all concerned. Máel Sechnaill may bluster, but he does love his children and will forgive Rhiannon in time.'

'How much time?'

'It depends, but he has a soft heart for romantic passion.' Rand scratched the back of his neck. 'Bridget used that knowledge to convince him to allow us to marry.'

Svanna's face became devoid of emotion, which meant she most likely disagreed with him. 'A love story for the ages. One that *skalds* can sing about. The proud princess who will only have the sell-sword and defies her father to get him. Then they live happily ever after.'

'Like many tales, it contains only an element of truth but didn't allow it to spoil the story.'

'Your Bridget knew, which is what mattered.'

Almost too good to be true. Rand hated the unbidden thought, except he knew it had merit. He had not questioned Bridget's devotion at the time, but later when they'd quarrelled during her first pregnancy, she'd claimed she'd only married him to prevent her marriage to the elderly petty king. She'd tried to unsay the words later, but he'd never forgotten them. It didn't mean he'd loved her less, but he'd loved her for what she was, even if he hadn't understood that at the time. And he'd had the family he'd longed for with Bridget, but fate had decided to take his wife, leaving only Birdie.

'I can't alter the past, Svanna. Máel Sechnaill forgave Bridget and me, but will he forgive Rhiannon and Thorarinn, particularly if they are not there to demonstrate their love and appeal to his well-concealed romantic streak?'

She tilted her head to one side. 'Interesting that your father-in-law, who knows the full story behind Bridget's marriage to you, decided to send you to ensure the marriage of another daughter to an elderly man.'

He hated that on one level what she said had merit. Why had Máel Sechnaill decided that he should escort Rhiannon and ensure a marriage happened? Other warriors were more suitable. He'd argued as much to the king. 'Máel Sechnaill weaves many webs. While he may forgive his daughter in time, he is very unforgiving of disobedient warriors.'

'Agthir's court bore some resemblance to a snake pit while the usurper was in charge. I survived that with my honour intact. Tara holds no fear for me.' She linked her arm with his. 'I can spin a pretty tale, Rand. If we work together...'

He firmed his jaw. Svanna had never encountered Máel Sechnaill or his fury. It was fundamental to his scheme to produce the errant pair, both showing the appropriate contrition. But he suspected he would be wasting the spit it took to say the words.

'Easier if it happens my way,' he said instead, disentangling himself from her arm. 'Trust my reasons, Svanna. You don't want to be there when Máel Sechnaill's temper explodes.'

Svanna didn't attempt to cling and wheedle as Bridget would have done but walked over to the embers and gave them a stir with a stick. Rand watched the curve of her neck and pushed the comparison away as being unworthy. Svanna would be unable to resist meddling, and he'd have to pick up the pieces.

'Do you have any idea where they have gone?' she asked when the fire burst into life. 'How long will it take to find them? We don't know what Turgeis has planned. He was bold enough to attack Sigmund.'

'Several ideas.' He shrugged and tried not to think about the scenarios that kept him awake last night. He'd little doubt now that the raid had been carefully planned, rather than a spontaneous decision. 'But they are only hunches.'

'No firm knowledge what else might be planned, nor indeed if, fearing for his bride, Thorarinn has turned to Turgeis for assistance?'

He raised a brow. 'Thorarinn has no great love for them. He rescued me from my beating at their father's hands and was beaten himself for it.'

Svanna gave the fire another stir. 'Alliances alter and shift, Rand.'

'Not with my cousin.' Rand shook his head. 'He is completely loyal.'

Normally, people understood his tone and backed off.

'Perish the thought.' Svanna made a cutting motion with her hand. 'But my purpose when I married you was to act as a peace-weaver between Agthir, Islay and Tara. I would like to speak with your king as quickly as possible. Turgeis might be plotting more mischief.'

Her words cut him more than he'd thought they would, but at least they were honest. He'd hoped she'd married him in part because she wanted to be with him.

'Will you never put yourself first?'

'If I do not fulfil my duty, I lose my honour. And without honour, is life truly worth living?' She bowed her head. 'A lesson I learned many times since my real mother first asked me that question back when I was younger than Birdie.'

'I see. Honour is everything to you.'

'Which is why I must humbly ask in the wake of what we know that we proceed to Tara.'

'And my cousin?'

She tilted her chin upwards. 'Trust your cousin to appear back here. For some reason, he or his bride want Birdie with them when they confront your father-in-law. It is why she should travel with us.'

The small curl of fear which had lurked in the pit of his stomach ever since Birdie had mentioned the trip tightened. That Svanna recognised what he did. 'What do you mean, "want Birdie with them"? How would it help them?'

'His bride promised Birdie a trip to Tara. I suspect they intend to make that trip happen. She would be a counter for them to ensure that the King hears their plea. She is the only living child of his favourite daughter. I'm not the only one who sees how that could soften her grandfather's heart.'

'Not going to happen.' Rand banged his fists together. 'Birdie is protected here. Measures exist.'

'Measures which your cousin and bride know. The only way you can ensure her protection is to keep her with us. She must come to Tara with us.' She stretched out her hand, but Rand ignored it. 'The most prudent option.'

He shook his head. 'She is safest here.'

'Is she? After what she confided? We could keep her away from her grandfather, but you would rest easier, knowing she was with us.'

He knew her words were sensible, but if he lost his trust in his cousin, his world became a carefully constructed lie. 'If you believe they will return, then we must wait.'

Her lips thinned to a white line. The Ice Princess had returned, making his decision easier. He'd little intention of blindly obeying authoritarian demands, even if an inner part of him protested that her ideas had merit and she was certainly not made of ice.

'You and I are needed in Tara. Agthir's peace depends on my success.'

'The monk will spread the news of our marriage. I suspect it has already reached Tara.' He allowed his eyes to roam all over Svanna, taking in her curves, her blonde hair and her finely drawn features, but he knew deep down that he wanted her fighting as hard for his family as she was prepared to fight for Agthir and Islay. Until that happened, he had to follow what had worked for him in the past. 'Máel Sechnaill will understand if I tarried on the road after he encounters you.'

The colour on Svanna's cheeks rose to a delightful crimson.

'What if the monk holds his tongue?' she said to the fire.

Rand rolled his eyes. 'The words were said to make his tongue wag faster. I know the man. He likes imparting gossip.'

She bent closer to the fire. 'Games of double bluff seldom work.'

'Says the peace-weaver. Playing games is what you do.'

She rose and turned towards him. Her eyes showed her fury and passion, even if her voice appeared to be chipped from a snow-capped mountain. 'We adjust but we hold what is ultimately important in the forefront of our minds.'

He disliked her reasonable tone. He could deal with the squalls of anger that Bridget had indulged in, but Svanna's emotions were on a tight leash.

'I begin to understand why you remained unmarried,' he said to provoke a response.

'Why? Because I have a brain and am unafraid to use it?' she said, putting her hand on her hip. 'Fancy that, a woman who dares to speak and point out flaws in your thinking. The first duty of a peace-weaver is to ensure her husband understands where he has made an error.'

'Who said that?'

'Astrid.' She tilted her chin upwards and her eyes half-closed as if she were reciting something from memory. '*A wife should never be afraid to speak her mind to her husband, particularly when the safety of her country is involved, but she does it in private so as not to humiliate him.*'

'Truly? And she put this into practice when?'

'Many times with her second husband. I saw her confront him within the confines of their chambers. I was there when she bargained for her life as well. Much scarier than the saga makes out. He'd sworn to kill Ingebord. I thought he'd kill me. I knew he would if he ever discovered the trick, including when the life ebbed from him. The usurper was like that.'

Rand stared at her. Her bravery made something in his throat catch. 'But he didn't.'

'I never knew why.' She held out her hands. 'Sometimes in my dreams, I don't get the wording right and bring the entire edifice down.'

Her voice held a sing-song note. She might be speaking brave words, but she was very nervous. It made him admire her bravery even more. He itched to take her in his arms.

'And this is why you feel you can speak to me like this? Your foster-mother told you that this was the correct way to behave? Do you think I am a danger to you?'

She hugged her waist. 'In private, and not shaming in front of servants or others. When you think on it, Rand, quietly and dispassionately, you will see I am right.'

Rand raised a brow. 'Will I?'

'You are angry with me because you're frustrated with Thorarinn. Because you need a person to be angry with and I'm convenient. I'm trying to help you, but I refuse to be used in that fashion.'

He stared at her, open-mouthed. His earlier frustration at her faded like snow in the morning sun. How did this woman suddenly understand his innermost struggles better than he did? He was more than frustrated with Thorarinn. If he felt able, he would shake him until his teeth rattled and a modicum of sense entered his brain. Worse, he'd nearly alienated the woman who had proved herself to be his biggest ally in this battle against Turgeis. When his late wife had raged at him for something her father or one of her sisters had said, he'd hated it even if it had led to some of their most passionate lovemaking. In the end, he'd wondered if she'd provoked the quarrels to provoke the aftermath because their lovemaking had dwindled to those times.

'*Frustrated with Thorarinn* is a good way to put it,' he said in a low voice, hanging his head. 'He can be most irritating at times. Selfish.'

She gave a wry smile. 'I haven't met the man, so I will take your word for it.'

He walked over to her and laid his hands on her. Her arms were shaking, and he suddenly realised the enormous effort it must have taken her to defy him in that way. Particularly as the alliance was supposedly the most important thing to her and the easiest way would have been to humour him. 'I apologise. Wrong of me. None of this is your fault.'

She gave a stiff nod. 'Apology accepted.'

'I don't want to fight, Svanna. I had enough of that with Bridget.'

'We were having a discussion, not a fight.' She lifted her chin and stared directly at him. 'I'm a grown woman, not a child. Discussions are allowed to become heated.'

'Life would be dull if they didn't.'

'Exactly. No need to walk on eggshells, but use your anger productively.'

He drew her into his arms and rested his cheek against the top of her head. She put her arms about him. 'You do appear to enjoy a lively discussion. I shall remember that for the next time.'

'As do you,' she said, glancing up at him.

Her eyes were large and fringed with a forest of lashes. Her lips had become a deep rose shade. Looking at her like that, he had trouble remembering that he had considered her an Ice Maiden, devoid of passion and only interested in strategy. He gave in to temptation, lowered his mouth and drank. Her arms went around his neck and for a long time they stood like that.

'What do you suggest we do?'

Her well-kissed mouth turned up at the corners. 'After that demonstration, I suggest sending several of your men out to search while we remain here, resting from the sea voyage. If they discover no trace of them, then we come up with another plan.'

He looked at her solemn face and knew she spoke the truth. He'd been fighting this so long on his own that it seemed odd to have an ally. 'A thoroughly sensible suggestion.'

Her smile lit her entire being. 'Thank you for considering it.'

Rand put his arm about her. 'After that, I want to show you my chamber where you will be resting.'

A dimple flashed in and out of her cheek. 'And why might that be?'

He nipped her chin. 'Guess. I shall hold you to that earlier promise.'

Chapter Twelve

'Do you think they will find the runaways in time?' Svanna asked after Rand had sent several groups of his men out with instructions to search the countryside for the missing couple.

She had to admit that sending search parties out was one solution and resting here in Donaghmoyne would not be a hardship. After doing that, he had loudly proclaimed that she appeared tired, and he would escort her to their chamber. The remaining servants had nudged each other and laughed until Svanna knew her cheeks burned.

Rand paused in latching the door to his well-appointed chamber. 'If they wish to be found, they will be. I only hope…'

Svanna kept her eyes focused on him rather than looking off at one of the many tapestries which adorned the room. Or worse, the bed piled high with furs. Everything about the room spoke of Rand's old life, the one he'd shared with Bridget—a timely reminder that she was the interloper here and could never command his heart. 'Hope what? That for some reason your cousin has not gone to seek aid from Turgeis?'

His tight smile told her all she needed to know. 'Hope persists when much else fails.'

'Forget I said anything,' she said, and tried to alter the subject. 'Your room exudes comfort.'

He shook his head. 'Better that you say it than I do.'

'Important to consider all the possibilities, but your cousin knows their fury.'

He caught her hand and raised it to his lips. 'At times, my cousin has the recklessness of an inveterate gambler, and I fear like you that this could be one of those times.'

She withdrew her hand from his much larger one. 'He'd be foolish to trust them, knowing what he does.'

'Agreed.' Rand watched her from under hooded lids. 'But my men will catch up with the pair and return them, forcibly if necessary. Only a limited number of directions for them to travel in exist.'

'Is the last for my benefit or yours?' she asked with her eyes dancing.

'If they are not found within two days, I promise to take you to Tara, and you may say your piece to Máel Sechnaill.'

She bent her head and fiddled with her cuff. The last thing she required was another quarrel, but she also knew she had to speak her mind. 'Remember Birdie. I refuse to leave her if they haven't been found. It would be reckless in the extreme to expose her to that type of danger. Her father's sword arm will be enough protection.'

'And if they have?' His quiet voice held a stern note.

'We make an assessment together.' Svanna put a hand on her stomach. She didn't want a repeat of their quarrel. She loathed quarrelling with people, but there was something odd about the aunt's promise to the girl.

She hoped in time the little girl would trust her enough to give her more information about the promise, but until then she acted on instinct and drew on all her skills of diplomacy.

'I know you'd rather she stays here, but my gut tells me

that she is an important piece in this game of *tafl* we appear to be playing with Turgeis.'

'A counter? Why?'

'I don't know, but the best way to keep her safe is to ensure she remains with us.' She forced a smile. 'She longs to be with her dear papa.'

'Are you any good at *tafl*?'

She concentrated on the table, where a game of *tafl* was set up. It looked as if Rand had been playing with someone as the game appeared half-completed. Who? She hoped that it was not some sort of memorial to his late wife, but feared it could be. How could she ever compete against a ghost? She pushed the thought away. Theirs was a strategic marriage and not about passion or love. She hated that a growing part of her hoped for the impossible. Dampening it down and concentrating on making the marriage they'd agreed to work on was the only option for avoiding a broken heart.

'My foster-mother and her second husband loved playing. My skills have been well-honed.' She gestured towards the board. 'I can demonstrate if you wish.'

'Well-honed?' Rand stroked his chin. 'We shall have to see about that.'

'Right now?' She went over to the table but deliberately did not pick up any of the pieces. 'Do you want to reset the game? Or shall I? I would hate to interrupt anything.'

Rand stared at it for a long time as if weighing his options. 'Why not? That game has gone on way too long.'

With a swift flick of his wrist, he sent the counters flying. In her heart, she knew the game must have been one he was playing with his late wife, and it made her unaccountably sad.

She said nothing and picked up the pieces, setting the game anew. 'Do you wish to be white or black?'

He laughed, a noise that rasped across her already taut nerves. 'You are amazing, Svanna.'

'Because I know where the pieces go?' She shook her head and chose to misunderstand. 'You must have very low standards if you think I wouldn't. I can play, Rand. If you are serious, we will have a match, but be warned, I play to win.'

He quirked an eyebrow. 'Something like that.'

She went to pick up the black king piece, which had rolled under the bed, but he caught her wrist. 'I'll do that.'

She dropped the piece into his palm. 'If you like…'

He placed the piece down and then drew her into his arms. 'I do very much like, but I would like this more.'

She wet her suddenly parched lips, hating the way her entire body thrummed with anticipation. 'Like what more?'

His mouth descended on hers. It was a different sort of kiss to the ones she had experienced before. Far darker, as if he was trying to expunge his demons as his tongue plunged into her mouth, demanding a response from her.

She tore her mouth from his. 'Are you frightened to play with me?'

'I prefer this sort of game right now. A game where we both win.'

He lowered his mouth to hers again. And she discovered that she wanted him desperately. To emphasise the point, she wrapped her arms about his neck and held him close. The pressure of the kiss intensified, and she moaned in the back of her throat.

He scooped her up, carried her over to the fur-covered bed and gently set her down. She fell back amongst the furs.

He carefully undid the brooches which held her apron up and placed them to one side before palming her breasts. At the gesture, her nipples instantly tightened, rasping against the rough linen of her under-gown.

'I know we should undress, but I need you too much.' He caught her hand and placed it on his member. Underneath his trousers, he was hard and thrusting.

She closed her hand about him and gently squeezed. He threw back his head. 'Undo me.'

She fumbled with the laces but managed to get them untied without knotting them and he sprang free.

He lifted her skirts and his questing hand nestled in the curls at the apex of her thighs. Round and round in a figure of eight until she was slick with wanting.

Then he opened her thighs and thrust home hard. Her body trembled before unfurling about him. She grabbed his shoulders and they rocked back and forth until they reached the shuddering peak together.

He collapsed down on her as if some great storm had passed and appeared to fall instantly into a deep sleep.

She stroked his back and he tightened his arms around her, murmuring some indistinct pleasantry she wanted to assume was meant for her.

She knew she couldn't ask him what it was or why his demons had suddenly gripped him. She had to wonder if it was somehow connected to the *tafl* game he'd destroyed. She only hoped that she had brought him a small measure of solace. She pressed her fingertips to her temples. What she did, she did for Agthir, not because she had feelings for him, but she had trouble remembering that and greatly feared that what she did, she did for Rand as well.

His steady breathing indicated that the crisis had passed.

'Are you going to trust me with the reason?'

His only answer was to murmur something indistinct and clutch her closer.

Her heart squeezed because she knew she was starting to care deeply about him and hoped he'd start to care for her, but he'd warned her against that possibility. All she had to do was to look at this room to know where his heart lay.

Unfortunately, her heart refused to listen, even though she knew it would most likely lead to tremendous hurt and humiliation in the future.

Chapter Thirteen

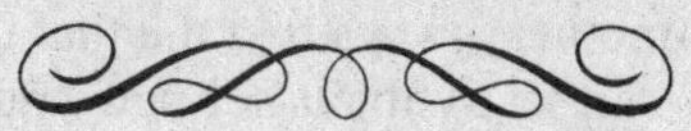

Svanna's entire being tingled from their exertions, but her mind refused to rest and kept going back over the problem of the missing couple and why they wanted Birdie. She levered herself up on her elbow.

'Rand? I want to see that loom your sister-in-law left behind, the one Birdie mentioned. Is that possible?'

He murmured something indistinct and turned over, clutching the pillow. Svanna frowned. He appeared to be in a deep sleep, the sort he'd sworn he never had. Worrying that she might wake him, she rapidly dressed and went in search of Birdie's nurse.

In the round tower's main room, Birdie was awake but clung to her nurse's skirts and hid her face as soon as she spotted Svanna. 'She's from the North.'

'Like your papa,' Svanna said.

Birdie appeared to think about this for several heartbeats. 'Like my papa? Truly?'

'Yes, truly.'

Birdie wrinkled her nose. 'I'm not sure I like you.'

Svanna inwardly sighed but resolved to win the girl's affection with patience. 'You have just met me. Liking a person takes time. We will have time.'

The little girl stuck her thumb in her mouth and peeped out at her without saying another word.

'You didn't bring a servant with you, did you, my lady?' The elderly nurse gave a quick curtsey. She clearly wanted to smooth over any awkwardness. 'Begging your pardon for my forwardness, but why?'

'My foster-mother always told me that the best way a peace-weaver can learn about her new country is to ensure she has servants from that country, rather than relying on servants from her old one,' she said, taking care to pronounce each Gaelic word carefully. Making sure she could speak the language fluently was imperative, particularly if she hoped to provide a shield for Birdie at court, but she didn't confide that to the nurse. 'It means I will learn to speak your language more quickly. Hopefully, there is a woman who will be willing to assist me.'

The elderly woman's eyes widened. 'You wish to learn our language? And you trust me to find you a servant?'

'You and Birdie surely must know of someone.'

Birdie tugged at her nurse's skirt and then whispered in her ear. The nurse nodded.

'Yes, that can be done. Birdie knows a woman, the sister of a friend of mine. She would be a good choice, I think.'

Svanna clapped her hands. 'I'll mention the new arrangement to Rand when he wakes.'

'My papa is asleep?'

'Very tired after his journey.'

The little girl nodded. At her nurse's gesture, she ran off to play with her doll.

'Can you explain to me, my lady, why you wish to learn our language? Many from the North don't,' the nurse asked when Birdie seemed absorbed in her game.

'Avoiding the language and taking refuge in a companion from home is a mistake I hope to avoid, as I shall be living here for the rest of my life.' Svanna carefully shrugged. 'Both my mother and foster-mother were peace-weavers. My late nurse drummed into me its true importance.'

She paused, gasping for air but pleased that she'd managed to say such a long speech in Gaelic.

The woman curtseyed. 'My late lady was determined to avoid your fate. Her father dangled her in front of many noses. In the end she engineered her marriage.'

Svanna kept her face completely blank. The elderly woman had obviously been Bridget's nurse as well as Birdie's.

'How fortuitous she found Rand,' she said instead of questioning her more closely. 'I understand the marriage brought a great deal of happiness.'

'I don't hold with carrying tales, my lady.'

'Rand speaks of her with a great deal of love and told me of his grief.' She forced a smile. She hated how her heart gave a pang. She might not be his great passion, but he was rapidly becoming hers. 'I know he already experienced the great passion of his life and does not seek another. Strategic marriage only.'

The woman nodded sagely. 'My lady's death altered Lord Randolfr. He used to sit and rock that child's cradle with tears streaming down his face. Say what you like about him being away all the time, but it is far from his choice. Our king makes demands even if he worries about him.'

'Birdie is Rand's sole heir. It's right that she remains where her father wishes.' Svanna fought to contain her growing excitement. The roundabout questioning had yielded much-needed background information, including that the nurse's loyalty lay with Bridget's family rather than with Rand.

'A wise woman, my lady.' The nurse curtseyed again. 'Where did you say you come from?'

'From Agthir. Perhaps you have heard of it. They say that some men from there now lead the Dubhghaill, the Northmen who threaten Gaels.' She willed the nurse to divulge more.

The woman glanced over to where Birdie sat crooning to her doll.

'I don't know much about politics, me,' she finally muttered.

'I believe their father was responsible for Lord Randolfr's facial scarring many years ago. He wrongly thought Lord Randolfr had dishonoured the Queen's daughter.'

The woman's mouth dropped open. 'Rhiannon never said anything. I wonder if she knows.'

'Rhiannon, as in Birdie's aunt? Did she speak of them?' Svanna tried to control a sudden rush of excitement.

The woman wrinkled her nose. 'She may have spoken once or twice about them, particularly one called Turgeis, whom she considered quite handsome, but nothing after she encountered Lord Thorarinn.'

Svanna stared at the woman. Was this an explanation? She had thought Turgeis was saluting her, but what if he'd been taunting Rand? What if he'd expected to see Rhiannon there? Was he saying instead that he knew where Rand must have hidden Rhiannon? She attempted to think logically and dispassionately instead of assuming that it was all about her.

'Did her silence come after she fell in love with Thorarinn?'

The nurse backed away. 'I've no wish to get anyone in trouble.'

'Will my papa go away again?' Birdie asked, running back with the doll in her arms. 'I'm sad when he goes.'

'I think he is sad as well. Maybe we can find a way to keep you with him.'

'If I go to court with my auntie, maybe he won't leave.'

Svanna gave the nurse a hard look. 'Who has been putting stories in her head?'

'She never asked for such things until her aunt arrived. Now it is all she will speak of. About how if she goes to court, she will truly have a family.'

Svanna hunkered down and held out her hand. The little girl hid her face in her nurse's skirt, but Svanna patiently waited.

Eventually, Birdie peeked out again. 'You talk funny.'

'I suppose I do, but will you help me to talk better?'

The little girl straightened. 'Me?'

'You're the daughter of the house. It is your honour and your duty.'

Birdie's grin became radiant from ear to ear. 'Oh, my saints and all the angels, yes.'

Svanna stifled a smile, knowing from the look Birdie's nurse gave her who used that phrase. 'I must try to remember that one—Oh, my saints and all the angels. Did I get it right?'

'Say it again.'

Svanna obliged.

Birdie waved her hand. 'It will do, I guess.'

'I do hope you will help me with getting my words right. Soon, no one will guess that I muddle my words.'

The little girl nodded vigorously.

The muscles in Svanna's neck relaxed. Her stepdaughter was more adorable than she had hoped. She wanted to do so many things with her and make her feel part of a family, instead of being used like a counter. She glanced about the room and saw a small loom was set up for making braid.

'Did your aunt teach you to weave this?' she asked, going over to it. The braid's weaving was more complex than she'd thought it would be for such a young child.

'She did that bit.' Birdie pointed a chubby finger at the pattern. 'I'm supposed to do some, but I like playing with the cook's new kittens better. They are going to grow up to be mousers.'

Svanna narrowed her eyes and tried to remember where she'd encountered the pattern before. Agthir, and a while ago. A chill went down her spine. Turgeis's mother wore this sort of braid. 'Unusual.'

The nurse hurried over. 'Something her aunt was doing when she first arrived. She'd apparently seen some braid like it.'

'But she tired of the pattern after she fell in love.'

'My lady knows.'

Svanna nodded. She could be misremembering, but it was if the other clues pointed in the same direction. 'A fun challenge to try and recreate braids. Ladies in Agthir's court wear a lot of braid.'

'I'm sure I wouldn't know.'

Svanna inclined her head. 'Maybe, one of these days, we'll all take a voyage there.'

The nurse went pale. 'I shouldn't like to travel there.'

'It is a very beautiful country, with waterfalls and deep lochs. Birdie's father spent some time there. I believe Thorarinn as well. Rhiannon was not thinking about going there, was she?'

The nurse looked anywhere but at Svanna. 'She failed to confide in me.'

'But if Rhiannon comes to say goodbye to Birdie, you both will let me know, won't you?'

* * *

Rand sat up in surprise. The golden light of morning shone on his face. He had trouble remembering when he had last slept for this long. His sleep had been remarkably untroubled.

Destroying that *tafl* game, the last one he'd played with Bridget, was the right thing to do. A new start. In due course, he'd change the tapestries and the position of the bed. He didn't want to erase Bridget, but he no longer wanted to look backwards.

When Svanna had stood there, looking at him in dismay while the pieces tumbled to the floor, he'd known that he wanted her with every fibre of his being. He'd needed to lose himself within her. The need remained unquenched, which added a whole new meaning to fear. The hurt, grief and guilt he'd experienced at Bridget's death had nearly destroyed him. He had no desire to experience that again and had actively avoided it, except the fates had mocked his hubris. They had tossed in his path the one woman who could reach inside the ringfort he'd built around his heart.

He stretched out his hand, hoping to find Svanna's warm body and draw her to him, but the pillow was cold beside him. He frowned. He sat up and looked about.

He swore loud and long. The *tafl* board had vanished.

He rapidly dressed and went in search of her, rushing through the ringfort with purpose and refusing to be distracted. The sun hitting the top of the round tower's door showed he'd slept even longer than he'd initially thought.

He entered the tower and discovered Svanna teaching Birdie how to play a simplified version of *tafl*. His neck muscles relaxed. Svanna was fine.

He watched, soaking in the scene of his newly made family and marvelling at Svanna's patience with the little girl as she slowly explained the move, obviously not for the first time, to Birdie. His family. Like he'd dreamt of as a young man. The blood pounding in his ears slowly receded and he regained control of his thoughts.

'Is Birdie old enough for *tafl*?' he asked when he trusted his voice.

Birdie gave a squeal and upset the board, sending the pieces tumbling to the rush-covered floor in her haste. 'My papa! My papa!'

He hugged her tight, drinking in her little girl smell.

'Mor Svanna is teaching me to play,' Birdie said in a loud whisper. 'I am…a…natural. But shh…a surprise.'

'A surprise? For whom?'

Birdie tapped him on the chest. 'You, silly Papa. You. You aren't angry with me for touching the *tafl* counters like Nurse claimed you'd be? On Mor Svanna's hair.' She scrunched her nose. 'Whatever that means.'

'How could I ever be angry with you, little one?'

Birdie nestled her head against his and sighed.

Rand looked over Birdie's curls to where Svanna was busy picking up the counters Birdie had inadvertently spilled. 'Mor Svanna?'

'Your daughter wanted a name for me.' She shrugged. 'I hope you don't mind me taking the *tafl* board, but I learned to play when I was about Birdie's age.'

'You thought to teach her without consulting me?'

'We are starting to be friends through playing.'

'Then I approve, but, Birdie, you must help Mor Svanna to clear up,' he said, lowering Birdie down. 'You were the one to upset the game. You can reset the board.'

'Will you help me, Papa?'

He reached for the king piece. It appeared warm in his hand, as if Bridget's shade somehow approved. He pushed the fancy away and set the piece down rather harder than he should have done. 'What if I play on your team against Mor Svanna?'

'*Mor* means mother in the Northern tongue,' Birdie said.

'I know it does, little one. I grew up there.'

'Oh, I'd forgotten.'

'Who is going to be the ultimate winner?' Rand asked after they'd managed to defeat Svanna on the second try.

'Birdie is rubbing her eyes, a sign of tiredness,' Svanna said in a low voice. 'Later.'

'You and I will settle it. Think about the appropriate forfeit.'

'A threat or a promise?'

Rand captured her hand and squeezed it. 'Most definitely a promise.'

At Rand's signal, her nurse came forward and gathered Birdie up, saying it was time to feed the chickens as they were her responsibility. Birdie's eyes shone. She ran to Rand, gave him a huge hug and then a more tentative hug to Svanna, who hugged the little girl back. A lump grew in his throat. Svanna was most definitely willing to play the mother to Birdie. Another practical reason why agreeing to this strategic marriage had been a good idea. Practical reasons, rather than reasons of the heart.

'Mothering comes naturally to you.'

'Does it?' Svanna said, sitting back on her haunches. 'I treat her like I wanted to be treated as a little girl. I know why you long to be with her, Rand.'

'How long did I sleep?' he asked, putting his hand to his head.

'You slept through the night and most of the morning,' Svanna said, walking over to a small loom. 'I didn't want to wake you to show you this, but I think you need to see it.'

Rand regarded the intricately woven braid with incomprehension. 'Don't tell me that Birdie is that accomplished. Even I know how hard it is to produce something of that intricacy.'

'Rhiannon was working on it when she first came here, but abandoned it.'

'Other matters in the south required my attention. I kept her safe here.'

'Thorarinn appeared at some point. They fell madly in love, scarpered, before returning here after you'd departed.'

'Speaking of which, have the missing pair been found?'

She shook her head. 'I'd have woken you. You required your sleep more than meaningless updates.'

'It has been a long time since I slept like that,' he admitted. 'Yesterday…'

She put her finger to her lips and shook her head. 'Behind us. Be grateful for small miracles. If any little thing I did enabled you to sleep then I'm happy.'

'How do you know that?'

Her lips turned up. 'The excuse you gave when you told me to drink that potion.'

He held out his hand. 'What have I done to deserve you? Let me give you a proper good morning kiss.'

She dipped her head and ignored his outstretched hand. 'The weaving first.'

He frowned. 'A jumbled mess.'

'Your sister-in-law apparently gave it to Birdie and told her to practice on it as she no longer had any use for it.'

Rand studied the length of braid. Svanna obviously wanted him to see something rather than pointing it out. 'What does it mean to you?'

'A design from Agthir, favoured by Turgeis's mother. A rune of his name.' Svanna bit her lip. 'Birdie's nurse said that Rhiannon spoke of Turgeis several times before Thorarinn arrived and not after that. She considered him handsome. I suppose some must, but he has very coarse features.'

Rand stared at the braid. In a certain light, it vaguely reminded him of the braids he'd seen in Agthir. 'What of it?'

'I fear we might have discovered Turgeis's spy.'

'Turgeis's spy?'

'Someone must have told him about your intended journey to Islay, and I don't think it was either of the missing kings. He waited for you. Was he going to capture your sister-in-law? Liberate her, as he'd put it?'

Rand resisted the temptation to roll his eyes. 'A pretty tale from this bit of braid.'

'Indulge me. Could Rhiannon have encountered Turgeis? Has he ever been at court?'

Rand pressed his fists into his eyes. How would he know? 'Rhiannon only has eyes for Thorarinn. I returned from the South to find them cuddling together. Thorarinn said that he was offering her some comfort. We left here together and stopped overnight. At which point, they disappeared. I sent word back to Donaghmoyne to welcome them but keep them there. I had to ensure I arrived for the gathering of the kings.'

'Does this happen to him frequently?'

'Not as often as it used to.' Rand stroked his jaw and then rejected the suggestion. Why would the woman run away with Thorarinn if it wasn't all-consuming love? Like a worm which refused to die, he could hear Bridget mockingly saying that he was in the right place at the right time for her rebellion and love had only come later. 'Part of me is pleased that he finally discovered someone who adores him.'

'But could she have had a flirtation with Turgeis at court?'

He shook his head. Svanna was worse than a dog with a

bone when an idea came into her head. 'A remote possibility, but I don't understand why it matters.'

'Turgeis holds grudges,' Svanna said quietly. 'Your cousin has spirited two of his prey away. First you. Now Rhiannon. He is unlikely to forgive that. We need to find that couple before he does.'

'My men are searching for them.'

'The same men who were supposed to keep them here if they reappeared?'

Rand winced. Once again, Svanna had a point. 'Where do you think they have gone? Speak plainly, Svanna.'

'Hopefully, your cousin doesn't see Dubh-Linn as a safe place from which to catch a ship to the North.'

'He has more sense than that. He has a deep loathing for the sons of Drengr and a finely developed sense of self-preservation.'

'But a deep love for his bride. He thinks you'll be angry with him.'

Rand stared at the braid. He didn't want to tell her about his sense of foreboding. The scouts should have returned by now with some sort of news. If Turgeis knew Svanna was at Donaghmoyne, would he target her? He rejected the notion as unlikely and the defences would protect her, unlike if they were out on the open road.

'I did the only thing that could be done, which was to go to Islay. I intended to go after them when I returned. I left an order for their detention.'

'Did Turgeis expect to see Rhiannon with you? Could that be why he pointed the sword straight at you?'

'How should I know?' Rand pinched the bridge of his nose, trying to think logically. His sister-in-law had always been flighty, flitting from one man to the next. Bridget had confidently expected her to settle as she grew older.

The scenario Svanna described sounded implausible, but it did explain. He hoped for Thorarinn's sake that Rhiannon hadn't suddenly developed cold feet or had been playing some elaborate game.

'What does Turgeis know about Donaghmoyne?'

Rand shrugged. 'She might have come here because she thought it was the last place anyone would look for her.'

'Why did they go abruptly? Why did this messenger turn up and what did he say?' Svanna tapped her finger against her mouth. 'We're playing *tafl* but can't actually see the board.'

'I wish I knew,' Rand said, pleased to be able to admit a weakness in that way. 'I wish I knew where my men were as well. I'd hoped one of them would return with information by now.'

'If Thorarinn knew Turgeis expected Rhiannon to travel with you, then he might have been waiting for a signal that Turgeis had returned and went to ground. I presume it is well known that you keep your most precious belongings, including your daughter, here.'

Rand hated the way his insides twisted. Thorarinn would never intentionally put Birdie at risk. He was many things, but he never turned his back on family. 'He wouldn't do that. You speculate wildly.'

'They left. Your men have yet to find them. From everything you have said about him, I don't think Thorarinn is a traitor. I suspect that Rhiannon is frivolous, with few thoughts in her head beyond her own requirements.'

'How did you form that opinion?'

'From what Birdie and her nurse said, and what they left unsaid.' Svanna spoke slowly, as if attempting to explain something blindingly obvious to a child. 'It was an early lesson my foster-mother taught me—to pay as much attention to what isn't being said as to that which is being said.'

'And I didn't?'

'You failed to notice the fatal attraction the two shared.'

Rand pinched the bridge of his nose and attempted to control his temper. Svanna made it sound as if it was his fault for being concerned with other matters. He'd known nothing about the love affair until the couple eloped together. He shifted uneasily. He wasn't entirely sure that he would have stopped it if he'd known. He might have counselled a different course, but ultimately, he knew Bridget had greatly desired her sister's happiness. She'd loathed the way their father used all his daughters as counters in his quest for power. All Rhiannon had to do was mention her fears to him and he'd have helped her, but she'd failed to. He stilled.

'Máel Sechnaill's game-playing with his daughters must stop,' he muttered.

'Playing *tafl* or dice is fine in its place, but real-life consequences hurt,' Svanna said softly.

He caught her hand and raised it to his lips. 'Forgive me for being in a foul temper. I'm worried. It has nothing to do with Agthir or your appointed task.'

'Has it truly been too long?'

'It depends on how they find them or where. My cousin can be stubborn when he gets a notion in his head. I hope you are right and that they have not headed towards Dubh-Linn, but away from it.'

A loud banging resounded on the door. 'My lord, you are required in the yard. News about your cousin, my lord.'

The muscles in Rand's back relaxed. 'See? They have been found and all is well.'

'You should not have to face these things alone.'

He watched her under hooded eyes, wondering what he'd

done to deserve Svanna's loyalty. Maybe it was simply her notion of duty, but he knew it would be easier to face whatever he had to with her at his side, and that knowledge made him wary—both of her and for her. If Turgeis or anyone else wanted to hurt him, it was possible that they would use Svanna.

And what would happen when they were vanquished? a little voice asked. Would Svanna have any reason to remain in the marriage? Was that why she'd asked for a Northern marriage, one which could be dissolved? Having just found her, he wanted to keep her, and that chilled him to the bone.

Chapter Fourteen

Svanna, praying to any god who listened that the pair had been found unharmed and were now here, or if not precisely here, very close, linked her arm with Rand's. 'We show a united front, no matter what.'

He smiled down at her and patted her hand. 'Thank you.'

Several of Rand's men milled about the yard, talking in low voices, but no one else. When Svanna and Rand entered the yard they stopped talking and shuffled their feet.

'What is this all about?' Rand asked in a measured tone but she could feel the tension in his arm. He had guessed as well as she did that their absence from the yard was not good news. 'Have you found them? Bring them to me.'

'My lord.' One of his men brought a horse forward with a bundle of bloodied clothes. 'We discovered these neatly folded under an oak tree down by the fork before the Emlagh Bog. I fear for Lord Thorarinn and Lady Rhiannon.'

'Did you find any horses?'

The man shook his head. 'No horses. Just the cloak.'

Rand held out his hand and the man put the cloak in it.

'I've seen Lord Thorarinn wear that cloak many times, my lord. No mistaking it. He'd never willingly abandon it. He used to tell that story about the time in Constantinople…'

Rand gave the briefest of nods. His throat worked up and

down, but no sound emerged. Svanna patted his back, but he moved away.

'Do we know who did this?' Svanna asked, realising that he was struggling. He gave her a grateful look. 'Is it a notorious area for thieves or bandits if it is near a peat bog? Remember I am a stranger here.'

The man who had carried the cloak shuffled his feet. 'I assume it was bandits, my lady.'

'We haven't had them here in a good few years,' Rand said. 'One good thing I have done.'

'Must be a new lot. You ain't been around here lately, what with the King's business and all, my lord. Meaning no disrespect, sir.'

Rand raised a brow. 'Why do you think bandits? Why not men from the North?'

'We found a North-made sword quite near to these bloodied clothes,' another man piped up.

'Why would bandits leave an intact sword?' Svanna said, tilting her head to one side. 'A good sword is hard to come by, normally the last thing anyone leaves and the first thing people take.'

Rand gave her a curious look. 'My lady speaks true. Why would bandits leave any metal?'

The questions swarmed in his head like bees around honey. If no bandits existed in that area but Thorarinn had run into difficulty, who was he meeting? Why had it gone sour?

'Perhaps they were disturbed, my lady,' the man answered with a frown. 'We found the corpse of a heavy-set man in the undergrowth, but no one we recognised. Maybe he was from the North.'

'Did anyone think to bring the dead man?' Svanna said.

'What good would have that done, my lady?'

'What good? All the saints and angels preserve me!' Rand thundered. 'Where did you leave your brains? My cousin is injured or possibly dead.'

Svanna put her hand on her hip. 'I'm trying to help. The corpse is important. If we can work out who he is, we might be able to figure out where your cousin and his bride are.'

'I didn't mean you, Svanna. This lot bring my cousin's cloak but leave this corpse.'

The man flushed. The other men still shuffled their feet. 'We wanted to get back here as quickly as we could. If there were bandits about, we didn't want to stay. We had a quick look round, like, but no other bodies, no nothing.'

Rand's scar throbbed and he appeared to be clinging onto his temper. 'You found a Northern sword, but didn't think to bring that?'

'We brought the sword.' The man gestured to one of the others, who proudly carried it over.

Rand turned it over. 'Kaupang or Agthir, Svanna?'

'Did this corpse have any markings on his face?' Svanna asked, trying to keep some sort of order. 'Can you remember that much?'

The man's mouth dropped open. 'What sort of markings, my lady?'

'Hatchet marks on both sides of the face, for example. Or filed teeth?'

The man's brow furrowed. 'Come to think of it, there were markings but I didn't look in his mouth.'

'Who do you think it is, Svanna?' Rand asked in an undertone.

'I've seen a sword like that before,' she said. 'It belonged to the eldest of Drengr's sons, purchased two warring seasons before in Kaupang. When I last saw him, he was heavy-set and sported a series of hatchet marks on his face. He had filed his teeth as well.'

Rand put his hands on the top of his head. 'Why would he be this far North? Why would he and his brothers risk a war with Máel Sechnaill? Outlandish tales help no one.'

'There is my theory…about Rhiannon and Turgeis.' She concentrated on the sword's hilt, trying to keep a smooth face. 'Go and retrieve the corpse and have a look around. Maybe the pair are hiding.'

'You read my mind.'

'Take plenty of well-armed men,' she said. 'We'll be fine here.'

He rolled his eyes. 'The day I can't handle myself…'

'Is the day you flee from Agthir,' she said, concentrating on keeping her hands from shaking. She hated that the pressure to get this right kept increasing because the possibility of Rand looking at her with disgust or disdain if she was wrong was too terrible to contemplate.

Rand started laughing as his men watched open-mouthed. 'You're going to ensure I always remember that.'

'Any reason to forget?'

'The intervening years have increased my expertise.'

Svanna made a noise in the back of her throat. 'They and their father bested you once, Rand. Don't allow your arrogance to get the better of your caution.'

She waited, knowing that she risked provoking his temper when she had little idea of how he'd react.

'What are you going to be doing?'

She tilted her chin upwards. Her fingers itched to demonstrate her value. A small part of her wanted him to be proud of her, even if he'd never love her or want more than a strategic marriage from her.

'Ensuring this household is ready in case Turgeis arrives in your absence.'

'Turgeis doesn't have a death wish.'

Svanna kept her smile firmly in place. 'When you return, Birdie and I will accompany you to Tara and you can personally ensure our safety. The high king must know of this outrage without delay.' She willed him to agree with her. 'Unless you have a better idea.'

He gave a sudden smile, one which demanded a true smile in return from her. 'When I return, we need to speak. There is much I want to discuss…about us. About Birdie.'

Svanna's stomach went into knots. Inadvertently, she'd built dreams where she shouldn't. Tantalisingly, she'd caught a glimpse of what her ideal life with Rand and Birdie could be like. She wanted to be valued instead of being the second-best, but her wishes had a way of failing. 'Tackling one situation before attempting another works.'

He put his hand to her cheek. 'Until then.'

After he'd left, she realised that he hadn't kissed her goodbye. He deliberately had not kissed her goodbye. Her heart ached at the knowledge that her small dream was unlikely to be fulfilled. She smiled wryly. When would she learn that believing in impossibilities was the surest way to get hurt? Concentrating on practicalities was the only way to keep safe. Rand must never know about her growing feelings for him, because she refused to take the risk of being that vulnerable.

After riding hard and trying not to think about Svanna's suggestion about taking Birdie with them when they went to Tara, or how much he wanted to be a real family with her, Rand dismounted and surveyed the clearing, which was off a narrow and disused track. The signs of disturbance were everywhere. But no sign of Thorarinn or Rhiannon or indeed the corpse. It made little sense why Thorarinn would choose this route, unless he was truly attempting to escape by going the arduous route to Dubh-Linn. Rand shook his head at the folly.

Was Thorarinn running towards something or away from it? Either way, he was moving towards danger. Why hadn't he trusted the defences Rand had put in place at the ringfort?

Rand examined a pile of leaves, but he suspected any tracks were muddled by his men.

'Bandits, my lord?' one of his men called out.

'A funny sort of bandit who can defeat a band of Northern warriors.'

'We only found one body.'

Rand clung onto the shards of his fraying temper. The ride out to the clearing had been more arduous than he'd expected. More than a dozen times, he'd discovered things he wanted to speak to Svanna about and get her opinion on. 'If you'd brought said body with you, we would be further on.'

'Over here in the ditch. I'd have sworn that it was in the centre of the clearing before.'

Rand marched over to the ditch. The body did appear to have been dragged there. He turned the body over. The features of one of his tormentors stared up at him. Rand could clearly remember his fist slamming into his stomach while he protested that he had no idea what they were talking about and that he was meeting a serving girl, Svanna. He hated that he had blanked that out. He had not meant to, but he had inadvertently caused Svanna to suffer.

'Svanna was right.'

'My lord?'

'The eldest son of Drengr took an incredible risk. Why?'

'Spying out a route for an invasion?'

'Thorarinn knows,' Rand said through gritted teeth. He also suspected Thorarinn knew far more about that long-ago attack in Agthir. A vague memory surfaced of Thorarinn confessing about receiving gold in exchange for information about Ingebord, the gold that had helped them escape. Bile rose in his throat at the consequences of those actions, even if Thorarinn hadn't deliberately meant to hurt Svanna.

'Show me where you found the clothing.'

The man pointed to the base of a large tree. 'All folded nice and neat.'

Rand frowned. Svanna was right again. Bandits did not leave swords, nor did they fold cloaks. They also didn't drag corpses to ditches after search parties had departed.

Rand walked over to the tree. The niggling thought that had plagued him throughout the long journey here, the seed that Svanna had planted, burst into full flower. Thorarinn wanted to disappear and didn't trust him to protect him and his bride. He had asked someone to inform him when Turgeis left, or possibly returned. This meant that Thorarinn must have suspected Turgeis would come looking for him.

A bleak coldness settled over him. Thorarinn and Rhiannon had departed to save their own skins. Was Thorarinn that selfish and devoid of all feeling to put a child in danger? He knew what Svanna's answer would be and hated that the evidence gave it credence.

Rand narrowed his gaze, methodically searching for any clue to what had happened to the missing lovers, ruthlessly turning his mind from Svanna and the peace he'd found with her.

The ferns were disturbed a little further away.

'I believe we have picked up their trail.'

'Whose trail?'

'Whoever Thorarinn has fallen in with.' Rand unsheathed his sword.

'You doubt he is dead.'

'He wants me and others to think it, and that bothers me. Shall we go and properly search this time, instead of making assumptions, men?'

'What do you wish, my lady?'

'We are going to do two things,' Svanna said, settling Birdie on her hip. After her father had left, the little girl demanded to be near her Mor Svanna. But simply sitting around and playing with the little girl was not going to ease her mind. Someone was coming and Donaghmoyne needed to be ready. 'First we prepare for a feast, including bringing all the animals in and making sure they are properly fed.'

'Who might be attending the feast?'

'The high king.'

The nurse's eyes narrowed suspiciously. 'Why do you think he might be coming here?'

'A possibility, no more than that, but if a rumour reached me that my daughter had married, I would want to speak to her and discover what was truly going on.'

'Why do you think the rumour has reached the King?'

'We don't know why Thorarinn and Rhiannon left and must plan for all eventualities. If I was Rhiannon and had gone against my father's wishes, I'd make sure there was a spy who could tell me if my father was on the move,' Svanna concluded.

The woman's cheeks became entirely pink. 'Oh, my, the King coming here! I hadn't even considered it. Now it makes sense why Rhiannon was speaking about our Birdie going to court.'

Svanna held up two fingers. 'But it also could be Turgeis

and a small war band coming. Either could happen. Someone made Thorarinn and Rhiannon scamper. We don't know who, as Thorarinn failed to leave a clue.'

She fancied a new respect in the woman's eyes. 'I see that. We should also prepare for siege.'

'Preparing for a siege is much like preparing for a feast, in my experience.'

The nurse smiled. 'I like you, my lady. You keep your head. More importantly, Birdie likes you.'

Svanna smiled back before pressing her nose into Birdie's hair. Birdie put her arms about Svanna and hugged her tight.

'You won't leave me, will you, Mor Svanna? Everyone always leaves. Papa left. Auntie left. Why?'

'I won't leave, Birdie. You can go with me when I do, though. Your papa and I will have a little discussion about it first.'

The little girl gave a sigh. 'I love my papa.'

Svanna rubbed her back and resisted the sudden urge to say that she did as well. He had not asked for the love, but her heart refused to listen.

'I think she probably needs a nap, my lady,' the nurse said, holding out her arms. 'Always when she gets like this, I know she is tired. She needs to go to the round tower, where she can be quiet like. I'll look after her there. The tower is the most secure place at Donaghmoyne.'

'She isn't a burden.' Svanna rocked Birdie gently as the little girl snuggled down into the crook of her neck.

'Even a cup of ale is a burden if you must hold it aloft for an entire feast.'

Svanna reluctantly handed the little girl over. 'You do have a way of putting things.'

'You are all right for a North woman,' the nurse said. 'I will ensure the high king knows that when he arrives.'

* * *

When Rand spotted a charcoal burner's hut with a tumbledown roof, a short way from the clearing, he gritted his teeth. 'Please tell me that someone bothered to check the hut.'

His men shook their heads. 'The body distracted us. We found it and the cloak and scarpered.'

'I didn't realise my men were cowards.' Rand marched over. His gaze swept around the hut. Little signs of recent occupation, like fresh ash and breadcrumbs on the swept floor, were evident. 'Thorarinn, come out and face me.'

No answer, but he heard a faint scuffling noise. He motioned to his men to go around the back. In the gloom, he spied a small cave with artfully draped ferns.

He strode over. 'How are you going to play this, Thorarinn and Rhiannon? You can come out with dignity, or we can come and drag you out. I want answers and I will get them one way or another.'

Some shuffling at the back of the cave. Rand prayed that it would not be a wild boar which trotted out.

Eventually, a dishevelled Rhiannon emerged.

'He has been hurt in the side,' she announced, sticking her nose in the air. 'He is going to need help. I can't move him any more. Rand, you must do it.'

Rand motioned to two of his men to go into the cave and bring Thorarinn out.

'He was the one to kill the Northern warrior?' he asked in a low tone. 'To protect you?'

She nodded. 'We were supposed to start a new life in the North, but that man arrived and began issuing orders.'

'Orders—like what?'

'He wanted us to separate.' She raised her chin defiantly and Rand could see the resemblance to the King and his late wife. 'I refused to be separated from my Thorarinn. We belong together. Thorarinn fought back.' At the sound of a loud groan, she hurried over to the cave. 'You be careful with him, you hear, or you'll answer to me.'

'He became rough, unlike his brother Turgeis.'

Rhiannon stiffened. 'Who told you about Turgeis and me?'

Rand silently blessed Svanna and her instincts. 'You had a flirtation with him, didn't you?'

Rhiannon chewed her bottom lip. 'He wasn't Turgeis's brother, was he?'

Rand narrowed his eyes. Rhiannon appeared to think she could play games with him. She knew who Turgeis was and he would get the truth out of her before they left this place.

'He was, but why should you worry? You broke with Turgeis.'

'Not exactly, cousin,' Thorarinn said, emerging from the cave, supported by Rand's men.

'Did you know Turgeis expected to marry Rhiannon?'

'Not marry!' Rhiannon laughed. 'Obviously not. I married Thorarinn, the only man I've ever cared about.'

Thorarinn gave her a ridiculous lovesick grin.

'You told him secrets, like the fact that your father wanted to marry you to an old man. If you require help with Thorarinn, I require the truth.'

He waited. Rhiannon finally sighed.

'And that the dowager Queen and her daughter from where he had to leave were there,' Rhiannon added. 'He and my father were particularly interested in that fact.' She deliberately yawned. 'Who cares about some old woman and her daughter, who I bet is ancient as well?'

Rand struggled to control his surprise. Máel Sechnaill

had known that Svanna and Astrid were there, but neglected to inform him. 'I'd have found it interesting.'

'You too?' Rhiannon put her face in her hands. 'Trust me. I'd no wish to marry an old man.'

'Ingebord, the Queen's daughter, was indirectly responsible for Rand's scar,' Thorarinn said quietly. 'I swear that I didn't know she'd be there, Rand. I'd have warned you. That gold enabled us to get away, remember that. We escaped together.'

'Her name is Svanna,' Rand said, not commenting on the fact that if Thorarinn had kept quiet, Drengr and his sons would never have attacked him.

'You and your Svannas.' Thorarinn gave a feeble laugh. 'You went on about one in your delirium after you were beaten. Some serving girl eager to open her legs, I suppose. Don't worry, Rand, she will be long married.'

'The Ingebord whom we encountered in Agthir bears the real name of Svanna. And no, she was never eager to open her legs as you ungraciously put it.'

Thorarinn's mouth dropped open. 'How do you know this?'

Rand put his face close to Thorarinn's, struggling to contain his temper. An ice-cold fury descended on him. Thorarinn did not care about anything or anyone except his own skin.

'Because Svanna is now my wife. And she was a virgin when I married her. Clear enough for you?'

'A virgin? But the gossip…' Thorarinn turned his head away and retched. 'Lied…'

'Thanks to your wagging tongue, Svanna was attacked and abused in that garden the day we departed. Thanks to her dog, she wasn't raped,' Rand continued relentlessly.

Thorarinn went pale and scuttled backwards. 'I didn't

know, Rand. Honestly, I didn't. I mean she was beautiful. It made sense that she would have serious flirtations. Everyone did in Agthir. Virginity was not prized like it is here.'

'Her virginity mattered to her.' Rand bit out each word with care. 'That is what counts. Don't you think I knew the difference?'

Rhiannon grabbed Rand's arm. He shook it off. 'Can't you see that Thorarinn is injured? You are upsetting him.'

'Something that he must live with. His selfish actions caused this.' Rand touched his scar. 'He caused an innocent young woman to be sexually abused and forced her to live in fear.'

Rhiannon put her hand over her mouth. 'You married this Svanna, the one who pretended to be Ingebord? Bridget used to say that you had unfinished business with a Svanna and until you had finished it, you were never going to be free.'

He stared at her in astonishment. 'How would Bridget know her name?'

She put her hand on her hip. 'You spoke her name several times in nightmares. My sister did confide in me, Rand.'

'Bridget spoke a lot of nonsense,' Thorarinn said, holding out a hand to Rhiannon. 'Come here and assist me, wife, instead of repeating gossip. I congratulate you, cousin, on your marriage.'

Rhiannon chewed her bottom lip. 'Where is your bride?'

'At my hall with Birdie.' He noticed the startled glances the pair gave each other. 'Surely you don't think Turgeis will go there. Tell me that Turgeis does not know the secret escape routes.'

'He was expecting to find me on Islay,' Rhiannon said to the ground. 'I told him I'd go with you.'

Rand stared at her. Svanna was right. Turgeis's salute had not simply been for her, but also for him. It signalled that the game was on. He thought Rand had been complicit in hiding Rhiannon. His mouth tasted of ash.

Thorarinn patted her hand. 'He won't know where you went, my dear.'

'But his brother…greeted us on this back road to Dubh-Linn. He must have known. And he thought I'd go willingly with him. Not bloody likely.'

Rand went cold. 'You left my daughter there to save your skins?'

Rhiannon shrank closer to Thorarinn. 'Nurse wouldn't budge. I knew enough not to waste my spit. Turgeis wouldn't harm a child.' Her voice became barely audible. 'He paid attention to me, promising to drape me in gold, but he also bit me, hard.'

Rand stared at Rhiannon in astonishment. The full import of what she was saying hit him. Svanna, Turgeis's long-time obsession, was there. 'Svanna is at Donaghmoyne.'

'Birdie and your Svanna will not be in any danger.' Thorarinn gave one of his laughs, the sort Rand remembered from the early days, which Rand used to call laughing in the face of danger. 'Turgeis only wants Rhiannon.'

Rand gritted his teeth. The fates were laughing at him. They had shown him what his life could be like if he could convince Svanna to alter their bargain, and now were going to dash it away. He tightened his grip on his sword. Not if he had any say. He would rescue Svanna and explain his growing feelings for her. He'd ask for the chance to begin again.

'You're no oracle, Thorarinn.' He inclined his head. 'You have decided your own fate.'

'Leaving us?' Rhiannon jabbed her finger at him. 'Your cousin is injured. We require help.'

'I will leave one horse and order two of my men to take you back to my hall. Then you will go to face your father,

Rhiannon, and confess what you did and the trouble you have caused. You'd best bring that corpse with you as well. Something to bargain with, Thorarinn.'

Rhiannon put her hands on her hips. 'Where are you going? Abandoning us like this! I am the high king's daughter. I command you to stay!'

'You command nothing, my lady. Be grateful your husband remains alive.' Rand inclined his head and silently gave thanks for Svanna, her good heart and even better sense. His neck muscles were tense to breaking point, but one thing he knew was that others had failed Svanna in the past but this time he would be there for her. 'I go to ensure my wife's safety—a safety which you and Thorarinn, in your unique ways, have compromised.'

Doing little things helped to keep Svanna's mind off whatever was coming next. The preparations for the feast were well in hand. The cattle and other livestock had been gathered inside the fort. She had made sure all the warriors had gathered their weapons and kept a proper watch. Little things kept her occupied and did not allow much time for speculation about the future or indeed her relationship with Rand. She'd freely entered the bargain, and she had to keep to it, even if her heart refused.

'Noisy,' Birdie said, covering her ears. Birdie had woken from her nap and insisted on seeing her Mor Svanna. Svanna suspected the nurse wanted to have a good nose around the preparations.

Svanna scooped her up and positioned her on her right hip. She touched Birdie's nose. 'Soon your papa will return. Your papa loves you.'

Birdie nodded and seemed to accept the reassurance. She rested her head against Svanna's. Svanna marvelled at how natural holding the little girl felt. She knew she loved her for her own sake, but also because she was Rand's. She clutched Birdie tighter at the realisation. She'd done what she'd vowed not to do—she loved Rand.

'The child will become spoilt,' the nurse said, shaking her head and bringing Svanna back to the here and now.

'She is rapidly becoming the child of my heart.'

The nurse nodded. 'A child who is easy to love.'

Svanna knew that she couldn't confess that she loved the child in part because she loved her father. Her feelings for Rand were far too new and private, particularly as he'd made it clear that love from her was the last thing he desired. With Astrid, she'd become the second-best daughter. She was Rand's second choice wife and wishing for anything else was not going to happen, even if her heart screamed that for once she wanted someone to love her for her own sake.

'I assume you have the appropriate hiding place picked out in the round tower.' Svanna forced a smile and waved her free hand. 'All a precaution, you understand. Lord Randolfr will return shortly with the errant pair.'

'Whatever happens, we will celebrate your marriage.'

'Precisely. Sometimes marking these things matters. It will be a feast that is long discussed.'

The nurse made a curtsey. 'I hope you are right. I would hate for it to be remembered for the wrong reasons.'

A loud banging at the gates made Birdie cry out. Svanna handed her to the nurse. 'Go quickly where you must, but stay by her side. Don't leave her in the dark to cower.'

The nurse promised to remain with Birdie until either Svanna or Lord Randolfr came to get the girl.

Svanna concentrated on smoothing her gown, before she went to the ramparts above the gate. Turgeis and a small band of fully armed warriors stood there. Her knees threatened to give way, and she felt physically sick. She put out a hand to steady herself and bade the feeling to go. She forced herself to look again. That number of warriors would be unlikely to besiege this fort for long.

'My lady, is everything well? You should not be here. My lord would object,' Rand's helmsman said.

'Is there a secret entrance?' she quietly asked. 'A way to escape?'

'Known only to a few.'

'Is it guarded?'

The man shook his head. 'Only shared with those whom Lord Randolfr trusts implicitly and my late lady, of course.'

Those Rand trusted and who would never betray him must include Thorarinn and Rhiannon. She fought against the rising tide of panic in her throat. The small gathering of men at the front could be a feint, as Turgeis had done on Islay. They could be going through the tunnel, if Rhiannon had betrayed them. And how far to trust the nurse? She kept taking Birdie away for her so-called naps. She had to act on instinct until Rand returned.

'Guard it now, block all the tunnels you know about, and keep a guard on Birdie's nurse.'

'My lady, we won't be able to get out if we're overrun. Go now.'

'Don't question my orders.' She raised her hand. 'Send word when it is done. Stay with the child, but get her to somewhere else besides the round tower. In the hall with the other children.'

The more she considered, the more she suspected that Rhiannon must have told Turgeis where the hidden entrances were. Turgeis's swaggering pose screamed that he expected to win, and she knew Turgeis only won through treachery.

'My lady, I've seen how you care for that child as your

own, carrying her about.' He bowed his head. 'I'd give my life for that child. It will be done.'

'Thank you.' Svanna turned back to the gate and concentrated on the figure glaring up at her. 'Why do you remain here, Turgeis? Why? Only death and destruction await you here. You don't have enough men for a prolonged siege.'

'Are we going to knock this gate down?' Turgeis called. 'You give me whatever I want, and I go. That simple, Ingebord. You've no choice. Whatever game you and your mother thought you were playing, you've been outplayed.' He kissed his fingers. 'The sweetness on top of sweetness.'

The words sent a distinct chill down her spine. Turgeis knew more than he was letting on, or wanted her to think he did. He hadn't expected to encounter her here though.

Whatever else she did, Svanna knew she must keep his attention focused on her, until she received word that Birdie was safe. She silently prayed that the nurse had not hidden her deep within a tunnel or indeed had decided to escape with the little girl, straight into Turgeis's men's arms.

'Give me what I require and your men can go, alive with their swords and honour intact,' Svanna called back down in Norse. 'We're not playing silly games, Turgeis. I'll not make this offer again. A small trifle from you. Non-negotiable.'

Turgeis gave a half-smile. 'What is this small trifle you require?'

'Your immediate surrender.' Svanna leant forward over the rampart. 'Your days of attacking peaceful communities are over. You must answer for your many crimes.'

'Never!' Turgeis's features contorted. 'I will never willingly surrender, not when I'm winning.'

'Are you winning?'

'Why are you here, Ingebord? I thought you'd have been

in Tara, making eyes at the high king, hoping he will hear your petition about Agthir's potential peril.'

Svanna tried to keep the fear about what he could do to her and to Birdie tamped down deep inside her. 'I could ask you the same thing. Why are you here? In a country which is hostile to you.'

'My needs outweigh the risks.'

'Do your men know the bounty on your head?' She cupped her hands about her mouth and repeated the words in Gaelic.

Turgeis gave a cruel smile. 'You have dispensed with hospitality. Good.'

'Hospitality is only given to those who come in peace.' She inclined her head. 'You've never come in peace, Turgeis. Not at Agthir. Not in Islay. And most definitely not today.'

He yawned. 'I have had enough of womanish wittering. Let me speak man to man with your husband.'

The men behind him laughed as if this was a good joke.

Svanna went cold. Had Rand ridden out into a trap? Were they now holding him? Or, worse, was he lying dead in some ditch? It did not bear thinking about, particularly as she knew how much he was starting to mean to her. What if he never knew that she loved him? Why hadn't she taken a risk and said something? All she could hope was that, somehow, he was on his way back, realised the situation and sought reinforcements from the King. They could hold out until then. And when it was all over, she'd try to explain a little.

'Rhiannon despises you.'

The warrior started and all amusement fled from his face. 'What do you know about Rhiannon and me?'

'That you care for her, or think you do.' Svanna ticked the points off. 'You met at her father's court. You probably thought she'd marry you, but her father rejected your suit.

She confided in you the plan to marry her off to an old man and begged you to save her. Maybe she let slip that the dowager Queen of Agthir and her daughter were visiting him. And the dowager Queen was working hard to get him proclaimed the high king of Islay.'

Turgeis's eyes widened with surprise. 'How did you know he rejected my suit?'

Svanna forced her face to stay smooth. Her words had hit a raw place. In his way, perhaps he did care for Rhiannon, but she doubted that they'd ever be happy. Turgeis possessed far too cruel a nature.

'I know many things, Turgeis,' she said, trying to keep her voice level. 'You came to Islay to rescue her, because you thought she'd gone meekly with the man Máel Sechnaill sent to negotiate the marriage like you suggested. You bided your time in the far harbour, waiting for her arrival.'

Turgeis made a turning gesture with his hand. 'Go on. I seem to recall your fascination with stories, Ingebord.'

'We thought you were waiting for the gathering, but that was merely a bonus distraction while you sought your true prize—Rhiannon, the woman you desired.' She waited and allowed the words to sink in. 'But she never got on that ship. She never wanted to marry you. When she met a real man, one who cared deeply for her, she eloped with him, even though she knew the scheme you'd concocted.'

Turgeis's face contorted, becoming red, and Svanna could see a vein in his forehead pulsing. 'You lie! Lord Randolfr never allowed her to board.'

'Rhiannon tricked you. She only wanted a way out of a political marriage. When she encountered someone more to her taste, she abandoned you.'

'No one ever abandons me!' Turgeis shouted, his voice becoming ever shriller.

'Why didn't she travel to Islay? Why has she fled?'

'I'll tear this fort down stone by bloody stone to find her where she hides.'

'Rhiannon is no longer here, Turgeis.' Svanna raised her hands. 'I swear upon Var. She and her new husband departed. Your eldest brother tried and failed. He now lies dead in a clearing.'

'Details fail to matter. And you lie about my brother.' Turgeis smiled. 'All in all, you have saved me a lot of bother. You and I have unfinished business, business from years ago, to settle.'

'Any business between us finished years ago,' she shouted back, giving in to her anger. 'You repulse me.'

'Pity there is the little hostage to consider. Perhaps you will change your mind.'

Ice crept down her back. Hostage? What hostage? He hadn't been expecting her. Who? That person must be Birdie. Turgeis knew the location of the secret passageways. She silently prayed that the man she'd sent had secured Birdie first.

'Let me see this hostage of yours, Turgeis. I know you of old—all whispered threats but no actual substance.' She clapped her hands together. 'Produce this hostage.'

'All in good time, my lady Ingebord. I dare say the hostage might learn a thing or three about pleasing men. Awfully young, but we can play our little game your way.'

Cold sweat prickled her back. He intended to harm Birdie and punish Rand as well as spiriting Rhiannon away. Rand would never forgive her if she allowed that to happen. She'd never forgive herself. 'You call this a game?'

Turgeis yawned. 'Merely the taster before the actual meal.'

Svanna put out a hand to steady herself. She had to wait and give the guard time. 'You're insane.'

'My lady, what you wanted done has been done,' one of Rand's warriors whispered in her ear, plucking at her sleeve. 'I was told to tell you this. The nurse isn't happy, but she complied finally. Both in the hall. Come away now and leave it to the warriors. Don't put yourself in danger.'

'Rand must have time to return,' she said in an undertone while Turgeis was still ranting. 'This one loves the sound of his voice, but he has brought too small an army for a prolonged siege.'

The warrior smiled. 'You are quite right about that.'

'Shall we give him a small taste?'

'At your command, my lady.'

She nodded and turned back to Turgeis. 'You'll come to regret this, as your father came to regret what he did. Why do you want someone who blatantly does not want you?'

'You know nothing.' Turgeis raised his sword. 'Time's up, Ingebord. Surrender or death?'

Svanna spotted a small movement on the horizon. Help? Or something worse? She glanced upwards and made a decision. 'What else can I choose but life?'

Turgeis smiled, the sort of smile which said she was a fool. 'Then open the gates and we shall conclude our business.'

Svanna raised her right arm and stood poised on her tiptoes. 'Never. We shall fight and win.'

When she dropped her hand, the archers unleashed their first volley of arrows.

Chapter Fifteen

Rand urged his horse forward towards Donaghmoyne. Its flanks were flecked with sweat and mud. Any other time, Rand would have stopped miles ago and rested, or at least changed horses, but not today. He kept the horse going onwards until he felt that he had never been out of the saddle. Far more than the need to see his daughter, whom the nurse would keep safe, his need to see Svanna and hear her reasoned and calm views drove him. He wanted to apologise for seeming abrupt and discounting her and then confess how he truly felt about her.

His group of men trailed behind, barely keeping up. The landmarks—the twisted oak, the bog on his left and the small pond—had all become more familiar. Normally, his heart lightened with each new sign of his approaching home, but this time the sense of foreboding only increased. There should be cattle in that field and sheep in the next, but the fields were empty, as if someone had given the order to prepare for war.

His horse stumbled. Rand reached and patted its neck.

'Keep going. My family is in danger. I know they are.'

'My lord. We need to rest. Our horses are far too tired. Donaghmoyne can hold out for days.'

'No one in their right mind would attack, but I suspect

our opponent isn't.' He pulled his horse up. 'Can you hear that?'

The men listened.

'Someone is trying to batter down the gates!' one shouted.

'My lord, we are but a handful.'

'Who would bring that large an army this far north?' Rand said, trying not to panic. Svanna and Birdie would be safe if they stayed within Donaghmoyne's walls. The defences he'd strengthened would hold and there'd be no need to use the secret passage from the round tower. A sudden paralysis gripped him. Rhiannon knew the passageways. She could have told Turgeis about them, and Turgeis would exact his revenge. He'd inadvertently put Svanna in danger. Despite all the promises his head had made, she'd burrowed deep in his heart. He had to ensure her and Birdie's survival.

'My lord, what should we do?'

'We don't know who attacks or why.'

'I had to ask, my lord. My wife and children are there.'

Rand knew he would have to make a choice—either to go in via one of the tunnels or to seek to draw the attackers off. On balance, given that the cattle and livestock were most likely inside, he had to assume Svanna had some warning and had acted. What had he done to deserve a wife like that?

That brief spell of being a true family clung to him. He knew he wanted that with all his heart and had to discover a way to convince her that they could have a proper marriage.

'Increase our pace. We will rescue them.'

Svanna directed the archers to launch another volley of arrows. Thus far, the arrows had failed to deter Turgeis's men, who were now using a fallen tree as a shield and starting to ram the gate with greater vigour. All she could do was watch and pray that somehow Rand would return and be able to rescue them. Somehow. But she also suspected that he'd have too few men to break through on a frontal attack. If he tried that, he could be cut down. Fear for him clawed at her throat and insides, but she drew on years of hiding her emotions to keep that fear contained.

'My lady, Birdie's nurse is demanding to see you.'

Svanna looked at the warriors manning the barricades. 'Can you hold out?'

Their leader fitted an arrow and shot one of the attackers in the leg. The ramming ceased. 'I believe so.'

'Send word if anything changes.' She hurried down and into the great hall, which teemed with people.

Birdie immediately ran to her and hugged her hard, exclaiming again and again that she'd come back. Svanna picked the little girl up and placed her on her hip.

'My lady, I must protest.' The nurse bustled up, resembling a wet hen. 'Birdie should be in the tower. Lord Randolfr left orders…'

'Lord Randolfr left me in charge.'

'Please, come with me. Let me show you that the round tower is safe.' She lowered her voice. 'Birdie doesn't like crowds, my lady. Neither do I.'

Svanna sighed and knew she'd get no peace until she'd viewed the tower. 'I will go, but Birdie remains here where she is safe.'

Svanna gently removed Birdie's arms from her neck and handed her to a woman who promised to entertain her along with her own daughter. Svanna indicated to a warrior that he should keep watch.

The nurse curtseyed. 'Thank you, my lady. You will see no danger exists.'

They crossed over to the tower. The sounds of the battle

were strangely muffled, but it did not appear to be intensifying.

Svanna nodded to the warrior guarding the entrance to the tower, and he allowed them in. The main room was eerily silent compared to the busy chatter in the hall.

'Birdie will be fine here,' the nurse said, gesturing about her. 'She can sleep. She will come to no harm here, if you take my meaning. I want to be able to look the King in the eye when he comes, see.'

Svanna frowned. The room appeared untouched. The *tafl* board stood in a corner, next to the small loom, signs of normality amidst the chaos of war. The trunks and stools remained where she had last seen them. 'There is at least one escape route here.'

The nurse reluctantly nodded. 'Only the family knows.'

'Not blocked, like I ordered.'

'That warrior wouldn't allow us to stay. Why should I tell the warriors? Lord Randolfr might choose to come back that way if he saw us being besieged.'

The fear clawing at her subsided. Rand had a way in. He'd arrive, and she'd see him again…

'Only the family knows, including Rhiannon,' she said, hoping to banish the thought.

'Rhiannon would never do anything to harm Birdie, my lady.'

'Not intentionally.' Svanna held out her hand. 'But I worry. Show me. I'm Rand's wife.'

'I suppose so.' The elderly woman pointed to the far wall. 'The fourth stone moves and there is a long tunnel. Built by my late lady's great-grandfather.'

As Svanna watched, the stone appeared to move.

'See!' The old woman positively radiated with glee. 'I suspected Lord Randolfr would come in this way.' She rushed over to help, moving the stone. 'Thank the gods you have arrived, my lord!'

Rand failed to emerge. Instead, the middle of Drengr's sons poked his head out of the hole. He appeared as surprised as the nurse was to encounter her.

A cold calm settled over Svanna. She looked about for a weapon, anything, but her limbs appeared frozen.

'You remain a wolf's head.'

'Ingebord?' he said, his eyes widening with shock. 'Why are you here, not the little girl?'

The nurse's scream echoed throughout the tower, freeing Svanna from her paralysis.

Svanna grabbed the heavy *tafl* board and slammed it into his face, knocking his helm sideways. The man's face registered shock. Svanna brought the board heavily down on his head, breaking it in half. He gurgled and ceased to move.

'Good,' Svanna muttered, tossing the boards to one side. 'Next time, use the front door instead of sneaking in.'

'You kill him?'

'No, his lungs fill with air.' She dragged the unconscious man into the room. 'Hand me the loom. I can use the braid to tie him up. And get help!'

The nurse needed no further urging and ran to get the guard. Three rushed in with drawn swords.

'Shall we dispatch him, my lady?'

'No,' Svanna said, from where she stood guard. Thinking strategically instead of emotionally was vital. As much as she might like to see him breathe his last, he was too valuable as a hostage, particularly if she had to bargain for Rand. 'Only living hostages are worth something. Tie him up properly. Put him somewhere secure but uncomfortable. Keep a guard on that hole in case anyone else tries.'

She went out into the courtyard and put a hand over

her eyes. Her entire body started to shake. She'd bested a son of Drengr and had not given way to violent anger. She wanted to collapse in a heap, but more than that she wanted to know where Rand was and that he was safe. She knew then she'd sacrifice everything for his life. She froze. *Strategically instead of emotionally* seemed to work for everything except Rand.

'My lady?' the nurse said, curtseying low and interrupting Svanna's thoughts. 'I was wrong. I'm sorry. Your quick thinking saved everyone.'

'Thanks to you, we have an important hostage.'

The nurse screwed up her face. 'I suppose so, but I remain sorry. I thought Birdie would be safe here.'

'Horsemen are coming, my lady,' came a shout from the ramparts. 'At speed.'

Svanna scrambled up onto the ramparts. Her one consolation was that they were unlikely to be late-arriving supporters of Turgeis. 'Do we know who they are?'

'Not yet, but Lord Randolfr would come in through one of the tunnels, not risk a flanking movement.'

Svanna narrowed her gaze and looked at the lead horseman. Every fibre of her being knew Rand must be the lead horseman. 'But then you would be very wrong. Rand is risking everything to rescue us. We need to give him a chance.' She slammed her fists onto the ramparts. 'Redouble your efforts. Use every arrow. Make a lot of noise. Turn their attention to us. Give him a chance.'

When Rand glimpsed the besieged Donaghmoyne with the black clouds towering over, it appeared to be a vision from one of his nightmares, the sort that always plagued his sleep when he was away. He'd known this day would arrive when he would have to fight for his home. What he'd failed to realise was that he would also be fighting for the two most important people in his life—Birdie and equally Svanna. His family. His mouth dried. Svanna belonged to him in a way he didn't want to think about, but he needed to ensure his family and particularly Svanna were safe.

He unsheathed his sword and urged his horse forward, yelling for his men to follow. Immediately, the defenders of Donaghmoyne started shouting and firing arrows.

The attackers appeared utterly amazed at the cacophony and started to run.

'Stand and fight like men!' Turgeis shouted from where he stood, directing the attack.

'Your men appear to have a problem with that,' Rand remarked, pulling his horse to a stop. 'They act fiercely and then run like the cowards they are.'

Turgeis bounced from foot to foot. 'Come down and say that to me!'

Rand swung himself off his horse. 'Gladly. Shall we have at it?'

Turgeis advanced a step and then retreated. 'You'll regret this.'

'This reckoning has been a long time coming, Turgeis. Overdue.' Rand swung his sword. 'Fight me like a man or prepare to die like the vermin you are.'

Unable to tear her eyes away, Svanna watched Rand advance towards Turgeis. Sweat flecked the flanks of his horse and his movements were stiff, as if he'd spent a long time on horseback. From the cheers on the ramparts, she doubted anyone else saw the little signs of Rand's weariness, but she did.

She inwardly cursed. Rand had had a long ride. He had to be tired. She had Turgeis's brother as hostage. They could have negotiated, but she doubted that Rand would have even considered that. He was worried and frantic about his daughter's safety. She wished one day that someone would be that worried about her. She winced, hating that thought.

Far too late for them, in any case. She balled her fists.

Turgeis hastily raised his sword. Steel met steel. Around and around they went until Rand half-stumbled and sweat poured down his face. She knew his muscles must be screaming in agony.

A fierce pride in what he was attempting to do filled her, but she also knew he'd taken more punishment than most men could.

'Live,' she whispered. 'Live because there are many things I want to tell you, many things I want to do with you, many years I want to spend with you. I want to fight for the loving marriage I deserve with you, not a soulless one based on duty.'

She shut her eyes, knowing what she wanted was hopeless and she should have taken the chance to tell him that she wanted a real marriage when she had it.

When she opened her eyes again, Turgeis suddenly pivoted and charged forward. His tired muscles aching, Rand ineffectually swung. Missed.

'You are pathetic. You always were.' Turgeis wiped his hand across his face. 'I can remember you pleading with my father. Pathetic. "I've done nothing to her," you said. You had her, I know you did.'

'You were there, were you?'

'I saw how she looked at you when you were in the training yard. How she wanted it, but she wanted it from a real man like me. And she will get it this time.'

Svanna stuffed her hand in her mouth. Turgeis was taunting him. He knew Rand was close to the end.

'Survive,' she whispered again. 'Do what you have to, but survive.'

* * *

White-hot anger surged through Rand, anger such as he had not experienced in a long time, giving him fresh energy. He wanted to live for Svanna's sake.

He struggled to retain focus. The surest way to get killed or seriously injured was to lose control. Even with his late wife, he had not been in danger of losing control in the way he was with Svanna and those who threatened her. He focused hard on his sword and the way it would swing next.

He waited until Turgeis charged again. He sliced his sword forward and connected with Turgeis's arm. 'You are disgusting. You forced yourself on an innocent girl.'

'She wasn't innocent,' Turgeis snarled, bearing his fanged teeth. 'She enjoyed it. Women always enjoy my attention. If she said differently, she lied.'

Anger washed over Rand, but he knew what Turgeis was up to with his filthy lies. He wanted Rand to suffer and make a mistake in their fight. However, Svanna had been innocent when they married, something Turgeis was unaware of.

Rand raised his sword and gave his battle cry. Turgeis's lips twisted up into a smile and he charged.

Rand neatly sidestepped the next charge and landed a blow on Turgeis's upper arm. 'You are deluded.'

'Deluded? I am the one getting the better of you. I will take all that once was yours. I will enjoy it. What is more, they will enjoy it as well.'

'I think not.' Rand swung his sword with all his might and hit Turgeis's wrist.

Turgeis's sword arched out of his grasp. Rand kicked it away, where it was retrieved by one of Rand's warriors.

Turgeis fell to his knees and raised his arms. He appeared to shrink. 'I'm defenceless. You wouldn't kill me in cold blood, would you?'

Rand stayed his hand. Turgeis wasn't worth it. It had to be Svanna's decision what she wanted done with her former tormentor. 'I should run you through, but I won't. You might still have your uses.'

'What are you going to do to me?'

'Turn you over to my wife. She can decide. You had best hope that she has a gentler nature than I. Personally, I would like to feed you piece by piece to the dogs for what you did to her all those years ago.'

'I… I could be of use to your high king. I know things about the Dubhghaill.'

'Of that I have no doubt.'

He nodded to his men. 'Secure the prisoner.'

They hurried to obey as Turgeis bleated on and on about how he could be of assistance and should not be killed.

Rand picked up the fallen sword and held it aloft. 'Your leader has surrendered. Surrender now and you will be spared.'

He looked up at his ringfort. A shaft of light broke the dark clouds, bathing Svanna in its golden glow. Despite what looked to be bruising to her cheek and the circles under her eyes, Rand thought she'd never appeared more beautiful. She was alive and safe. All the things he wanted to say to her could now be said, but not in front of other people. Svanna was too private a person for that.

'Svanna, I have returned! I have brought you a gift.' He shoved Turgeis forward and hoped that would do to begin with. 'Yours to decide what to do with.'

'Indeed you have! I…that is…we were watching and cheering you on!' Svanna called from the ramparts. 'Truly marvellous.'

Rand saluted her with his sword. 'Pleased to have put on a good show for you.'

'I have a gift for you as well.'

He tilted his head to one side. 'A gift? What sort of gift?'

'A hostage. Another son of Drengr. I fear for the *tafl* board though.' She tilted her head to one side.

Rand went cold. If Svanna had captured him using the *tafl* board, he must have entered through the tunnel in the round tower. Rhiannon's betrayal was total. 'Is my daughter safe?'

'She plays in the hall with the rest of children.' Svanna looped a strand of hair about her ear. 'Luckily, I considered the problem before the situation turned sour. Thanks to her nurse, I was in the tower when your gift attempted to break in.'

Rand did not bother to blink back tears. Svanna's precautions had worked. It could have all ended differently but for his beautifully practical wife. He wanted to tell her how much she meant to him and how he wanted to start their marriage again as a proper one, but when they were alone without prying ears. He had to give her a choice, something few had given her in the past.

'I suspect King Máel Sechnaill will appreciate both gifts,' Svanna called down. 'Alive for him to do with as he wills.'

The knot in his back eased. Svanna, ever pragmatic, had not gone for revenge, but for a result that would benefit all living in this country. It was the correct thing to do, but he knew he would have made a different choice.

'My brother has been taken?' Turgeis squeaked, turning pale and interrupting the conversation. 'How is this possible?'

'A heavy *tafl* board to the head,' Svanna called down. 'Amazing what it can do.'

Rand gave his prisoner a contemptuous look and pretended to count on his fingers. 'Three brothers. All met with mishap. Careless.'

'Why don't you get it over with and kill us?'

'Because my wife has spoken. It was her decision, not mine. You can thank her that she has chosen mercy.' Rand motioned to his helmsman. 'Take him and his brother away. I intend to enjoy my family.'

He walked through the open gates and enfolded Svanna in his arms, burying his nose in her hair and making a memory. He'd left her without telling her how much he cared for her and how much he wanted them to be a family. 'I'm back. Did anything happen while I was away?'

A shadow of a dimple played in her right cheek. 'One or two small things, not worth mentioning really.'

He laughed. 'But I want to hear about them.'

Her brow puckered. 'Did you find your cousin?'

'Alive. Although I suspect he may live to regret his choice of wife. Rhiannon is a little more managing than he is used to.' He shrugged. 'They and the corpse of the third brother Drengrson travel more slowly.' He stared up at the sky, knowing that he needed to get his words right. There had to be a way that he could make a fresh start with her. 'I owe you an apology, Svanna. Many apologies. You guessed correctly about who was responsible.'

'Oh, my papa! My papa!' Birdie barrelled out from the hall and threw her arms tight about him before Svanna replied. 'I missed you, but Mor Svanna let me stay in the hall. One day, I'm going to be big and brave like she is.'

'That would be a good thing, little one.' He lifted his daughter up but knew his chance of putting things right with Svanna was slipping away. 'Do you think I could speak to Mor Svanna alone?'

Birdie gave a long sigh. 'If you must…'

'There are things to be done, Rand,' Svanna said with a frown. 'The aftermath must be sorted properly. Indulgence must come later.'

He caught her hand. It trembled within his. The words refused to come. He had already made too many mistakes. An indulgence? He knew his late wife would have seen it differently, but Svanna was not her. He knew then that he loved her for caring about others. 'Later. We can have privacy then. There are things you need to understand about my cousin and Agthir to help you decide.'

He closed his eyes. He'd said it, letting her know that he knew the full truth and that he was going to give her a choice.

Her smile became forced. 'The sooner things are accomplished, the sooner we can go forward into our future.'

She slipped away from his grasp, and he knew he had to let her go.

His words must be for her ears alone, and they needed to be perfect. He needed to find a way to make it up to her for all that she'd endured because of his cousin and his lies. More than that, he needed to find a way to make her love him and to begin the marriage afresh. She needed to be able to choose for herself, but he knew her answer could crush his hopes.

Chapter Sixteen

Svanna did her final round of ensuring all the injured were tended to. The last item on her long list of what one did after a raid, and then she knew she'd have to go and speak to Rand alone. She had thought doing the small tasks would allow her to regain control and stop wishing for things which could never happen. It had taken all her self-control not to blurt out how much she loved him, how worried she'd been and how she wanted their marriage to become a loving one. She wanted to go forward and not have the past burden her. She started across the now-deserted yard.

'Is this what Lord Randolfr calls hospitality?' a loud voice boomed from the far side of the yard.

She turned to see a simply dressed man with a head of flowing copper hair heavily laced with grey streaks and fierce blue eyes. Five other men dressed in simple hunting gear stood behind him.

'It depends, King Máel Sechnaill,' she said, sweeping into a low curtsey, 'on whether or not you arrive after a major battle.'

The man arched a brow, bearing more than a passing resemblance to Birdie. 'You are aware of who I am?'

'You and your granddaughter share the same eyes. I presume your late daughter had those eyes. I've yet to meet Rhiannon.'

He frowned. 'Rhiannon isn't here? I was reliably informed that she had appeared with some man in tow.'

'She is apparently slowly making her way back with her beloved. Rand discovered them and left several of his men to help with their safe return. I believe they may require some medical treatment when they do arrive back as her man, as you call him, had to fend off one of the Drengrson brothers.'

'You appear remarkably well informed, my lady.' The king tilted his head to one side. 'Have we met?'

Svanna bobbed another curtsey. 'Svanna Guthardottar, the dowager Queen of Agthir's foster-daughter.'

'I understood her foster-daughter sat upon Agthir's throne.'

'You were misinformed. Her real daughter sits. I was the substitute for a while, but now I've other duties. Lord Randolfr and I made a blood alliance, uniting Eire, Agthir and, in time, Islay.'

Máel Sechnaill appeared to digest the information with some surprise. 'What are you to this place?'

'Svanna is my bride,' Rand said, slipping an arm about her waist. 'This hall is now her hall. It stands in no small part thanks to her and her quick thinking. I was lucky to find her.'

Svanna leant into him, basking in the glow of unexpected praise. Her heart kept whispering that she could have more if she asked for it. Then she moved and his arm fell away. She knew it had been for show and hated that she wanted it to be real.

'You married?' Máel Sechnaill turned to his courtiers. 'Why wasn't I informed of this? My son-in-law has contracted a second marriage with the Queen of Agthir's foster-daughter. I expect better service from my little birds.'

'I presume Birdie's nurse sent word that Rhiannon was here, directly after the couple arrived and you set off immediately,' Svanna said.

The King's mouth dropped open. 'How do you know I am in communication with her?'

Svanna rolled her eyes. 'My foster-mother taught me well.'

He gave a barking laugh. 'All right, I confess. The nurse does send messages from time to time. I want to know what is going on. When I received word that my daughter was missing, I was beside myself.'

'Your granddaughter will be delighted to see you. She bears no small resemblance to your side of the family.'

Máel Sechnaill's lips became a thin line. 'I came to find my daughter, not to visit my granddaughter. My granddaughter's fate must be her own. I've had more heartache than a man should bear.'

'But my daughter would love to see you,' Rand said, putting a firm hand in the centre of Svanna's back.

'Birdie makes any heart lighter,' Svanna added, trying not to lean into him. 'She is in the main hall, playing with the other children.'

'Go and see her,' Rand said in a low voice. 'Bridget's spirit lives through her. The spitting image.'

Tears swam in the older man's eyes. 'Does it? I'd like that.'

'A feast has been prepared. You will be feted at the high table,' Svanna said. 'You must visit your prizes afterwards. Today is an end of Turgeis and his brothers menacing us—Eire, Agthir and even Islay. We must celebrate.'

'What are you going to do?'

Rand laced his fingers with Svanna's. 'Speak to my wife. Alone.'

The high king laughed. 'Who am I to come between a determined man and his bride?'

Svanna knew her cheeks flamed, but she allowed Rand to lead her away to a secluded barn, even though she feared what must be coming.

'Are you sure that was wise?' she asked. 'The King complained about the hospitality, and he is uncertain about Birdie. I won't have her upset, Rand.'

'Very sure,' Rand said. 'Because first the King and then my cousin and his wife will arrive. By the time everything is complete, you'll have something else to do. Are you avoiding me?'

'I'm trying to play my proper role, the one we agreed when we wed—a peace-weaver bride. To keep to our bargain.' She willed him to understand and let her go. She hated that she longed for his love, but she'd learned a long time ago that the moon would never be hers.

'What if I would like you to play a different role?'

Svanna's mouth went dry. 'A different role? We've an agreement.'

He raised her hand to his mouth. 'I've done you a great disservice, Svanna. Before we go any further, you must know this: For years I believed my cousin saved my life, but I know now he was entirely at fault for what happened in Agthir that day.'

Svanna tilted her head to one side and tried not to panic. She hated that she wanted to be married to him whatever shape that marriage took. 'The past stays past, Rand.'

'Its shadow will always fall between us unless I explain.'

She wrapped her arms about her waist and nodded, bracing her heart for whatever came next.

Rand rapidly explained what had happened in truth. How Thorarinn had made a wild guess to pay off his gaming debts, and then, after receiving the gold, had learned who was being beaten. When he'd finished, he caught her hand and raised it to his lips. 'Can you forgive him? Or would you rather not have anything to do with him? I know how much you've suffered.'

Her heart turned over and she knew she was sliding further in love with him, but it had ceased to matter. What he'd confided showed that he did care a little for her. Maybe they could work towards making a proper marriage.

'No gold would have been on offer if Turgeis had not invented the rumours.' She shook her head. 'The people who bear most of the blame were Drengr and his sons. I will hear no more of this. It happened, but I bear your cousin no ill will. You survived. I survived. I will go on surviving.'

'We both have scars, Svanna. Mine on my face and you…' He touched her chest. 'Deep in here. I can't undo them, much as I would like to. Now we need to renegotiate our marriage bargain.'

The sound of her heart pounding nearly drowned out his words. 'Negotiate our marriage contract? We married because it was the right thing to do for both our countries. Simply because we defeated the Drengrson brothers does not mean the need for our alliance will cease.'

'I find I want more than a bloodless alliance, a strategic marriage, I believe you called it. It won't suit. It won't suit at all. I want a family like I dreamt of having as a boy, one where I spend time with my wife because I want to, and we raise our children together on a farm. I grow weary of war, Svanna.'

Her mouth went dry. He wanted a real family. More than

that, he wanted her because of who she was, not because of her relations. 'Your heart is buried with your wife.'

'The man I was ceased when my family was buried. That man's life had been far from perfect. I spent far too much time away and we lost sight of our dreams. In my heart I knew when she'd gone that we'd somehow lost each other long before.'

He paused. The hope growing in her breast threatened to overwhelm her, but she drew on all her training to remain silent.

'But I didn't die,' he said, finally breaking the silence. 'I lived for my daughter. In the beginning, her nurse told me that because Birdie had struggled to breathe at birth, she was too fragile to survive. Days, months and then years passed. My daughter who seemed weak and helpless grew into a sturdy little girl. But I stubbornly refused to see the goodness life could hold until you came into my life. Suddenly I find old dreams have returned. I want that family again. I believe in second chances now, Svanna. Can you?'

'Are you trying to say you no longer have need for an alliance?' she whispered around the fear that clogged her throat. Did he want to end their marriage?

'I thought my heart was small and incapable, but you came into my life, making demands, and my heart grew stronger.'

'What are you saying?' she whispered, hardly daring to believe what she was hearing.

'I'm willing to release you, Svanna, if you don't want forever. But will you begin our marriage again? Not for Agthir's or Islay's sake, but for yours? Because you want, above all things, to be my life-partner, just as I long to be yours.'

She turned her face into his palm. 'You want forever? With me?'

'The man I am now loves you, Svanna, with all his heart. The youth I once was, maybe he would have grown to love you in that garden. I don't know. My carefree youth vanished that night in Agthir and what is left of me is scarred, but I want to be with you for ever. Not because it makes sense for either of our countries, but I want to start my day with your head next to mine on the pillow and end it with our lips pressed together.' He paused and ran his hands through his hair. 'Sigmund may have called me a silver-tongue, but my tongue is tied where you are concerned. Will you have me?'

'You love me?' She shook her head in wonderment. He wanted her for herself? 'But you said your heart was buried. You told me not to expect or hope for anything other than simple regard.'

'I've said many stupid things in my time, but none as foolish as that. How the angels, saints and even the Norns of my youth must have laughed at my words.' He caught her hand and raised it to his lips. 'I want to live fully, Svanna, but to do that, I must know that you want this sort of marriage as much as I do. You need that choice because no one else has given you one.'

'A long time ago, you were a fantasy, something that I clung to in times of trouble, but then you came into my life, and I discovered that the reality of you was much better.' She cupped his face with her hands. 'I love your daughter, Rand, as if she were mine but, most of all, I love you. You make my heart soar. You give me hope for tomorrow. Yes, I want a true marriage with you.'

'We agree. Good.'

'Sometimes, Rand, you talk too much.' She lifted her mouth to meet his and for a long time neither spoke.

'Excuse me?' a quarrelsome voice sounded behind them. 'Why is no one paying me any attention?'

Svanna jumped and saw a dishevelled woman leading a horse with a body slung over its back. A man leaning on a stick was walking a few steps behind. Her heart sank. Rand and she seemed destined to be interrupted. She pasted her best smile on her face and stepped out of Rand's arms. 'You must be the missing Rhiannon. How wonderful that you are finally here.'

The younger woman wrinkled her nose as if to say Svanna was beneath her notice and ignored her outstretched hand. 'Did you tell your new wife, Rand, that we were bringing a valuable hostage for ensuring peace? One of the fabled sons of Drengr.'

'Never be rude to my wife again.'

Rhiannon blinked her eyes slowly several times. 'I've travelled a long way.'

'Svanna will tell you that the only hostages worth anything are the ones who are alive.' Rand inclined his head. 'Turgeis and his other brother are now in our custody, waiting for your father's judgement.'

Rhiannon opened and shut her mouth. 'When my father hears of this... You forced me to bring this corpse.'

'Go in and speak to him now.'

'He is here?' Rhiannon shrank back. 'Thorarinn...he's here.'

Thorarinn turned pale, but he attempted to stand straighter. 'We will face him together, Rhiannon.'

'Take your husband to the priest. He'll heal him,' Svanna said, taking pity on them both. 'Then go into the hall. Your father longs to greet you. Beg his forgiveness. He came here because he was worried and is a romantic at heart.'

'You are truly generous. It's far more than we deserve, Rhiannon,' Thorarinn said. 'Let's take her advice.'

'You must do what you like,' Rand said. 'But my wife and I will leave you here.'

'Why?'

'Because I am taking her to bed, where she can have a well-deserved rest, away from other people's demands. Someone must look after the weaver of the peace as she refuses to.' Without waiting for an answer, he bent down and picked Svanna up. 'We are most definitely not to be disturbed for a long time.'

Svanna put her hands about his neck. 'One of your better ideas.'

'You wait, my lady fair, I have many more where that one came from,' Rand said against her ear in a voice full of promise.

Islay. Eight weeks later

'Our mother looks the loveliest bride of all,' Maer said, linking her arm with Svanna's as the cacophony of getting the bridegroom settled with the bride resounded. 'It appears the entire island has turned out for the wedding.'

'Thankfully, our mother knows how to plan a feast.'

'I think she had some help from you...'

Svanna inclined her head, acknowledging the fact.

Svanna and Rand, along with Birdie, had arrived over a week ago on the island in preparation for Astrid and Sigmund's wedding, but Maer, her husband and two young children, had only arrived on the tide before the wedding. Maer looked more serene than ever. Being Queen suited her. And she and her husband appeared to be very much in love.

Maer had genuinely been delighted to see Rand again. They'd both agreed that they had had a lucky escape from each other.

'I did what I could,' Svanna said modestly. 'You know how she is.'

'You are the only one she'll listen to in these matters.'

Svanna laughed. Maer was giving her far too much credit. 'Our mother had it all in hand. The women here adore her.'

'Isn't it funny how it all turned out? We three all found the loves of our lives, even if it took some of us time to realise it.' Maer nodded towards where their mother stood with Sigmund receiving congratulations.

'But all is right with the world now.' Svanna paused, thinking how they'd received word from Tara before they'd left that somehow Turgeis and his remaining brother had managed to meet with what was being called a fatal accident. Svanna wasn't tempted to enquire too closely about the details. 'I was sorry to hear about Tippi. She lived far longer than anyone could have hoped for. Hopefully, one day, I will get Birdie a dog like her. A companion for all the seasons of her life.'

'Then I hope you will take this little one as a small token of my gratitude.' Maer signalled to her husband, who was standing chatting to the swineherd. 'Time, darling.'

'Time for what?' Svanna asked.

Maer accepted a large basket from her husband. The basket emitted a few yips and made a scratching sound.

'I knew when Tippi's great-granddaughter had a litter of puppies that one of them had to be destined for a special person.'

Svanna gingerly lifted the cover. A little black nose touched her hand. 'A puppy? She looks like Tippi. Maer, I could not have asked for a kinder present.'

'A little girl puppy. Hopefully for you and your little girl. I know how much joy and comfort Tippi brought to you.' Maer smiled. 'I thought you could use a familiar face as a belated wedding present.'

Svanna took the puppy from the basket. The puppy licked her face. She was instantly transported back to that day when her world had fallen apart and her only comfort was a small dog nuzzling her palm, promising all would be well. Now, another small dog had entered it, asking for no more than a little love and affection.

'What do you have there, Svanna?' Rand asked, slipping an arm about her waist while Maer and her husband went off to greet old friends. 'That puppy seems to be a lively thing.'

Tippi lunged out and licked his fingers.

'Maer's private gift to celebrate our marriage. Tippi the Younger.'

'She is perfect. She will be the right sort of companion for our daughter to go exploring with.'

'I love how you say *our daughter*. Birdie truly has become the daughter of my heart.'

'You are her Mor Svanna, the lady who saved her and became her real mother, like she wished on the moon for.'

'Birdie and her notions,' Svanna said, laughing.

'And she is very excited. Apparently, the saga of the usurper King of Agthir will be sung tonight and she will get to hear how her mother saved everyone's life.'

'You know that story has been altered.'

'But you saved lives, including mine. Why allow the truth to get in the way of a good story?'

'Why, indeed?'

Rand gestured towards where Birdie was excitedly speaking with Sigmund. 'Now shall we go and show her the newest member of our family?'

Tippi the Younger gave another excited yip and Svanna knew she had the family that she'd always longed for.

* * * * *

If you enjoyed this story, then you're going to love
Michelle Styles's latest historical romances

Tempted by Her Forbidden Warrior
A Viking Heir to Bind Them
Secret Princess for the Warrior

And why not pick up her Vows and Vikings miniseries

A Deal with Her Rebel Viking
Betrothed to the Enemy Viking
To Wed a Viking Warrior